FORGETTING THE ALAMO,
OR,
BLOOD MEMORY

Chicana Matters Series
Deena J. González and Antonia Castañeda, series editors

Chicana Matters Series focuses on one of the largest population groups in the United States today, documenting the lives, values, philosophies, and artistry of contemporary Chicanas. Books in this series may be richly diverse, reflecting the experiences of Chicanas themselves and incorporating a broad spectrum of topics and fields of inquiry. Cumulatively, the books represent the leading knowledge and scholarship in a significant and growing field of research and, along with the literary works, art, and activism of Chicanas, underscore their significance in the history and culture of the United States.

Forgetting the Alamo, Or, Blood Memory

A NOVEL

By Emma Pérez

UNIVERSITY OF TEXAS PRESS
Austin

Third paperback printing, 2010

Requests for permission to reproduce material from this work should be
sent to:
    Permissions
    University of Texas Press
    P.O. Box 7819
    Austin, TX 78713-7819
    http://utpress.utexas.edu/index.php/rp-form

∞ The paper used in this book meets the minimum requirements of
ANSI/NISO Z39.48-1992 (R1997) (Permanence of Paper).

Library of Congress Cataloging-in-Publication Data
Pérez, Emma, 1954–
    Forgetting the Alamo, or, Blood memory : a novel / by Emma
Pérez. — 1st ed.
        p.   cm. (Chicana Matters Series)
    ISBN 978-0-292-71920-0 (cl. : alk. paper) — ISBN 978-0-292-72128-9
(pbk. : alk. paper)
        1. Mexican Americans—Texas—Social conditions—Fiction.   2. War
and society—Fiction.   3. Texas—History—Republic, 1836–1846—
Fiction.   I. Title.   II. Title: Forgetting the Alamo.   III. Title: Blood
memory.
    PS3566.E691324F67 2009
    813'.54—dc22
                                                2009014400

For Scarlet and Luzía

And in memory of
Vincent Maurice Woodard, friend, scholar,
poet, visionary and soul mate to so many.
April 21, 1971–February 4, 2008

ACKNOWLEDGMENTS

The kernel of this novel came to me more than ten years ago, and I have been fortunate that friends, family members and colleagues have weathered the decade with me, continuing to offer advice and consolation as I conducted research and traveled throughout Texas to imagine my characters in the nineteenth century. Two informative primary sources that assisted my imagination are *Texas: Observations, Historical, Geographical, and Descriptive,* by Mary Austin Holley, and *The Evolution of a State or Recollections of Old Texas Days,* by Noah Smithwick.

From its inception, my writing bud, Alicia Gaspar de Alba (B.C.) and I held private writing workshops that helped my story and characters materialize. Always willing to listen and always willing to give suggestions, Alicia kept me on track. The novel has profited from her keen talents as a writer. Catriona Esquibel read the first draft of this novel, one I tossed (no, she didn't retrieve the manuscript from the garbage, although she is a serious archivist of all things Chicana lesbian), and she has eagerly read many incarnations since, pushing me gently with her questions. Michael Topp, a loyal friend who mirrors my dysfunction, enthusiastically read drafts and gave worthy observations. My sisters, Yolanda Pérez, Cris Pérez, Sonja Pérez, and my brother, José Roberto, listened good-naturedly, more or less, as I rambled. Cris and Sonja read drafts and never gave up on me. I thank las diosas for my remarkable, beautiful siblings. My nephew, John Michael Rivera, also read an early draft and fell asleep, leading me to conclude that the plot demanded tension. Sandy Blandford has been an exceptional researcher who sent me books on the history of the West, including an amusing book on saloons.

At the University of Colorado, Boulder, friends and colleagues were generous with their time. Elisabeth Sheffield offered valuable suggestions.

Vincent Woodard gave detailed comments, and even when in the hospital, he remembered to ask about the project.

I revised preliminary chapters of the novel in A. M. Homes's fiction workshop at Columbia University in the spring semester of 2000, in Sands Hall's novel workshop at the Iowa Summer Writing Festival in 2001 and at Tom Jenks's advanced novel workshop, held in Denver in spring 2005. All were considerate, discerning mentors.

I also owe much to colleagues and friends, scholar/activists, who excavate our past to confirm that as a people of many nations, villages and tribes, we have always traversed and occupied the Americas, north and south. I list here those who have helped me shape this work of fiction: Arturo Aldama, Antonia Castañeda, Ernesto Chávez, Ward Churchill, Arnoldo De León, Elisa Facio, Juan Gómez-Quiñones, Deena González, Ellie Hernández, Linda Hogan, Katie Kane, Thomas Kinney, Yolanda Leyva, Alma López, Arturo Madrid, Rafael Pérez-Torres, Gregory Ramos, Vicki Ruiz, Chela Sandoval, Rosario Sanmiguel, Sandy Soto and Deb Vargas.

Thoughtful and incredibly efficient, Theresa May at the University of Texas Press is everything an editor should be. I'm fortunate that the series editors, Deena González and Antonia Castañeda, took an interest in a historical novel. I also thank staff members at UT Press who assisted with details, large and small.

My familia tejana is too numerous to name individually; however the stories that describe the lives of my mother and father (Emma and José Pérez), abuelas y abuelos, tías y tíos, primas y primos continue to inspire me. In Denver, the following spaces kept me sane and nourished: Highlands Vital Yoga, DJ's Berkeley Cafe, and Urbanistic Tea and Bike Shop.

For the last decade, Scarlet Bowen has put up with my bipolar moods, my intense anxiety, my ruthless demands and my unwillingness to change lightbulbs. She brought to us our miraculous daughter from another planet, Luzía Etienne Bowen-Pérez. You are my anchor, my net, my serenity.

After sleep, after amnesia, after inhabiting different worlds, I no longer know what truth there is in memory. I believe things I didn't believe before. About what is outside us. About what is inside. It is a new geography, that of the forgetting body and mind, the remembering spirit, a new landscape.
—LINDA HOGAN, *THE WOMAN WHO WATCHES OVER THE WORLD: A NATIVE MEMOIR*

FORGETTING THE ALAMO, OR, BLOOD MEMORY

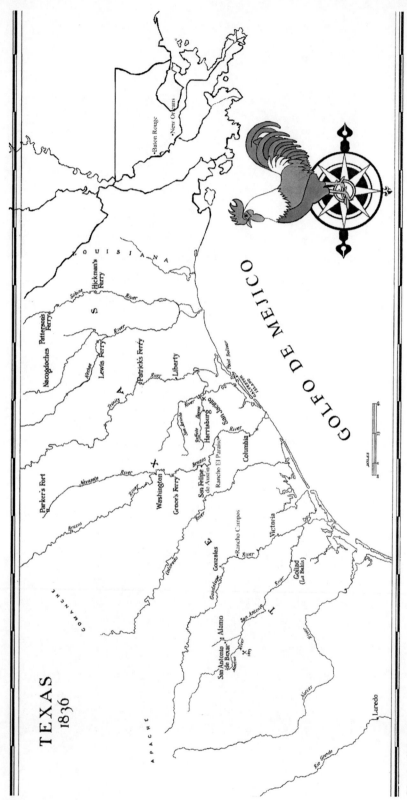

TEXAS
1836

LOUISIANA

Baton Rouge
New Orleans

GOLFO DE MEJICO

Nacogdoches
Patterson's Ferry
Hickman's Ferry
Lewis Ferry
Patrick's Ferry
Liberty

Parker's Fort
Washington
Grace's Ferry
San Felipe de Austin
Rancho El Paraíso
Harrisburg
Columbia

San Antonio de Bexar
Alamo
Gonzales
Rancho Campos
Victoria
Goliad (La Bahía)

Laredo

Sabine River
Angelina River
Neches River
Trinity River
San Jacinto River
Buffalo Bayou
Brazos River
Navasota River
Colorado River
Guadalupe River
San Antonio River
Medina River
Rio Grande
Nueces River

COMANCHE
APACHE

Point Bolivar
Galveston Bay
Galveston

MILES

Map by Alma López

CHAPTER 1

Everyone said he was lucky but I didn't believe it. Not for a second. Jedidiah Jones wasn't lucky; the angels of clemency had forsaken him but the devil, the dim-witted devil of injudicious earthly things, whispered in his ear that he was a good boy and Jed confused the imp on his shoulder for an angel. My cousin, half white, half Mexican and full fool, was lucky at cards. That's all. Just lucky at cards. And tonight was no different. He leaned back in his chair, tilting the legs the same way he would tilt his hat back on his head until it seemed it would fall but it didn't. He leaned back and smiled big the way only he could whether he had a bad hand or a good hand. He loved the game and so did I but he thought he was the better player since he was so good at pretending to be good. And even when I tried to do as he did, I went unnoticed while he went home with all the winnings.

The year was 1836. Battles were behind us and more were before us and many spoke of a war that would change our lives but none of that mattered to my cousin. Jedidiah Jones sloped his long, tapered chest into the table, peeked at his hand and winked at me across from him. Another card from the dealer caused him to slant his hat farther back on his head. I recognized that tip-off. He was about to win big or lose big. Either way, all eyes were on my cousin because he had a way that obliged you to watch him.

I was the plain opposite. No one watched me and at the time I might have taken advantage of my unexceptional character more had I known that I could have used it to my gain, but I lacked confidence and envied what I didn't have and that was Jed's style for winning even when he was losing. Me, I was impatient for victory, the kind of impatience that makes you look nervous to others, especially since I didn't know how to risk all that had to be risked if I was to be the victor. I fidgeted, twirling strands of hair, or I bit my nails but I never threw myself wholly into the game. I was young and scared but too stupid to know I was scared so instead I feigned a self-possession that carried me through my young life like the lie that it was.

I think back to that infamous day for no other reason than missing Jedidiah Jones. I ask myself plenty why I bother yearning for my conceited cousin but when I imagine his white teeth glinting from that idiot grin, I pine for him more. Nearly a decade has passed since our many battles with each other and I still get mad at myself for the way I feel. Of course, the years have taught me some things but what I am not yet sure.

What I do know is that I held him responsible for every consequence that followed the events of the day that changed our lives for eternity and beyond. It was nothing but one small poker game but it tainted all things known to us. He never admitted that game's meaning. He couldn't. It would have meant different choices and realizations at a time when boys like Jedidiah Jones had their fair-haired futures handed to them. I remember every detail of that day because every detail played over and over in my head for months after as I tried to make sense of what had happened, but mostly I was obsessed with how it happened. Never the why of it. Why was too big a venture and anyway, I've come to appreciate that "why" is not worth mentioning since it's only an excuse for those who need one. Me, I'm tired of excuses.

The game started out easy, with my father, Jed and me playing to pass the time. None of us wanted to get back to the ranch so early on a Saturday afternoon. I guess Jed won enough times off of my father to get to feeling confident so that when three ugly strangers entered the saloon in our small town of El Pueblo, Jedidiah Jones swaggered from the bar back to our table waving to the newcomers to come play.

I gawked at each one, memorizing their vile faces without knowing that's what I was doing at the time. The leader of the bunch had a short stub of a nose with scabs falling off, looking like his snout had only recently been chopped back. As the strangers sat down, the stub-nosed leader elbowed another man equally as ugly with an ear half gone as if someone had cut it but neglected to cut clear through. The third of the trio, with a craggy face and yellow teeth, wasn't as homely and I hardly noticed him since he put down his cards and folded for the first game. Stub-nose and Half-ear winked at each other and for a moment I thought they were cheating.

"I'm out." It was Half-ear.

"Hell, you give up too easy, Runner."

"I ain't lucky like you, Rove."

"I ain't lucky. Just sure of myself." The stub-nosed man named Rove looked at Jedidiah, wheezing hard. "I'm gonna go all the way on this one, son. You sure you wanna stay in?"

Jed squinted his already beady eyes and pushed his hat farther and farther back and chuckled out loud. "Do what you want, old man. I'm ready for you."

"I got a horse outside says you're bluffing."

"How bout that? A horse? You betting me a horse?" Jed grinned. "Fine. A horse for a horse."

"I'm all in myself," I said but I might as well have not spoken.

"I got a horse outside myself." This time I whispered since I was lying. I had no horse and neither did Jed but somehow his lies were more convincing than mine.

"You're bluffing." Jed singled out a piece of straw from his shirt pocket and chewed.

"Well, how bout I show you mine if you show me yours?" Rove winked at Jed.

"How bout you go first, old man."

"Ain't you a gentleman? Somebody sure taught you some good manners, son."

Rove laid his cards down and showed three kings. "How do you like that?"

Jedidiah Jones fanned out five cards. He was showing three aces. The stub-nosed man got up at high speed and I cringed until I saw him retrieve a leather pouch from his back pocket and slam it on the table.

"Take it. It's all I got. But dammit, son, don't take my horse. I need my horse. You a patriot, ain't you?"

"That depends."

"On what?"

"On who I'm being a patriot for."

"General Sam Houston, that's who. I cain't go into battle for the General holding nothin but my dick. I need my horse, son."

He sat back down and fingered his six-shooter, pointing the barrel at my cousin. I felt myself go red but my dark skin's color hid my flushed cheeks and my long, crimped hair fell forward, hiding my face. My hands shook and I secured them by laying one on top of the other and fanned my cards wide across the table. The man named Rove poked his pink nose stub with his gun barrel as if to scratch what wasn't there and then he peeled off fat brownish scabs and let the skin fall on the table near my cards. He didn't see my full house. Three queens and two jacks. No one looked at my hand or at me but they sure gawked at each other.

Under the table, I kicked my cousin but he was distracted because a gun had been aimed at his head, forcing him to rush a decision that he clearly preferred to mull over. This man's horse was worth a lot more than a leather pouch of coins, which would be valued at almost nothing this time next month if Sam Houston whupped Santa Anna, and all were keen for that lesson to be consummated. But if Jedidiah accepted the coins, he would dodge the prospect of this stub-nosed man stalking him to steal back his horse. Or worse. Jed snatched the leather pouch, turned it upside down and dumped Spanish hammered dollars on the table. He stood, pocketed a pile and buried the pouch in his back pocket.

"I'll take both," said Jed.

"Why, you little sonovabitch."

"Thank you kindly for the game, boys. I'd like my horse if you don't mind."

"You little sonovabitch. You'll regret this."

"Maybe. Maybe not." Jed grinned wide and self-assured.

"The coins will do just fine," said my papi. "Keep your horse, Rove."

Jed's grin did not diminish and that's when I realized how much the boy loved to bluff, even after the game was over. He headed for the door with my father by his side and the gambling men all followed.

I sat in my place. That no one had bothered to look at my full house was expected and yet still I wanted more from my cousin. But expecting more from Jedidiah Jones was like hoping for the devil to change his wicked ways and I have to admit, at that time when Jed and I were young I thought he had it in him to transcend the evil that was all around us and growing to be sure. More than once I plainly realized there was no wisdom in my weakness for Jed.

"Get on out of here, sweet thing." The bartender didn't bother to look at me when he spoke. "We don't want no trouble. Go on with your pappy. Girls don't belong in here. Now get."

I slipped my winning hand inside my sleeve, got up and skipped through the swinging doors and saw my father with stub-nosed Rove, who poked papi's chest and lectured something I couldn't hear.

Except for those gambling boys, the town was quite nearly emptied of white folks, but even so I was not surprised when Miss Elsie popped her head out from under a wagon as if to check the tension of the wheels. Jed hovered over her and his voice sounded loud and frustrated.

"Mamma, I'm telling you, it ain't safe."

"It ain't up to you to tell me what I can and can't do, Jed." Miss Elsie rose up from her haunches and her skirt fell down around her knees. She saw me and shouted out to me.

"Get on over here, girl, and give me a hug. I ain't seen you for some time. You're looking more and more like a full-growed woman."

Miss Elise pulled me to her bosom and I smelled her rose water perfume, so pungent and sweet I wanted to flee for fear someone might suspect how much I liked being buried at her chest. But it was Melina, one of Miss Elsie's girls, who made my head spin in ways it shouldn't for another girl even when I did my level best to ignore her. Melina was such a sweet thing. Ever since she had arrived at Miss Elsie's saloon at only thirteen years old after being abandoned by her father, the girl stayed close to Miss Elsie's side. And if Melina was like an adopted daughter, Jed was Miss Elsie's adopted son, which made for a peculiar relationship between the two, who did not consider each other family relations.

"You look more like your mammy every day." Miss Elsie slapped my backside and I felt myself grow red. "Got the same wide hips growing back there too." From the corner of my eye, I saw that Jed was enjoying the comedy of my womanhood but his brow was furrowed in his concern for Miss Elsie.

"You don't got to be so stubborn, Mamma. I'm telling you, it ain't safe with Santa Anna in the vicinity."

"And I'm telling you, I got to get back to Bexar. That ole sonovabitch General ain't gonna strike twice in the same place." She winked at me. "Life's too short to run and I ain't about to start now."

"Let me fix your hair for you, Micaela." It was Melina and as she spoke she stroked my curls and untied the grimy twine that fastened my hair.

I pulled back and regretted my panic immediately.

"I won't hurt you. I promise," said Melina. "You just need a trim and maybe some bangs to show off those pretty gold eyes of yours."

Jed laughed out loud and Miss Elsie finally butted in.

"I reckon she likes to hide behind those long curls. Leave her be, Melina."

"Yeah, leave her be, Melina. She belongs in that old ugly pigtail of hers," said Jed.

Melina and Jed strolled off together and whispered in a manner that made my gut hurt. His back faced me and every now and then she would glance toward Miss Elsie and me.

"How's your mammy, Micaela?" said Miss Elsie.

"Getting on."

"Don't give her no trouble, you hear me? Times are hard right now and a woman like her has got enough trouble to tend to."

"Yes ma'am."

"Tell her to come visit me in Bexar. Things ain't so bad as everbody says. Hell, we'll survive and so will she. You tell her that."

"Yes ma'am."

"Melina, leave my boy alone and let's git. We got to git back to town sometime before next year. I hear Santa Anna's on the prowl." She winked at me again, I thought mostly to mock Jed.

"Jed, you stay out of trouble, you hear me?" Miss Elsie wagged her finger at him.

Jedidiah chewed on his straw as he watched Melina's backside.

"Did you hear me, son?" She repeated herself louder.

"I hear you, Mamma, I hear you. Dang, can't a man get some peace and quiet in his life?"

"You ain't a full-growed man yet. Don't go getting big britches."

Miss Elsie waved at me and then climbed up on her wagon with Melina at her side. They rode off, Miss Elsie at the reins.

I lagged behind Jed and we loaded the wagon with a single sack of flour and a few other items for the farm. He sat himself down on the wagon's seat and I hopped up beside him.

"Take a look." I fanned out my cards again.

He nodded.

"You see?"

"A good hand," he said.

"But I won. That's my money in your pocket."

He laughed. "Just try to take it, cousin."

"How about you give it to me?"

He grinned.

My father mounted his horse and leaning forearms on the pommel, signaled with his chin to Jed, who picked up the reins and clicked his tongue but our mule wouldn't budge. He smacked the reins down against the animal and clicked his tongue louder. The mule picked up its front right leg and set it down again. I pulled my hair back and tied it with the same grimy string, then hopped down and heaved on the mule's mane in a tug-of-war until the animal retracted his stubborn ways momentarily and plodded beside the horse.

We rode serene and as we reached the outlying acres of my papi's land, I tried to set my mind to rest that the fate of our home would not be threatened by any imminent war. At dusk the ranch and the land that my father had inherited appeared transparent and vast through the clearing. Eleven sitios. Nearly forty-nine thousand acres. A lot of land for a young boy whose people had inched their way up the valley two centuries prior, moving slowly at first from the central valley, then north each time they shifted, each time farther north to prairies, crossing rivers and streams. Monclova had been home for a while but two hundred years felt like plenty of time, so they picked up and moved north again, crossing el río Bravo, traveled some more and stopped and settled in for what they thought would be another two hundred. They came in groups, my papi said. Tlascaltecas and Otomí with the Spanish and the Spanish Moors with the Mexicans and the Mexicans with Apache and Comanche mixing into a brown race journeying through land expansive with bloodred horizons until they stopped and looked around and settled into what was already in our blood. Movement. Settlement and movement. Back and forth our ancestors trekked rivers and streams blending and interbreeding with tribes and making families and villages in deserts, plains and groves. Tribes of families and villages of mud huts sank into the landscape where buried vessels and bones became soil and clay. I felt proud to be a part of that ancestry, convinced that one day it would all be mine and Jed's provided he stopped gambling.

It was late when we arrived at the ranch and I could already sense Walker Stephens hanging back in a corner of the barn. Darkness shrouded his face but his bare feet stuck out with veins so blue we did not miss seeing him swinging a kerosene lamp back and forth.

"What the heck are you doing, Walker? Come on out and put my horse away." My father addressed him harshly but never meant it that way.

"I ain't your slave. Get that damn boy of yours to help you."

"What the heck is burning you up?"

"How long you been gone?"

"Well now, Walker, I got myself a wife for that kind of nagging."

"You bring my hoes?"

"In the wagon."

Walker gathered three farm hoes, nuzzled them under his arm, then picked up his boots and scuttled in his bare, blue-veined feet out of the barn. Jedidiah and I raised eyebrows at each other thinking the same thing: "There goes one nasty sonovabitch."

"Walker? Where you going? Get on back here." Papi yelled but Walker was far beyond hearing him.

"One of you go and fetch him."

"I ain't going after him," said Jed. "Man hates me."

"Put this horse away for me, Micaela. Jed, let's see what's aching your papi"

"He ain't my papi."

"He is."

"He ain't."

"Fine." My father dusted his pants with his hat. "Feed that mule. And take that sorry sack of flour to your Tía Ursula. Tell her it's the best we could do."

He ran out of the barn after Walker, who was already slogging in his bare feet to his hut about a mile down the road.

"Tío is too dang loyal," said Jed.

"Can't say the same for Walker." I brushed my father's horse and glanced at my cousin sideways. "Or his son."

Jedidiah dropped a bucket of water intended for the mule and the creature bayed.

"Now look here, Micaela. Nobody invited you to play in that game. You got yourself a winning hand that nobody was gonna listen to 'cause you're nothing but a girl. You got that? Now learn your place."

I pitched the brush heavy and direct at his face and it thumped his nose firm. He bent over, face in his hands to catch the blood running from his nostrils and I was glad to see him in some of the anguish I'd already been feeling. Heaving the flimsy sack of flour for my mother on my shoulder, I darted out of the barn and into the house.

Jed and I were the kind of cousins with a history so thick and wide that it was destined to bind us in ways we never wanted and yet there it was. A past coming upon us like birthdays we were eager for when young but once older they became like a burden. The next generation would take on the weight of a past begun not with us as cousins but long before we were born and that weight endured into the next generation who would pick it up, measure it and say to each other, These are lies, all lies. Where's my real legacy? But they too realized there's no running from or evading, there's no stopping it or getting away because the burden of inheritance will follow them as it did us into the next and the next and the next generation. Jedidiah and I had inherited every possible birthmark, every familial trace that stained us as each other's. And days like today, when I looked in his eyes and saw my own hazel-brown color, I hated my cousin and I hated a destiny we were expected to carry out for the sake of a man we both loved, yet who himself was too loyal to see that the man pretending to be his friend was not a friend at all.

"¿Y tu papi?" My mother stood over the stove, stoking its fires with wood piled in the patio.

"Con el Walker." I pitched the flour sack against the wall of the kitchen.

She sighed at the sight of the puny sack and stirred a pot of chile with potatoes and venado.

"Siéntate a comer, Micaela."

I sat at the kitchen's worktable where at one time only the cooks and hired help ate their dinner but those times were long past. Now the family sat in the kitchen for the comfort of warm fires and spices from my mother's cooking. Jed straggled through the door, bloodied rag hiding all but his eyes, and sat across from me. I refused to acknowledge him because he only wanted to gloat the way someone does when they think they have the upper hand because you did something bad to them and they deserve to get you back when you're not looking. If I turned my back, he would get me because he always did.

My mother placed a bowl of chile stew in front of him and it spilled over with chunks of meat. She grabbed his bloody rag and handed him a clean washcloth.

"When are you two going to learn that family is family?" She looked at me accusingly and left him to his self-satisfied innocence.

Behind her back, he beamed at yet another victory and I hissed through my teeth and took a bite of gristle in my bowl.

Jed slurped crude and loud then reached into his back pocket for his leather pouch and spilled coins on the table.

"Gracias, mijo."

She pocketed the coins and Jed stuffed the empty bag in his back pocket, grinning his usual goofy grin, the one that drove me crazy because days like today I hated the dim-witted idiot for breathing.

"I'm going to bed." I wiped my mouth clean with the back of my hand and marched out of the kitchen.

CHAPTER 2

On the day I was born my father said I puckered my lips into an O and whistled into his face to greet him. He laughed, kissed my mother's cheek and announced, "She's mine all right." Growing up, I had curly hair and a dimpled chin that resembled his and although my disposition was a child's, I adopted his moods, laughing when he laughed, giving orders as he would and never crying since he wouldn't. I became the reason for my parents' battles. No matter how much they argued, what was clear to one was not to the other. My father could not comprehend what my mother had deciphered since I was old enough to convey my preferences saying out loud in as many different ways as she could without saying what she really meant.

"Agustín. Mira a tu hija," and my mother pointed to the patio where I messed about. "Es un machito."

"She'll grow out of it."

He looked out the window and saw what my mother saw but he did not recognize its meaning. I was a girl with no interest or inclination for propriety or clean habits. In overalls I squatted in mud and teased both cat and mouse, dangling the one by its tail in front of the other while the larger one batted at the one boxing for its freedom. The sight made him smile but my mother glimpsed my future long before I ever could and divined that I would never marry.

It was spring and I was long past fifteen, having turned eighteen the previous fall making me an old maid by most opinions, but it was the way my father treated me that may have confused us both. I was more like a son and less of a daughter but his propensity for proper rituals and tradition often plagued his common sense. I think there was a moment when he would have taken me with him into battle but humiliation at the Alamo coerced him to decide otherwise.

He had avoided going to Bexar, having heard of the carnage at the Alamo mission and undecided as to what he would do upon encountering destruction. But on Sunday morning, the day after the poker game, he woke me before dawn and handed me one of his prized firearms. It was a rifle decorated with silver filigree twisted into his initials, AC. He knew it was my favorite of his collection and I wondered why he was spoiling me so early in the morning. He wouldn't say even if I asked.

I didn't know if he had told my mother I was to go on the road with him and I suspected he had not, given our speedy departure. In darkness, we set out on horses that he packed for a brief journey. Bexar was a long day's ride if you tendered the horses with a chance to rest but if you raced them, you arrived long before Miss Elsie's saloon got rowdy and that was before suppertime.

My father was not one to talk much but when he did, he cussed you out, bossed you or spoiled you. I never knew which of those temperaments would emerge so I usually waited until he gave me a clue of some sort. The sun barely peeked through brightening clouds when he finally addressed the day.

"You're riding better than you used to."

"I am?" I was pleased he was in a spoiling mood.

"Sure are."

"Is that good?" I guess I wanted to hear more compliments and thought it was a good time to pursue them.

"I didn't say good, I said better. You're riding better. Didn't you hear me or do I got to repeat myself?"

"I heard." I would have preferred silence to his irritation and I got my wish because we rode hushed for another three hours if not more. The sun's heat inflicted a humidity that made me drip so much sweat I thought I might as well be bathing in hot springs. I took off my hat to cool off.

"You'll be wanting to put that back on," he ordered.

"Yes sir."

I felt his gaze on me and it made me nervous. I stayed quiet then heard him laugh out loud.

"You look more and more like your mamá," he said.

I wanted to ask if that was a good thing but refrained.

"Micaela, ain't you asking me what's in Bexar?"

I wondered if this was a trick.

"Go on. Ask me."

"Why are we going to Bexar, papi?"

"Now then, I didn't say to ask why, did I?"

I could see that he had no intention of sharing his true purpose in San Antonio de Béxar so I entertained myself by exploring from my saddle the new path we trekked. We rode far north of Victoria along the Guadalupe River and just south of Gonzales we crossed unfamiliar oak orchards until I caught sight of the part of the San Antonio River that I usually rode when mamá and I traveled by wagon to Bexar. The route seemed longer than the one I was accustomed to but I decided not to question my father on his choice to take us farther north than I thought necessary.

We did not race our horses, putting our arrival time long past midnight. The streets were shadowy with the half-moon shining bright through trees and the stench of death was surely in the air. Less than a week had passed since the battle at the mission and with the siege in Bexar concluded, we dismounted our horses without hesitation or fear.

He led our horses to the town stable and after setting them right with a young boy who fed and brushed the tired creatures, my papi and I staggered bone tired into Miss Elsie's saloon. One dim candle shone from the table where Miss Elsie busied herself counting coins. My father grabbed a bottle of whiskey from the bar and sat himself down next to Miss Elsie and then ordered me to get myself a glass of milk and a piece of pie from the back room where Miss Elsie stocked provisions.

"I only got goat's milk, darlin, but there's peach pie and cheese in there. Bring some for your pappy too," she said. All the while she did not glance up from her tally.

It was pitch-dark in the back so I picked up the candle to light my way and left the two with only a slice of moon shining through the doors of the saloon. From the back room, I heard their whispers and it wasn't until I was almost completely in front of them that I heard my father teasing Miss Elsie.

"You're still a good-looking woman, Elsie."

"Shut on up, Agustín. Your daughter is here."

"She probably agrees with me." He continued to stare at Miss Elsie through the moonlight and I had to agree but only to myself that the light softened the weariness on her face and she resembled herself in younger years.

"How come you and me never got together?"

"Now you're talking nonsense, Agustín. I don't like that kind of talk and you know it."

"I'm paying you a compliment, woman."

"That ain't no compliment, that's a nuisance. I gotta put up with enough of that in this place. Got plenty of girls upstairs if that's what you want but I can tell you right now, Ursula ain't gonna like it none."

"Ursula stopped caring long time ago."

"You wanna tell me why that is, Agustín? One too many visits to places like this is one reason, I can tell you that." She took the pie from my hands and placed a heaping portion in front of my father. "Here's something you can handle. And don't be talking like that in front of your daughter. She don't need no ideas."

"Hell, you're the one confessing my life to her." He picked up the pie and bit off a mouthful. "I ain't that kind of man anyway. I been good to Ursula."

"Yeah, yeah, you been good. All you men who come into my place, you been good to your wives."

"Okay, okay, woman. Leave me be. I been riding all day and all night and this is the kind of reception I get." He finished his pie.

"I fed you and there's your drink. What else will you be wanting?"

"How do you know I'd be wanting something else?"

"You're here, ain't ya? Fess up. I ain't got all night."

"I got business with a boy named Rove. Said he'd meet me here. You seen him? Ole ugly fellow. Long, lanky. Got a stub for a nose."

"Ain't seen him and I don't care to see him. He's trouble."

"Elsie, who ain't trouble or in trouble these days?"

"Well now, Agustín, you need me to point out the difference in your reckoning?"

"I do not."

"A man like Rove may get himself into trouble but it don't likely matter since he brings bigger trouble with him, wherever he goes. And you know what that means?"

"I guess you're going to tell me."

"Means folks run from him."

"You sure think you know a lot, Elsie."

"I know what I know, Agustín. You best watch yourself. It's all I'm saying."

"Fine by me." He saluted her and headed up the stairs to one of the spare rooms Miss Elsie saved for family and other acquaintances.

I was permitted to sleep in her room on her bed, having done so since I was a little girl but now that I was older, the prospect made me uneasy. She was immune to my agitation and wrapped her arm around me and blew out the candle.

"My sweet baby girl, Micaela. Sleep tight," she said. And before I knew it her snores were so deafening I had to place my hands over my ears hoping to fall asleep before morning.

I must have slept more than I had thought possible since I awoke to an empty bed. I washed, dressed and ran downstairs assuming my father would be eating breakfast but he was not. Neither he nor Miss Elsie was in the saloon. I stepped outside and saw in daylight raw and clear what had been hidden in the night. Bodies heaped in muddy ditches and so much vile destruction I bent over and upchucked without fully capturing what I was enduring.

My father was not a holy man but in the distance he was on his knees as if to be praying. I approached slowly and saw he caressed a head, just a head with no body. I was further repulsed but more than anything troubled by my papi's reaction to the decaying skull in his arms and even more worrisome to me was my papi crying. He looked up at me and held out the skull as if a prized souvenir and I refused but fell to my knees in front of him and finally witnessed the spectacle that was before us. It was his brother. My Tío Lorenzo. The eyes had been gouged but the scar on his face was plain. I had known him all my life by his crescent scar. As a boy he himself had cut his cheek to show a big brother that he was as tough and mean as anybody. At least that was the story my Tío Lorenzo told me. Tears flowed down my face and I touched his branded cheek as if to solidify the memory of my uncle. Why he had been here at all was not such a mystery.

"I told him, mija. I warned him. Always the big shot, your tío."

We sat in mud with flies and other putrid pests in our midst and as much as I attempted to free my father from remnants of chaos that surrounded the Alamo mission, I could not. It was Miss Elsie who spotted us and lifted him from his knees and dragged him back to the saloon where she put him to bed and gave him whiskey to calm his choking tears.

I never found out the real reason we had gone to Bexar. My father never told me. I guess he stumbled upon his little brother when he stopped to survey trash and rubble at the Alamo and like so many who witness the wreckage of pointless wars, he too became immobilized by cadavers and bloodshed. Among that rubble, he hit upon his baby brother and never got to the business he came for. I'll never know for sure if that's how it happened and anyway, it didn't matter. What mattered was that another bad event was tied to an occurrence that entered our lives, evil and foreboding, and what I came to realize is that all the evil that ever happened to us was fixed to one man. Rove. If that stub-nosed sonovabitch had never walked into the saloon in El Pueblo, we would not have come to Bexar so soon after the battle of the Alamo and we would not have seen my uncle because he would have already perished into soil. We stayed a few more days to bury Tío Lorenzo, or the only part of him that remained to be buried, and I was grateful to Miss Elsie, who prevented me from losing my remaining sense of sanity since my papi disappeared from me in the way I had known him.

On our return to El Pueblo, my mother acted peculiar and although I suspected the reason, my father did what he always did and ignored her. She went about the house cooking and cleaning to keep her hands from strangling him, especially after I revealed the news of Tío Lorenzo. My father did not say a word about our journey and instead pursued another unsettling matter, one I hoped would never be revealed.

"El Viejo Barrera," my father said, "has he married again?"

"¿Por qué?" said my mother.

He left the kitchen without answering.

Every fall and spring, my papi traveled to the interior of Mexico to buy and trade what was unavailable in our far northern province of Coahuila y Tejas and it was then that I saw my mother become so lonely she began to invite El Viejo Barrera to visit more often than I would have liked. Dressed in clean, crisp, lacy shirts and polished black boots, he wooed my mother as he had when they were young before my father disrupted her needs making promises he could not render. With a shiny disposition El Viejo sweet-talked his way back into my mother's life bringing with him cabrito from his hacienda for nightly dinners and as they drank Mexican brandy my mother giggled and was made over into a young woman without worries of meager crops and a husband's put-on promises.

"I'm going to visit Barrera," said my father.

"Lorenzo is dead and you're visiting a man who isn't your friend?"

He squinted at my mother in a manner so disturbing I walked outside to avoid a confrontation but before I reached the edge of the patio, papi marched past me and joined Jed beneath a cottonwood tree. The two whispered and I heard every word but pretended I didn't. Lugging on my shoulder the rifle papi had given me, I peeked through the eyehole at my cousin who rolled un cigarrillo on top of his kneecap, brushed off lingering leaves and smoked, gazing up at the sky's slow-moving clouds.

I was envious that my father and cousin whispered secret pacts and as I watched Jed rise up and stand beside my father, I practiced my aim before setting my rifle down. I lingered lonely at the edge of the patio and thought, Fool—my cousin's a grinning fool, and I felt unease and turmoil in my gut over what was yet to come.

CHAPTER 3

On the eve of battle, I sat high up in the barn studying rain clouds through the hayloft doors. In my red leather-bound journal, I sketched scenes as if to document for myself what my memory would forget. Below in the courtyard, my father wandered over to my mother plucking feathers from a chicken whose neck she had twirled and wrung then chopped clean at the base of its skull. When she let the headless body loose, it scrambled and ran confused until it toppled with webbed feet quivering.

"It's time for her wedding."

"Estás loco, Agustín," she said. Plucking the chicken, my mother swerved her hips on a stool with her back to my father.

"When I return, we'll plan the wedding."

She yanked out feathers that drifted in midair.

"Barrera is ready for a wife," he said.

"Venustiano's an old man."

"An old man with land and money."

"Land and money," she sighed.

"He'll take care of her."

"She doesn't need taking care of, Agustín."

"All women need taking care of, Ursula."

"No conoces a tu hija."

"She'll do what I ask."

"You don't know your own daughter, Agustín."

"Tú dile. She's going to marry him."

When my parents married in 1814, the nearby battle in Medina the year prior had already changed lives for those who lost so many but papi was not one to stop when he saw something good and hopeful in front of him thinking he'd spite what was behind him. He looked ahead and promised mamá she would have a ranch filled with cattle and horses and fat chickens and hogs with servants and laborers. On a spring day in April hundreds came from nearby ranches to honor the bride with her groom and all feasted for days on roast pig, tamales and brandy. Most who came were Bexareños, families who had lived in Bexar for over a century and some centuries longer, that is, those who had married Comanche or Kiowa but kept the secret if they had money and didn't if they were poor since nobody cared who or what the poor came from.

The match was agreed upon, more or less, since my mother's father agreed but her mother did not. Their blessing didn't matter because when my mother saw my father round up cattle and burn wavy lines like a river on their loins, she already admired his agile hands roping steers and branding hide. By midsummer, they were a couple hiding behind cottonwood trees near the riverbank. My father's good looks made my mother breathless having bumped up against him often enough, letting him rest his thumbs on her belt. When his fingers circled midway around her waist, he grinned and she could not have known the grin meant he was pleased with a body robust and thick, perfect for babies, ideal for fieldwork.

It was said mamá was india and her grandmother on her mother's side was Tonkawa, a people descended from the wolf, but those who said this spoke in whispers. Others whispered she was mulatta, having inherited her great-grandfather's tanned skin of a Spanish Moor, but her father's family claimed she was Española, as pure and Spanish as they were meant to be, descendants of the Canary Islanders that arrived a century earlier. But my mother said she was Bexareña. Generations of her family were rooted in San Antonio de Béxar and she told me how the floods and droughts of the San Antonio River had tested them. It was on that river that she leaned her back against a tree and my father pressed against her, his brown mustache probably tickling her nostrils.

"Marry me," he said. In the spring, they married.

My parents built their farm on the Guadalupe River near a town that came to be called El Pueblo. That was in 1820. I was almost three years old and my mother had already miscarried twice. Years later, the twins were born. A boy and a girl. Ifigenia and Aristus. Then she miscarried once more. Her inheritance dwindled on a farm that barely yielded crops and her losses made her strong but with that strength came bile and resentment and soon my father became the one who felt rancor from his wife and soon another man's touch was far more consoling than a husband's, especially a husband too distracted to notice that his wife was too tired to be the woman he had married.

From up above in the barn's loft, I saw how papi scrutinized the chicken mamá plucked and they each watched the feathers sway in a dance, tumbling to the ground.

"The boy's coming with me," he said.

She yanked feathers silently.

"We leave day after tomorrow."

My mother's thighs weighed heavy on the stool. I could see how she felt the weight of the decades but my father refused to see what he had encouraged and she in turn dismissed his requests as anything but annoyances. When she announced almost daily, "Just lay me down here on this ground. Like an animal," my father only mumbled to himself and carried on with his day.

I saw papi take from his breast pocket a document he handed to my mother, the same document his own mother had handed to him decades before on her deathbed.

"¿Y esto?" she said.

"Keep it safe."

"Safe? Nothing is safe anymore."

Mamá unfolded wrinkled parchment, brown and ripped at the edges. Something had been spilled on the paper and the shape of the droplets resembled the wings of a crow or an eagle. My great-grandmother Campos had passed down to her daughter, my grandmother, the same piece of paper that had been stamped by the Spanish Crown when their family had claimed the land grant that would be tendered through generations. My grandmother had offered my father the title on the day she was to die having had no daughters to whom she could will the land. Papi was her oldest son and he had survived independence battles in Mexico's capital not because he had been quick enough to dupe death but because he had refused to travel south like his younger brother "to fight for a cause that was too far away for me to care," he said. On her deathbed, my grandmother bowed her head and handed him the certificate that bore the family name.

Mamá let fall the paper she had never believed in anyway, having

learned from tribal ancestors that land was not for giving and taking.
When she saw that papi had scribbled the name Jedidiah Jones as inheritor of his family's land, she said nothing and he answered with what was only on his mind.

"El Viejo Barrera. He's got all the land she'll ever need and more."

The chicken was bare and she cradled it in her arms, stood and walked out of the courtyard and into the kitchen.

The morning my father left for battle, mamá gazed at the sky and pointed out to me a cloud's image of papi in battle but I did not see what she saw: a ten-inch blade glistened in a flash of lightning, its pearl knob held by a man's shadow.

"You're going to die, Agustín. At that battle. You're going to die."

From the height of his horse, he looked into the distance and I sensed a bottomless sorrow in his stooped shoulders.

"Listen to me," she said.

"I'm listening, Ursula, I'm listening." My father sounded irritated.

"Then don't go."

He shook his head and bent forward, forearm on the saddle's pommel. "They killed my baby brother, Ursula."

The three rode away, my father and Walker up front, fixed on the horizon, with Jedidiah trailing. A dust veil stung our eyes and coated our throats.

"Hombres necios," my mother said.

"He'll be back," I said. I wrapped an arm around my mother's waist.

"No. He won't." My mother tore away and walked back to the courtyard leaving me alone to watch my father's cloud of dust fade away.

CHAPTER 4

"They came here often to see my girls, especially my meskin girls. Like you." Miss Elsie pointed a finger at my mother and pulled at a bodice that pinched the skin underneath her breasts.

I sat in the room and pretended to read hoping my mother would not send me away while she and Miss Elsie squabbled over men's liberties, the ones that made them do the kind of things that only set them back to a sorry way of being.

"I been in this business thirty-five, no, forty years counting the time I was back home. A fifteen-year-old pup, I was." She reached behind her back and unbuttoned her dress.

"Darlin, reach behind here and unpeel this darn thing."

My mother squeezed the bodice tight to undo each metal hook that marked an "s" on Miss Elsie's pale, freckled skin.

Miss Elsie sighed. "I been here a long time and I seen men come and go. Come and go. Thank you kindly, darlin." She aimed her thumb over her shoulder.

"Them ole boys at the Alamo? Some heroes. Some of them boys, I knew them back in Tennessee. Used to beat up on women. Don't nobody know that but me. My cousin Maddie. Why that poor girl, she's got scars on her back cuz them boys used to whip her and once they took a knife and cut her, thinking they wanted to brand her like she was an animal belonging to them. Got her good. Right here." With her index finger Miss Elsie touched her right breast just above the nipple.

"And that Bowie. Nothing but a damn drunk. And a thief to boot. Stole so much land you cain't even count how much. Them boys ain't heroes. They ain't no better than a buncha drunks who come here whoring expecting me to open up my doors when they want, waking up my girls when they're all filthy and smelly. Now folks are talking heroes." She turned around to face my mother. "And that little meskin baby? The other day in church? Did you hear about it? Hell, they shoulda hanged that gringo. They shoulda hanged him for firing his gun in church. They woulda hung him if a white baby hada been killed. I hate to say it bout my own people but they woulda. Like a meskin baby don't matter none. I swear it didn't use to be like this. Ten, twenty years ago, it was downright peaceful here. Quiet, peaceful, everbody worked hard." She paused and coughed, wiping brown spit from her lips with a lace handkerchief. "All them years of chewing tobacco." Miss Elsie stood in front of her bedroom window and with her arms resting behind her back, she patted the back of one hand inside a palm.

"So many changes," she mumbled. "So many changes."

My mother sat on Miss Elsie's bed, a four-poster Mr. Byron Jones had shipped through Kansas on the Mississippi River and then hauled on wagons to Bexar when he asked her to marry him. I heard that the balding middle-aged man had surprised her one day, took her hand and led her to her room and there it was. A cherrywood four-poster. She said to me that's when it hit her that he didn't mind who she was or what she did and so she accepted the gift and married the man. It was as if Byron forgave what a woman had to do to get by even if men and women judged her saying all she did was make these young women's lives harder by letting them into her whorehouse. None of them thought about how they were just girls running from husbands or fathers who beat them. None of them thought how much safer these women felt among others who were also running and looking for some kind of refuge, any kind.

Miss Elsie stared down at the callejón below, muddy with potholes from so many wagons, from so many comings and goings through town. Without turning around she addressed my mother.

"Now you're here telling me my boy is done gone again. Dang it, Ursula. Why'd you let him go?"

"There's no stopping a boy who thinks he's a man."

"I heard he's got a new pony." Miss Elsie turned and wrinkled her brow at mamá. "When you gonna tell him Lena was your sister?"

"He knows." My mother readjusted a frayed skirt that dug into her waist.

"You and I both know that there's knowin something cuz we think it and there's knowin somethin cuz we done been told that somethin out loud. Seems to me nobody never cared to talk to that boy and tell him what's what. All this guessing and them secrets, heck, no wonder he's done run off again, Ursula." Miss Elsie hovered over a clay vase and rearranged dangling wisteria blossoms. She plucked out the dead ones and threw them on the table.

"I've done my best with that boy and you know I love him like he was my own and I treat him like my own blood. He is my blood. He calls me Tía and that's the right thing because I am his tía. I say the boy already knows Lena was my sister. How can he look at his own face in a mirror and look at me and not see the resemblance? We didn't raise a fool. I've got my reasons for not saying what you want me to say to him. You may not like it but that's who I am and where I come from and I come from here and that's the way things are done in Mexico. This is still Coahuila y Tejas and no Anglo Texan heroes are going to change that. Not ever."

"Hell, Ursula, you ain't gotta tell me none of that. Who you think you talkin to? It's me, Elsie. I known all that for a long time but you ain't listening."

My mother raised her head. The thin parchment of flesh below her eyes was dark and puffy. She looked at Miss Elsie, who stood at the table fussing over wilting flowers. Drops of murky water dribbled from the tips of stems brown and stringy and dead.

"Don't matter now. He's done gone and I don't know when I'm gonna see him again. I bet he gets himself killed this time," Miss Elsie said.

"He's a strong boy."

"Lots of evil out there right now and you know it."

"I know but he's gone. All the men are gone and that leaves us here to tend the fires until they return."

"Only fires you ever tended were the ones for that old man."

My mother looked at the floor as if that would elude what had been said. She fiddled with the tight waistband of her skirt and loosened a button that stamped a circle on her skin.

"Micaela, go to the general store for some calico. I need a new skirt."

I walked out of the room, closed the door behind me and slid down to the floor listening to that which Miss Elsie and my mother wanted to protect me from.

"He's marrying Micaela. At least he thinks he is."

"I guess he's got your goat now." Miss Elsie giggled.

"At least he'll look after her."

"Ursula, your daughter ain't about to marry your old lover and you know it."

"Maybe. Maybe not. Doesn't matter now."

"You plan on carrying on with him? After your own daughter marries him?"

"Don't be a fool."

"Well, I'm just talking bout what I seen for years. You think I ain't got eyes? You can fool a man bout them things but you cain't fool a woman."

"You're talking crazy, old lady."

"Sure I am. I always talk crazy. Keeps me from going crazy. Alls I know is that you cain't go and keep them secrets and expect them not to creep up on you one day. Cuz they will."

"My life's my business, Miss Elsie."

"Hell, Ursula, I ain't one to sit in judgment. Look around. I'm a whore and I live in a whorehouse and what's more it's my whorehouse and I keep whores for the likes of men like Walker and old man Barrera. You think I like what I do? Alls I know is somebody's gotta give them poor girls a place to live cuz they been run out of their homes by some mean husbands or papas or brothers or uncles who raped them or beat them or expected them to be their dang slaves. Well, let me tell you, here they got a home and I ain't never let a man raise a hand to them and if them boys is gonna get a poke, well then they better pay up. I ain't proud of what I do but I'm sure pleased they ain't out on the street begging. And your sister Lena, well, after what your cousins done to her, it's a wonder she lived as long as she did with a smile on her face every now and again."

My mother's sighs seeped through the woodwork.

"Only sin that child ever made was to be borned a pretty girl in the likes of a family like yours with so many of them danged uncles and cousins who treated her like a puppy dog chasing her here and there and never leavin her alone. I tell you. What them boys did to her is sinful."

I could sense my mother getting angrier. Although she had told me I had a Tía Lena, I'd never met her since she was kept a secret from our family. It was Miss Elsie who told me stories she herself had learned from my mother about a time when two sisters ran and played in cornfields. My mother chased her baby sister until they stumbled tripping forward giggling and high-spirited. They were no more than eight and ten. Two maybe three years later my Tía Lena's eyes were circled with dark pouches from lack of sleep. Late one night as they made a tent of the bedcover, their heads braced the arc of a fresh scented sheet that fell around their heads, she displayed blotches on her skin. Lena pointed to her breast and to her crotch, scratching her skin with tiny fingers saying that she itched. Red spots covered parts of her body.

"You've got some misquito bites, Lena. Es todo."

But the red itchy spots on her breasts and crotch were the young girl's allergies to her uncles and her cousins. That's what Miss Elsie made sure to tell me. At age eleven the white lace dresses that she wore to mass were already tight around her breasts and when her nipples protruded through the cotton, she felt delicate and fine until her cousins cornered her in an empty room of the mission and they took turns rubbing grimy hands across her nipples dirtying her dress with fingerprints muddy and filthy. She ran home in tears, stopping at the well to dip her hands in water and she smudged the dirt into her dress to appear as if she'd fallen. My mother saw her coming up the path to the ranch and although she knew what was wrong, suspected what might have happened to her baby sister, she did nothing except to take her hand and lead her to the kitchen where they sat and peeled leaves from cornhusks. The silken strings fell to the floor gathering into a mound. They sat silently ripping off the skin and setting aside leaves that would dry and harden.

"Anyways, don't matter now cuz that poor girl is dead. None of your dang family came to her funeral. Hell, y'all made like she was some leper instead of a whore forgetting who made her a whore in the first place. Them dang cousins and uncles and any man who thought he had a right to. Don't think she didn't tell me, why she told me everthing."

I could hear my mother's sighs get louder.

"Let me tell you something. I listened to her when she cried and I gave her a home where she was protected as much as she could be."

"Ay sí. Some protection."

"Go on. Go on and say it all jus cuz you're the one feels guilty. Yep, it was my fault all right. I welcomed her here and I made sure she had enough food and clothes and love to get by. Just to get by. Cuz that's all this place is. It's a gettin-by place for girls like Lena who was only left with that sorry choice in life. Gettin by. Sure is a sorry way to live."

My mother came out of the room so quietly I didn't have a chance to hide. That I had been listening didn't rile my mother any more than she already seemed. She looked down at me on the floor and said, "Vámonos."

As we followed the river back to El Pueblo, the wagon wheels swayed with a squeak that hypnotized and when I glanced at my mother's face and hands, I felt sorry for the way each had grown more leathery with the passing cotton seasons. She worked fields and buried babies. Her own and others. Once they were born and in her arms, my mother loved instantly whether hers or someone else's. She loved babies, coddling and protecting newborns from meanness and she claimed her last one had died from meanness. She was sure of it although my papi denied it. Venom so strong had crept inside her belly that when the child slipped out, a feverish anger seeped from her womb and she could not comfort the baby, born tired and angry, the way she herself had felt for years, she told me often. And as her daughter I did not want to hear complaints against my father. But she had strength, my mother, a valor belonging to soldiers in battle. Somewhere between the death of her sister and the death of so many babies, she had become a warrior whose grieving my papi ignored but it was her strength that kept us all alive. At the time, I didn't know any of these things. All I knew was that on the day we returned from Bexar, those babies' cries echoed in the river and Miss Elsie's accusations rang clear for me in ways I'd never realized before. I guess I felt sorry for mamá, Tía Lena and Miss Elsie 'cause there was no way I would ever end up like any of them. I was so sure of myself that I must have seemed like a big-headed fool at the time.

When we arrived at the farm, I was so weary I crawled out of the wagon hoping my mother would leave me be but she yelled after me, "El Viejo Barrera is coming for you. Tomorrow, he's coming." I didn't turn to argue.

I don't know if my mother heard the tapping at her door as she sat in front of her dresser's mirror brushing her hair, but I did. She probably chose not to hear, suspecting it was El Viejo Barrera but he ignored her silence and crossed the threshold and from behind boosted her from the chair with his hands on her waist. He raised her skirt and even if she might have longed to expel from her body Venustiano's hands, she allowed him near. When he kissed her mouth, she turned toward the window, probably hearing my rustling outside. I guess she must have regretted what had just happened because she turned and slapped him more from decorum than anger, I thought. He grunted throaty and coarse, then smiled and left as abruptly as he had entered. My mother sat on the bed examining roughness on once silky hands and said out loud, "You're not marrying my daughter, Venustiano," but he was already gone.

It was the first time I had truly spied on my mother and her lover and it was the first time she was aware I knew her secret. I couldn't face her after the particulars I had witnessed. I longed for an excuse and there it was. The next day, I hopped on a pony and set off after my father to a battle my mother disapproved of.

CHAPTER 5

I don't regret not having stayed behind on the day marauders plundered our ranch. Regret is not enough. Regret only implies disappointment or remorse and what I bore after that day was more than any disappointment or remorse that might pursue me for years to come. I became hollow. Repeating the story even if only to myself inflicts emptiness so vast that I have yet to fill that void.

By the time I arrived at the San Jacinto River, I was ready to do battle but I witnessed instead remnants of an ill-conceived crusade in which death and conquest were strewn across a field. There were piles of brown bodies in muddy pools of blood and I became so terrified that I ran through the field searching for my father and Jedidiah, not caring or even wondering about Walker, but saw no one I recognized and doubted if I could have recognized them with so many poked-out eyes and faces smashed in.

The battle itself had lasted barely eighteen minutes. To the north Harrisburg was burned and looted and the bridge to the Brazos River was destroyed leaving no escape route for anyone on any side. I arrived at an execution accomplished and witnessed corpses and soldiers with Kentucky rifles hopping over those corpses and I heard the soldiers whooping and hollering, "Remember the Alamo, remember Goliad."

I wore myself out chasing ghosts until I sat on my haunches and rocked for what must have been hours of me sobbing. The sun set behind me and darkness came quickly. A soft mist speckled my face and arms but I could not move until finally my pony came to my side and nudged my head with his and I awoke briefly from my dementia. I stood and took his reins and pressed my head against his so as to feel warmth from something living, then walked him to the edge of a line of timber and I fell to my knees and dropped my body down hoping to sleep so I could start my search again at daylight. Three days and two nights, I rummaged that field determined to find my father and my cousin, never once thinking of Walker or his fate. I watched vultures overhead and steered clear of them as they swept down to eat guts from decaying corpses and I fed my horse the dried fruit I had packed days before, days that seemed like years to me now. I took only small bites of the dried peaches.

On the third day I saw him. My father. I recognized his brown suede jacket and I recognized his boots but I stood paralyzed wishing I were seeing things. But I wasn't. I stood ten feet from his corpse and falling to my knees, I crawled to him. There was the knife mamá had said would be his end. I pulled it from his heart and held it close to my chest and then something came over me, maybe ghosts or spirits because I didn't realize what I was doing nor did I remember having done it. It was as if a strong spirit forced my hand and I cut my cheek from eye to mouth in a crescent moon like my Tío Lorenzo's brand and blood dripped onto my hands and onto my father's chest. Then, and of this I was wholly conscious, I sliced off my long braid and tossed it into a ditch and right away I felt strength come over me. I heaved my father's corpse to pull off the jacket and I put it on. I was in some kind of dream state or nightmare and if not for some stronger spirit advising me I may not have mounted up and left that field behind me.

I rode into the night with face throbbing from where I had cut and the wound bled down the side of my body drenching me crimson until I arrived home the next morning. I surveyed the patio in such disarray with pots overturned and lard caked on the ground that I ran through the hallway nearly tripping, shouting for my mother. I shoved past Walker standing at my mother's bedroom door and gave him the nastiest look I could conjure and when he saw me I caught sight of fright on his face and realized that my blood-drenched clothes must have scared him. When my mother sat up in bed with a face bruised and stamped, her welfare concerned me more than having seen Walker alive and unblemished from battle. The shock on her face proved she loved me and I guess I needed to see that love from my mother. At that moment, I needed to know we were each other's family.

"Mamá, ¿qué pasó?"

She touched my blood-spattered cheek and held me tight and shook her head but her whole body shuddered with tears and grief.

"The twins? Mamá, where are the twins?" I darted past Walker and searched the hallway and the rooms screaming for Ifi and Rusty, returned to my mother and her gaze dropped away from mine.

"Who did this? Mamá? Who did this?"

"Leave her be. She's in shock," said Walker. He stood in a corner of the room not daring to approach her bed. Walker stood tall and crossed his arms. "He did his best."

"Who?"

"Your pappy. I buried him."

"You're lying." I stared into him as mean as I could.

He peered beady-eyed at me, grunted and strolled out of the house.

"Mamá, who did this?" I picked up a damp cloth from her bedside table, patted her forehead and brushed hair from her face.

She pulled me close and tapped the raw wound on my cheek with her finger. "¿Qué te pasó, mija?"

"Nada."

"¿Comó qué nada? And your beautiful hair? Ay, mija."

"Papi's dead, mamá."

"Yo lo sé."

"I saw him. He's dead."

"Sí mija. Yo sé."

She rolled her head toward the wall and fell asleep. I stayed and watched over her, not able to leave her side. On her bed I looked through the portal at sunlight that cast shadows from leaves on the shutters. I held my palms up on my lap and scrutinized scratches of dried blood that I had not seen before. The house was quiet. There were no shouts from the stream and no pots banging in the patio, only my muffled sobs echoing through the rooms.

Not for a few days did my mother gather enough courage to relate to me the events of the day the marauders looted our ranch. She told how three riders, scruffy and pale-skinned, came toward the ranch ready to pillage lone women, knowing all ranchers had gone to war.

The day had started out all wrong, she said, with no one except the twins to help with daily chores and when mamá rushed to milk the cows, she spilled milk returning to the house, then promptly burned the last of the breakfast beans. She handed a cold tortilla and a short glass of milk to each twin and they complained to have no beans until she shushed them. After breakfast, mamá marched to the patio, as she always did, gave Ifi a wooden spoon and bent over a cast-iron urn of lard and lye that bubbled over fire. As she listened for my brother, who splashed and paddled at the river, my mother sensed a presence and from the corner of her view saw two men heading toward the patio and just then a third stranger who had skulked around back slipped through the archway of the courtyard and snatched her by the waist. I imagine her still, flailing and screaming. She must have cursed me as I would curse myself for years to come. Ifi charged and struck the cursed marauder with her spoon and made him yell but when he jabbed her tiny body with an elbow, she toppled. He covered my mother's mouth and pressed against her bosom but she kicked his shins with the heels of her shoes and Ifi pounded on him with her fists. He snorted and the other two men stood on the veranda, chuckling and snorting.

It was Rove and his gambling buddies. I was sure of it. I still see the image of that sonovabitch scooping up my baby sister and in the distance Aristus running from the river shouting Ifigenia's name. My mother falls back unconscious to screams that echo prophecies she had hoped to steer clear of. Rove and his marauding boys rode out like three scavengers with farm-rusted tools stabbing at the sky.

I was not to know the particulars of this story, that it had been Rove, until later. Right then, I was preoccupied with a rising vengeance.

In the night, I fell ill. I fought cholera that stirred up inside me again, having beat it three years prior but my ailment had not rid itself from my body entirely. The sickness had taken many including ranch hands leaving papi's cattle to graze the outlying acres neglected.

Fevered, I went outside to stand in the rain.

"Come inside, mija. You're not well," mamá called from inside.

"I'm all right."

In the dark I hid at the rear of the patio and picked up a broken wooden spoon and slapped it over a knee until splinters spliced my skin. I stood naked and beads of rain trickled down my nipples and bony hips that would become bonier still with my illness. When I was a girl, I'd come out in the rain and break off a chunk of soap from the slab in the cast-iron kettle and scrub my skin until I bled. The bits of dirt and leaves that trickled into the kettle made the soap bumpy and my skin scratched red from too much lye in the mix. Only when it rained would I wash. I was all gangly and skinny then and wore the same pants and tattered shirt that hung loose from suspenders that held up one pant leg. The other pant leg scraped dirt when I walked and my matted brown hair was almost always caked with mud but I didn't care how I looked or stank. On the ranch, field hands bathed in the stream shaking off dust and animal smells and I watched them in their long underwear splashing about and they would call to me to get in. I watched in the same pants and shirt, my underwear stained and caked with girl's fluids. When the winds were calm, I stood composed in the patio and then a gust stirred the air and my mother would plead with me to bathe but my father would grin and say, "Let her be, Ursula, let her be." At midnight, when thunder woke me, I would go out into rain and take off my clothes, put them in a tin bucket and rub them with lye soap. Like tonight. I scrubbed and cried as I had never cried and my tears fell into the tin's cold water. My father was dead, the twins were dead and my mother was harmed by the devil that had invaded our farm. My tears did not ease the persistent ache in my bones and inside my skin pain breathed like a living thing. With soap in hand I rubbed harder until I broke my flesh and my blood mixed with filthy water and as the soap dwindled to a small lump, brownish scabs like the ones I had seen before on Rove poked out from the white cake to let me know what I needed to know and although the sign was measly, it was enough for me.

"Micaela, come inside, mija."

"All right."

The next morning, I stumbled from my room and followed the path to the patio and pondered my mother who was already strong at work. She dropped what she held in her hand and a spoon toppled softly to the grass. Mamá was a tall woman and when she rose up erect and stately, I often thought she could hover above clouds and no one could reach her heights or have the inclination to do so. My mother could be fearsome and I was not so stupid that I didn't notice when she was her most formidable. She gazed at sprawling cotton fields, stooped over and rattled an urn with a stick and grabbed chunks of soap that she hurled to the ground. White crumbs scattered onto grass and dirt.

"I know who did this," I said.

Mamá was silent.

"This is all Jed's doing. He never should have took their money."

My mother picked up a big chunk of soap and broke it in half.

"I'm gonna find them."

She broke half chunks into smaller pieces.

"I mean it, mamá. I'm gonna find them and I'm gonna make them pay."

She stood up straight and held her hands palms up. "Look at my hands,

Micaela. Just look. I'm tired of hauling water and planting cotton and
hoeing the same cotton and killing weeds and killing animals for you all
to eat and I'm tired of these hands scorched by lye and bloody with thorns
from picking cotton. Look out there. Look at those fields. We've got a lot
of work to do and nobody to help us and no money to pay anybody to help
us. All we can do now is take care of the land the best way we know how.
With hard work. Your papi is gone and there's nothing we can do about it.
We're lucky if Jed shows up to lend a hand."

"After what he did?" I said. "You're waiting on him? After what he did?
Your damn precious Jed?" My face went red and I had to wipe spit from
the corners of my mouth. I could feel the cut on my cheek sting.

"I guess he did no more than you. Disappearing."

My mother bent down to break more slabs of soap.

"You blaming me, mamá?"

"All I said is we need the boy to lend a hand. Just lend a hand. Walker's
all I got to help me out right now."

I stuffed my hands deep in my pants, wiggling fingers clear through to
holes that I ripped. My mother looked at the holes that needed mending
but wouldn't get fixed until I draped them over a chair and slept and she
would sneak in the room to patch up the pants and leave them dangling as
if they had never been touched.

"Help me slice up this soap."

I picked up a dull kitchen knife and cut squares and triangles, piling
them on the grass. Tears rolled down my cheeks and I wiped them with
my sleeve and I coughed to unsettle the ball in my throat but tears came
anyway and I wiped them on the tail of my shirt, hiding my face.

She straightened her spine tall above me, wiped her hands on her skirt
and marched toward the kitchen door.

"El Viejo Barrera. He's the father. To the twins," I said loud enough for
her to hear.

She walked back unhurried and with fists balled on her hips, my mother
studied my tears then reached up with her right hand and slapped me.

I rubbed my cheek's budding handprint. Mamá pulled me close and
buried my face at her breast. She stroked my wounded cheek and cut hair
and would not release me but I stiffened a body that must have felt like
bones in my mother's arms. I hardened and she squeezed and we endured
the sun for what seemed like hours to one and seconds to the other who
would not let go and promised herself that she would not until I, her

daughter, was grown and married with children of my own who would doubt and judge and come to expect more than any mother was capable of giving. But none of that was to be. My mother held firm as I struggled shaking my shoulders back and forth to pry free but her arms were vast and powerful and when I fought more she softened her grip until I finally tore away.

She bawled out loud calling me to come back but I ran through the patio to my room where I lifted my father's rifle and raced outside with the firearm flung over my shoulder aiming at the sky. At the corral I mounted one of papi's mares and rode into nearby fields. I conjured ghosts along the road but the ghosts were quiet, listening for prayers that might save them from hellish destinies of wandering and seeking that which was lost. The spring heat dampened my clothes and my shirt stuck to my back and my eyes moistened and stung. I veered off the main road and jumped down off the mare with reins in hand and walked to a huge live oak at the crest of a hill covered with bluebonnets. Beneath its shade I rested with my papi's rifle at my side and my hat covered my face as I breathed in musty sweat. I dozed off for what seemed like a second when I felt a tapping on the bowl of the hat and it slipped from my face. The sun shone in my eyes and I could have sworn my father hovered above me, elbows extended into an arc with hands in his pockets. But it wasn't. It was Walker.

"What are you doing here?"

"Your mamma got worried so I come lookin for you." Walker squatted leaning back on haunches.

"I can take care of myself."

"Shore you can." He chomped on a bit of straw and tipped his hat back.

"I can." I slumped against the tree trunk.

"I ain't disagreein with somebody so disagreeable." He got up and walked over to the mare and pulled hard on the reins and spread open the horse's muzzle to inspect the teeth and tongue.

"Why did you say you buried papi?"

He ignored me.

"Did you hear me? I said, why did you tell mamá you buried papi?"

He continued to ignore me, inspecting the mare further.

"What are you doing?"

"Takin a good look."

"Why?"

"She'll bring good money. For somebody who wants to breed her."

"You're not selling her. She was papi's favorite."

"Darlin, it ain't sunk into that thick skull of yours, has it?"

"What?"

"How do you think this farm is gonna keep runnin?"

"It's not a farm. It's a ranch."

"It's a farm. Never been a ranch."

"Still not yours."

"I ain't fightin no girl about that."

Walker Stephens handled the mare clumsily and the mare tossed her head, shaking and spitting. The way Walker broke a wild horse or branded cattle was clumsy and fumbled. He got mad and harsh and deliberate, laughing when he stood before the steer with a hot iron at its eyes and nose so it could see and smell the fire and then he scorched the flesh jamming the iron on its hide longer than it needed to be. He didn't meet the animal's eyes like my father who eased them and said, "It's going hurt for a second." Not Walker. Never once had I seen Walker look a horse straight in the eye. He yanked them by the reins and jerked hard so that the bridle rings bruised their noses but he didn't care. Didn't notice and didn't care. That was Walker Stephens.

"He gets the job done," my father would say. "He gets the job done and has time left over to go to town and have some fun."

"He's mean to horses, papi."

"He don't mean nothing by it. It's his way. He sees something that's got to get done and he don't let nothing stand in his way."

"He's not one of us."

"That don't mean nothing."

"He's from Tennessee."

"That sure don't mean nothing."

All we really knew about Walker Stephens was that he was a loner looking for a place to settle since his father had no use for him and his mother was someone he'd never known. If he had siblings, he never spoke of them and anyway, all that mattered to Walker was land and more land and hands to help him till the soil.

"You got no business selling her."

"Go on and shut up and let me do my work."

He yanked at the reins pulling the mare behind him and mounted on his horse and rode fast toward the main road into town.

I chased the man and my mare aiming my father's rifle at Walker's back, fired at the ground and powder bounced off the gravel road. A dense cloud like a ghost appeared between Walker and me and through waves of dust that coated me, I ran and yelled swallowing powdery dirt but he was gone. The dust cloud thinned and when I looked down at my boots and the pebbled road, then up again into the distance, a tiny cloud lingered. I flung the rifle across my shoulders, hanging my arms over the length of the rod, my hands dangling as I walked home resembling a crucified figure without a wooden scabbard to bolster me.

When I saw her hunched over the well, I staggered to my mother whose body was hearty and huge and ripe for babies but she was done having babies she said. I dropped the rifle and put my arms around her waist and laid my head on her broad back feeling the ripples of her spine and I bawled out loud and I was crying for myself and what I had lost but I was mostly crying because it was me who was to blame for what had happened on the ranch and I wanted my mother to scream it. To fault me and no one else. Not my father and not Jedidiah but me since I was the one who abandoned her and our sweet twin babies. I was the one who had committed the crime of bad luck.

She poured more water into the clay pot and twisted around hugging me and lulled my cries until I tore away from her body in the same way I had torn away steadily since the day my mother bore me.

CHAPTER 6

All night I crawled and cried on my bedroom floor like a gutless coward from the missing of Ifi and Rusty and when I thought about their murder, my skin ached and I shivered from fierce desperation. The birth of the twins had lightened burdens on the farm and for a while my mother and father teased and laughed as they had when I was a kid. When Ifi and Rusty waddled their baby butts through the patio, their giggles rose up and beyond the prairie and it seemed we would always be hearing those giggles to make us all smile some more. Now the calm all around us was excruciating but the funny thing was that even in the silence I heard their squeals and every now and then I could swear I saw their chubby bodies running through tall grass to the river and back. The hardest part was that papi was also gone. He wouldn't have thought twice about going after those marauders but me, I was feeling cowardly even though I knew it was what I had to do.

At dawn I sought out my mother to announce I was ready for my journey but when I found her hoeing Walker's fields as if she owed him her charity, I had not expected to see a Mexican girl who resembled my baby sister. It was not the resemblance that caught me by surprise; it was the girl's body protruding ever so slightly.

Walker lived alone and had been alone as long as I had known him and as long as he had known my family but today he had company. I whispered to my mother's pony, Lágrimas, patting the pinto's neck, smoothing my hand down his mane to a coat spotted with ivory patches like uneven water drops, and as we trotted through the passage leading to the shanty hidden from the main road, a breach in the clearing exposed Walker hoeing baby plants of cotton. Beyond him mamá worked with a family, or what looked like members of a family, each one stooped in an arc with arms branched out on stick hoes and the bodies and the hoes cut crescent moons. Two men, a woman and a slight girl with honey-brown faces were swathed in clothes from head to foot covering every inch of skin.

The girl looked no more than eleven or twelve and what was clear to me was that she was with child and didn't know it. When she cleaned around the plants with light downward swatting, she barely cleared any weeds at all and if not for the woman who stooped beside the girl periodically, the scrubs straggling above ground would have stayed rooted. Walker hung over them like a driver heeding their every move. Occasionally, he plodded backwards and the field hands plodded toward him so he could see them when he lifted his gaze from the ground.

I slid from the horse and tethered him to a tree, counted ten paces and faced Walker.

He stood straight up. "You here to help?"

"Hell no."

"Well then, git."

"I'm here for my mamá."

"She ain't ready yet."

"She is if I say so."

"You ain't her boss."

"You feeding them?" I nodded toward the family advancing quickly through the rows except for the girl who worked none too hard.

Walker threw down his hoe and it thumped on the ground. He scratched the back of his head with his thumb. "Girly girl. You is somethin, you know that." He rested his hands on his belt and tipped up his hat's brim with his forefinger's dirty nail.

"They get a good meal at the end of the day. Same beans I eat, they eat. And they can pick all the peaches and corn they want. To their heart's content."

"They sure look scrawny."

"Ain't none of your business. I got my own land to plow and I got my own cotton to harvest and I got my own field hands to work these acres. Anybody I want. Not like it's easy to find help what with Santa Anna scaring everbody away. Get on outa here and let me do my work." Walker spit and bent to pick up his hoe and started chopping weeds intruding upon the cotton plants.

I walked toward the girl and saw plainly her little belly punching out of her body, not like she was malnourished, not like that, but as though something was inside taking root and preparing to grow that much more in a month, maybe two. Her eyes were black and black strands of hair hung loose from a homemade bonnet and her smile exposed a big toothless gap on her upper gums. The older woman, who could have been her mother, worked up a sweat hopping from row to row as she scattered weeds that clung to roots.

"Where y'all staying?" I said.

The girl grinned a silly side-mouthed grin at me, then looked to Walker who hung about ten feet away with one ear pointed toward us.

"None of your business. I already told you," Walker yelled.

My mother handed me a hoe and I checked her for a sign but there was nothing to warn that she recognized what I could see and what she herself had lived in the fields. More than once I had seen blood trickling from my mother's inner thighs down to the soil she labored. She would stop briefly to mop blood from her legs with her skirt then rise from the ground braced by a hoe only pausing to gaze at clouds before returning to the demands of the farm.

When mamá finally followed my gaze, she saw what I suspected. The girl's toothless smile showed and I returned the courtesy attempting to be playful while anticipating my mother's reaction but she said nothing of the situation and continued chopping weeds alongside Tomasa, the woman who was matriarch to the men and child. They spoke about family and the children who would and would not carry their lineage to the end of something better. The girl Juana was her niece, her sister's daughter, said the matriarch. Her sister had died giving birth to another child five years prior and the child had been buried with her. They had come up from the south like my papi's family and they had planned to farm and ranch but fortune and God's will had not been with them. The woman herself had buried three children who died of cholera in '33.

"Three of my babies dead and buried," she said clearing weeds and mopping her face with her sleeve.

One man was her husband and the other was her husband's brother and when they came up together her sister was still alive. Two sisters and two brothers married with hopes of farming and raising children to tend the land and praise its offerings. Juana was the only reminder of her sister and she cared for her niece as well as she could but she neglected her ever since her own babies had died. Her brother-in-law was a good man but an ignorant father and he drank on weekends to quell his sorrows but she claimed it was his excuse to drink since her sister had been dead for five years now. Mamá listened with head bowed as they diced unwanted plants shoving them aside and tidying rows in which the cotton buds would swell.

"We have to help your niece," mamá said.

The woman Tomasa didn't ask why and either pretended that she didn't know or truly didn't know that her niece had been messed with. Instead she talked about her sister Angustias who had urged them to travel north from the lower region of Coahuila assuring them there was enough farm-land for them and the generations to follow. Angustias sang as they traveled by wagon and settled finally on land not far from Austin's colony. That was in 1825.

"White folk came from the east with slaves and Kentucky rifles and we came from the south, just our own backs to slave on the land but looks like we lost most of what we earned," Tomasa said.

"Squatters took what we had. And damn Mexican soldiers made matters worse all around. Killed off Comanches just like the white soldiers did. Killing was done for the sake of killing but nobody stopped to think about that." Tomasa continued working fast. "Angustias and me, our mother had Comanche blood. She wasn't full-blooded but she had that blood in her and it's in me and in the little one too." She pointed to Juana. "Back then, Comanches come down from up here to our village to trade. One time, our grandmother saw a fine Comanche warrior and she said she was going to marry him and she did. She left with him but she'd come back every now and then, our grandmother. She come down this one time with our grandfather and our mother was already born. They brought her to the village to meet her family. That's when some soldiers saw my Comanche grandfather and shot him dead. For no reason except that he was Comanche. My mother told us over and over how our grandmother couldn't stop crying and she wanted him buried right there in our village but his people said no, he belongs in the prairies, we'll take him home and so they did. We think they buried him up here somewhere in these prairies and hills. Our mother said that's what our grandmother told her so Angustias always said we're going to go there. To grandfather's land. And so here we are but we come across bad times. Now my sister's gone but she's happy here somewhere near grandfather and I promised I'd take care of that child of hers over there but sometimes I think she's no better than a stubborn mule." Tomasa stood and rotated her skirt's hem and paused at an unsoiled spot and wiped her face.

"She's with child."

"Who?"

"Your niece. Está embarazada."

Tomasa smirked as if a bad joke had been told, then glared at Juana and saw finally what she had denied because such a notion about a child was better left unthought. She hurled the hoe and stomped across shrubs to her niece and slapped cheeks already red and burning from the scathing sun. Confused or shocked or both the child rubbed her cheeks with sticky palms and cried.

My mother shoved the woman aside, clutched the child and held her close. "She doesn't know, you understand, she doesn't even know," mamá screamed at the woman who mopped her sweat and tears with the skirt's smudged hem.

In the far rows the men chopped and raked and did not look up. Except for Walker. He stood and gawked at the women huddled around the girl but the arguing and screaming and crying did not divert him. He hunched his shoulders, worked a row and started another but then he did something that made me suspicious. Walker stood up straight, pushed his hat far back on his head until it fell, deliberate like. When he picked the hat back up he grinned devilish so I could see and then turned his back on us all.

And that was how my duty to the girl Juana became a responsibility I could not abandon. I wasn't sure why I got so involved but I did. It was as if Juana was my baby sister Ifi in disguise and my heart hurt to see this girl's body ill-treated. When I watched Walker twitch and turn his back on us after offering up a devil grin, I realized he had put this little girl in a calamitous circumstance.

To fetch Juana from Walker's barn in the night and carry her on my pinto pony to la curandera's hut wasn't hard to do. It's not as if anyone cared about her that much, certainly not Walker, and her aunt Tomasa fretted but was preoccupied feeding her family. In her own way Tomasa was relieved that someone was tending to her niece and that someone turned out to be me.

When I arrived late in the night with Juana, la curandera only had to look at the girl to identify her condition. La curandera was someone my family had come to rely on for remedios when any one of us was sick. My mother often sent me to her and I would return to the ranch with herbs from la curandera's forest of shrubs and trees behind her hut. The healer could bring someone back to life or even take that someone's life if she so wished but that was rarely in her design. She preferred to heal she said often enough and the results of her handiwork deemed that statement true.

She examined Juana and said, "It's women who got to clean up them messes." She stooped over a pot's boiling mix, her round rump barely resting on a rocking chair. Her thighs seemed to burst out of her pants and I couldn't stop myself from staring at her neatly cut toenails wondering how she kept her bare feet unsoiled. The old woman's gray hair glimmered in the firelight and for the first time I saw the floor of the hut was packed down hard so that no dust lifted at all. I imagined her stomping on it daily with her muscled frame and bare feet.

She mixed concoctions and from that mix gave the girl a drink. Juana drank as if she had been offered honeyed water, then sat on a bedtick kicking her heels back and forth and humming a tune unknown to me. The humming grew softer and the kicking lighter, then she put her head down and fell into a deep sleep. La curandera rose from her chair and walked to a corner of her one-room hut, pulled on a sheet that hung from the ceiling's vigas and made an enclosure, promptly falling asleep behind the curtain.

When shadows flickered on the wall, I jumped and realized my own silhouette loomed over me in fragile protection. I blew out the candle and with the light went the shadows. In a light slumber, I woke to vomiting and howling and as my eyes adjusted to the darkness I saw la curandera's body, an outline of outstretched hands that held back Juana's hair as the girl vomited into a tin basin. A puddle of blood sank into the canvas tick where it sagged and Juana moaned and scooted from the sagging middle until she settled down and fell asleep curled on the edge of the tick.

At dawn, Juana's bedtick was empty and blood caked its edges. I got up fast in a panic from not seeing her.

"She's fine. Already playing outside. Young uns are fast cures." La curandera stood over a pan of water, dipped her hands and scrubbed her palms rough against one another then dried them on an apron.

After breakfast of stewed hare and goat's milk, Juana and I tagged along with la curandera into the backwoods and gathered yerbabuena, manzanilla and other leaves and roots unidentifiable to me. La curandera did not tell me their names and declined to explain their uses when I asked.

"It's too much responsibility. Knowing these plants way I do. You come on back sometime and I'll tell you if you're good and ready to carry on that duty."

The next morning we ate more stewed hare and drank more goat's milk and la curandera packed a lunch of fried rabbit, tortillas and peaches. At the bottom of the basket I found yerbabuena and manzanilla wrapped together in cloth.

"Give her yerbabuena after she eats and manzanilla to sleep."

"Yes ma'am."

"Go on now. She'll be fine."

The sun beat down on the crown of our heads as we rode Lágrimas back to the ranch and although la curandera foresaw trouble ahead for us, she would not tell her visions, maybe thinking we were too young and frail to carry more burdens and she refused to be the one to impose more than had already been imposed. La curandera waited until we disappeared into the morning light before she returned to her hut.

I delivered Juana to Walker's farm and Tomasa was grateful enough although she was consumed by the fields chopping more weeds. She called out to Juana to get to work and I left the girl behind but worried for her prospects and admitted I could do little more.

I returned to the ranch and from a tidy distance observed my mother kneeling over a clay tub in the patio and as I inched closer, I saw water filled to the tub's brim and dead kittens floating facedown with paws stretched out from the center of their bellies. I screamed but she only looked up at me and frowned.

"About time you got back." Mamá picked up a kitten and plunked it in the water where it sank then drifted up facedown, tiny paws whirling round and round as waves rippled from the drowning creature. She pushed the tiny head down lightly until the paws quit whirling and the water quit wrinkling.

"Mamá, ¿por qué?" I cried and kneeled before the tub and pulled them out, one by one. Their heads flopped from side to side and I guess I hoped I might bring them back to life so I pressed the creatures to my chest and cradled each one.

"We got enough animals to feed. Get washed. Your dinner's cold."

The black tomcat that had fathered the bunch watched from a corner of the patio and I sensed he was peeved at me for what I had allowed to happen. I saw him judge me in the way only an animal can and then he turned and scampered to the barn. I piled the litter into a cuddled bunch then dug a small grave in the garden and put to rest their furry shells and covered them with black soil. In the morning, I chased away a stray dog that hollowed out the graves and bit down on scruffs shaking mischievously as if some secondhand toys had been found. I was already fuming from my mother's massacre the night before but when I saw the dead creatures spread out on the grass, I was so riled I ran to the kitchen with the intention of shouting at mamá.

She sat at the table crying. I inched my chair close to her and she placed her hand in mine then caressed the cut on my cheek. She looked at me and in her eyes I saw that she was sorry but sacrifices had become a way of life for her and she expected the same of me.

"Ya te vas, mija."

That she didn't ask and stated instead what she knew I was about to do made entire sense to us both. She understood that I was serious about my scheme and that no one and nothing was going to prevent me from gathering up my father's rifle and heading out on a journey that could mean my own end. If I stayed, each of us inside our quiet anger would only find new methods to punish each other for all that remained unsaid. It crossed my mind that I could truly insult her if I stayed back to marry El Viejo Barrera but he wasn't done with my mother and her discretion had almost fully subsided since my father's death. There was no reason now for her not to marry him. I wanted to wish her well but my muted rage kept me from doing so. All that kept me alive was my conviction to find the men who killed the twins during a senseless battle that ruined our peaceful lives.

The town already swarmed with men and women who joked, triumphant and bigheaded after that last battle was won. Beyond the river, towns would be settled and plans would be made and what my mother had foretold about Tejas would come true but it was a long time before I knew how right my mother was and how wrong papi had been. Tejas was not changing for the better. Not for our kind anyway. But I was not prepared to give up. Not now. Not ever.

Before sunrise the following day I led the pinto Lágrimas by the reins and elbowed my way through brush feeling stickers prick my cotton shirt. I tripped on rocks in my path, regained my stride and hopped on my saddle. In the distance through a window, the glow of a candle flickered like a shadow on the curtain, then went out. It was either the wind or someone's breath but I couldn't stop to wonder who or what; I rode through darkness, fixed on a concealed horizon waiting for the sunrise.

CHAPTER 7

Jedidiah Jones stood tall at the battle of San Jacinto but he did not last long once Kentucky rifles were aimed above his head. He ran so fast from the scene that he didn't have a chance to witness the conflict and its crime but knowing my cousin the way I did, I gave him credit for having turned up at the battleground at all. The way I heard it, Jed rode all the way to the field near the San Jacinto River with my father and Walker but when bullets were fired, Jedidiah Jones escaped and nothing was going to keep him from running. Like I said before, I recognized my cousin was too lucky to get himself involved in a gambling prospect that could turn cold sooner than he anticipated.

In some ways Jedidiah Jones was just like his birth father, although neither claimed each other and having inherited few of Walker's features at birth, Jed refused to take the name of the man who only gave of his seed. Jed said often that he grew in a brown woman's body and she was the one he adored, loved, missed and ached for all his life but never for Walker Stephens. And unlike Walker, who was a bug-like-looking man, my cousin was good-looking and he used his good looks to get by. Jed's eyebrows furrowed when he laughed or frowned and the eyebrows lengthened above the skeletal bone into furry thickness. A blond strand lightened the darker brows and from a distance he looked darkly brown yet golden. His hair fell wavy and almost black framing round cheeks and when he looked down at the ground kicking gravel he tugged at his back pockets, burrowing his hands as if he was eager to proclaim something you didn't want to hear. At nineteen his eyes were golden chestnut slits and the beadiness of them made him appear suspicious. But he wasn't. It was his way, his look. A smile, a smirk, a grimace or a chuckle, all were the same since he was not bad-tempered and instead took pleasure in being even-tempered, performing card tricks for all to see. The furrowed brows and beady eyes told otherwise but he was not that other thing that was his father. The man who didn't claim him was white and greedy although known to be jovial when necessary to fool and in some ways the son had inherited this last trait. The fooling trait.

When my Tía Lena del Río was pregnant she spoke to her son in her belly, called him Jesús and rubbed the ball that stretched her skin thin like a balloon. "Jesús, mi hijo bendito." Her sweet, sacred son, she said.

Lena hadn't loved his father. He couldn't be loved. She liked him well enough and he made her laugh when he came to see her in the whorehouse but she never felt much more than a strange affinity to the man from Tennessee. Esteban she called him instead of Walker and he didn't mind so long as she said it in private upstairs in her "whorin boodwah" he said. Downstairs in the saloon, she called out Esteban once and he recoiled and slapped her across the face with the back of his hand but she kicked him in the groin and he doubled over and choked on his spit chortling and coughing until he caught his breath and took her over his shoulder climbing the stairs to her room.

On a cool fall day she told him she was embarazada. He grinned and said "good luck to ya" and walked out of her room, which had become their private bedroom because he paid for her keep with instructions that no other man could enter that room and no other man did. She saw him on Saturday nights in and out of Maribel's room down the hallway. He grinned and greeted her when he bumped her stomach in the narrow hall and said, "why you sure lookin fat these days Lena, fat as a cow." And he'd stumble downstairs to the saloon and drink some more, play a game of five-card draw until somebody thought they caught him cheating and beat the heck out of him but he'd just take his winnings, sometimes snarling sometimes chuckling. That was Walker Stephens.

Jedidiah came into light on a summer morning and Walker was nowhere near, making it easy to give Jed the name Jones after the proprietor of the whorehouse and saloon. Byron Jones was a good man with Miss Elsie by his side and they pitied the boy born where no child ought to be born. They swaddled him and cared for him the moment his mother died and Lena died the moment he breathed. The baby cried for months.

The makeshift father, Byron Jones, was a rotund baldheaded man with fat fingers who wore a greasy bloodstained apron every day of Jedidiah's life until the boy was eight and Byron died. He choked on a chicken bone. In the rear of the saloon, Byron wrung chickens by their necks and chopped off their heads with a butcher knife and the boy covered his eyes and steered clear of chickens stumbling headless and collapsing. Byron plucked their feathers and boiled them whole and made soup that he sold by the bowl to hungry drunks. He sucked on chicken feet and gave them to the boy when he was done sucking and Jedidiah would bury the toothpick limbs. The boy never saw him without that apron and he smelled the whiskey, sweat and chicken fat on the worn fabric when his father picked him up and sat him on the bar for all his customers to see. After Byron died, Miss Elsie finished with the raising.

For the summer months, Miss Elsie sent the boy to my father to learn ranching and farming and on the farm Jed became skilled at a lot of things but he especially learned to keep away from Walker. Walker saw the lanky body and chestnut-golden eyes but didn't recognize a thing not even the thick eyebrows and brow bones, the only features the boy had that looked at all like Walker but Walker never looked at the boy anyway. Never cared to look at him even when he visited the whorehouse in Bexar weekly. Not until Jedidiah turned eight after Byron Jones died did Walker see the boy and that was only because he was at the farm regularly.

"Why you got to bring that boy here, Agustín?" asked Walker.

"I promised ole Byron."

"That ain't his son. Belonged to that meskin whore named Lena. You're damn lucky Ursula didn't end up like her."

Papi pitched hay in the barn, making a pile in a corner.

"A ole dead meskin whore."

"Well now, Walker, seems to me you was born from the same kind of woman. Leastways, that's how you tell it," said Agustín.

"Never said no such thing. I was raised by billy goats, Agustín. I told you that. Mighty tasty too, them billy goats." Walker smacked his lips and Agustín grinned big and chuckled.

Jedidiah watched Walker branding steers and hauling hay while talking nonsense and hated him as much as he could and if he ever forgot that hatred, Jed told me all he had to do was summon something hateful about the man and the feeling grew big again.

Walker might have sensed Jed's loathing because he taunted him and sometimes threw a pitchfork at him until Jedidiah ran from the barn to the patio and wrapped himself around my mother's legs. I felt sorry for him those days but she protected and consoled him especially since my cousin was prone to crying just as Walker was prone to picking on him saying, "It'll make a man outa him. He ain't nothin but a crybaby. That's all he's gonna be hiding behind your skirts, Ursula."

My cousin grew up on the farm and in the saloon between two homes. He was as attached to the one as to the other. Each home was a part of him and he loved Elsie, calling her ma, and he loved mamá, calling her tía. Each September he climbed in the buckboard and waved good-bye to my mother and the twins, who cried, but when he waved to me I turned my back. Papi returned Jed to Miss Elsie's saloon in Bexar and he was happy to see her and didn't complain about leaving the farm and didn't mind that he worked in the saloon during the fall, winter and spring. That was his schooling. His education.

Jed worked the front bar and became acquainted with Walker's weekend visits to the whorehouse and they nodded to each other at first but when drunk Walker teased my cousin and called out to him from one of the rooms, "Come on in here, boy. Let's make a man outa you" and he'd chuckle and Maribel would say, "Leave that boy alone." Jed's cheeks turned pink. As he got older he shuddered from hate for Walker who repeated the words like a chant, "Come on in here, boy, I'll pay the whore for ya myself. Heck you sure is a sissy-boy. Where you get them curls on your face? Look like a dang sissy-boy."

Father or no father, one day he hauled off and punched Walker. He punched him and Walker fell on his back and Jedidiah jumped him and slapped him again and again holding his collar with one hand and slapping with the other. "Sissy-boy," Walker said through his chuckling and coughing and drunkenness, his chest rising and dropping. Jedidiah slapped over and over with the back of his hand and his silver ring caught Walker's eyebrow and ripped it and the skin flopped open through to the bone. The ring shaped like an eagle with spiked raised wings had been Byron's and it wobbled slack on Jedidiah's middle finger. As he stopped to examine the ring, Miss Elsie yanked on Jedidiah's shoulders and yelled at him to get up and "leave a drunk be cuz he was nothin but a fool and only a fool fought with a drunk and you ain't no fool, Jed." Straddling the father he wanted to kill, he rose from his knees and inspected the ring bloody with a clump of hair and a piece of skin.

"Come on and hep me," said Miss Elsie and together with Jedidiah and Maribel they dragged Walker by his legs and arms and shoved him in an empty room and shut the door.

"Sissy-boy, sissy-boy," Walker howled and held a bloody rag to his forehead and passed out.

Jedidiah reached for Maribel's hand to lead her to his room but Miss Elsie shook her head no at Maribel for Jedidiah not to see and she pulled away and went to her room and shut the door. He shrugged and descended the stairs and stood behind the bar and served whiskey to customers and swallowed shots of tequila, then joined the poker game, played a few winning hands, started losing and quit.

That was in February of '36. He was about to turn twenty and Texas was about to become a sorry, blood-ridden country and although I had days when I loved my cousin I mostly hoped I'd be rid of him for good but no such luck. He would enter my life story again and again and with each passing season we intensified our unspoken competition for any and all things or people we thought we could have or that would love us full and complete. We were cousins with an ax to grind looking for the best place to do the grinding. How could I have known early on that Jedidiah Jones was to father the children I would claim as my own?

CHAPTER 8

I rode into the next town incognito dressed up in my papi's buckskin jacket to bulk up my body and his black gloves to cover my small hands. In his study, I had found a hat that belonged to my Tío Lorenzo and I wore it over my eyes to hide any expression that might reveal a feminine look but I was certain that I was far beyond any femininity with my cheek puffy and oozing pus. At the far end of the road, I tied Lágrimas to a post and entered through double doors into the saloon knowing I was not welcome without papi or Jed by my side but I chose to walk through those doors alone to test my new identity.

The same bartender who was accustomed to ordering me out squinted his eyes at me. I inched my way to the bar and slapped down a coin.

"We don't take no meskin pesos no more. Ain't you heard?"

"I need some help," I said.

"Help? The days for helping the likes of you is done gone. Now get on outa here before I get you throwed out. Willy! Willy! Get this little meskin outa here."

He looked me up and down and I got nervous.

"You need a whore, son? I got a girl back there but she ain't meskin. Boys around here don't want no meskins. You can go on over to Bexar if you want a meskin whore but my place is clean. I got Hilda in the back if you're looking for a little taste of white meat." He chuckled.

"I'm not looking for that," I said. I gazed down at my feet and felt my cheeks flush. "I'm looking for somebody."

"Ain't no meskins in here. Didn't I say that?"

"I'm looking for some men. One had a stub for a nose. He's got two fellows with him."

"Old Rove and his boys? You best leave them alone." He inspected me and I felt him get suspicious about me.

"What would you be wanting with Rove?"

"He owes me money."

"Well get in line, son."

He bent down and picked up a rag, whipping it against a pant leg. Dust motes fell into a puddle of sun shining on the floor. He scratched his head to rub grease on his fingers, then rubbed the crescent discoloration again slipping and sliding across glistening wood where his fingerprints smudged and dulled the sheen. Then he leaned forward, arms folded on the bar and studied my face. "How you get that scratch?"

"Huh?" I scratched my itchy cheek and peeled off a layer of skin.

"Come here," he said.

I stood still hoping he'd let me be.

"Come here, son. I wanna show you something."

I drifted toward the bar until my chest was pressed against it.

"See this." He pulled back his apron and unbuttoned his pants.

A few of the men snickered. "That's right, Benny, go on and scare the poor boy."

"Shut on up, boys. Don't listen to them." He pulled the waistband of his pants down and showed me a scar the size of a snake winding down low to his leg.

"Comanches done that. You know why? 'Cause I had me some meskins. Working for me. When I had me a farm. Them Comanche come along and said those meskins had stole from them. Stole their horses. They pointed to them horses and them horses lifted up their ears like old friends had come calling. It was clear as daylight what them meskins had done. Can't trust a meskin, no sir. Can't trust them. They up and stole them horses from Comanche and them Indians got fighting mad and done this to me. I ain't even gonna tell you what they done to your meskin cousins. Lemme tell you they deserved it. Them thieving meskins. They make trouble and next thing you know, here come Comanche and if good white folk are in the way, why they come after us too."

He stared at me and said, "Look. I'm giving you a warning like I woulda given them old meskin boys who stole from Comanche. Before you start looking for trouble, you best be sure what you're doing 'cause if you're not, you're gonna end up like them meskin boys and they weren't lucky like me. I got away with this little ole scratch but not them. Comanche don't like meskins who steal their horses. Now, get on outa here."

The men who hung close by snickered and spit and one of them winked at me. I walked backwards out of the saloon until the swinging doors slapped my back and I caught myself from stumbling.

CHAPTER 9

For almost a month I crossed plains and prairies, entered towns and saloons in pursuit of Rove and his boys and thinking back I realize I was too young and too stupid to be afraid enough to stop my journey of vengeance. Oh, I was afraid, believe me, but not enough to keep me from doing what I was raw to get done. I was told more than once, "Them boys is in Louisiana by now. Bet you'll find them there. Gambling in New Orleans." But I doubted they had gone far. These men were not clever enough or guilty enough to leave Tejas and so I kept searching through towns and saloons, discreet inside my uncle's hat and my father's buckskin coat so that I would not be seen as a girl vulnerable to scavengers' misdeeds.

After weeks of frustration, I doubled back to the Brazos and galloped upriver thinking I might have missed them in one of the smaller towns. One day, without expecting it, I saw a familiar stride. A brown fleck of a man rode into the path's curves without hurry. When I gained on him I kept enough distance so that he would not suspect he was being trailed. Jedidiah Jones paused where the river was deserted and stripped down to his long underwear, climbed to a precipice and jumped into the water hugging his knees. When he spotted my hat nudging out from behind a cottonwood sapling, he waded to shallow water and yelled out.

"You a fool if you think I can't see you."

I hid behind the sapling's trunk.

"Dang, you sure is skinny, gal. You're about as skinny as a foal's stumbly legs."

An impulse to swim took over me and so I ran out from behind the tree, soared into the river fully clothed with heavy boots pulling me down. That I sank didn't surprise me because I couldn't swim but I guess I was optimistic that one day I would stop sinking. Jed swam to me, picked me up by the scruff and dragged me to the riverbank.

I leaned back on my elbows coughing and sputtering. "You damn near drowned me."

"You was already drowning, knucklehead." He inspected my face. "What the hell happened to you?"

"Battle scar."

"Battle scar? What are you talking about?"

"Not like I saw you there."

"Where?"

"You know where."

He rose and gathered his clothes that lay strewn across a berry bush and put on his pants and shirt over wet underwear. Tugging at his bootstraps, he tucked a small knife inside the right boot. When he had finished dressing, he seized his pony's reins and led him from the river.

"Ain't you glad to see me?" I said.

He continued into the forest of cottonwood trees, saplings among older, mature trees.

"Don't you miss your cousin?" I yelled.

"Sure."

I leaned back, yanked off my boots and water poured out finding its way back to the river.

"Now look. I got me some squishy boots. Thanks a lot, just thanks a lot."

He walked back to the riverbank, grabbed my boots and laid them in the sun. "Let them be for about a hour. They'll be damp enough to cool your feet when you head back home."

"I ain't going home."

"You are."

"I'm not."

"Dangit, Micaela, I don't got time for your stubborn head. You're going home and that's all there is to it."

"Nothing to go back to."

"Tío and Tía need you. Ifi and Rusty do too."

"You ain't heard."

"Heard what?"

"All dead. Except mamá. No thanks to you."

I wanted to wound him as cruelly as possible and saying the words like that achieved my objective. Jed slumped over and leaned on his haunches drawing circles on the muddy sand with a stick. I saw tears well up in his eyes.

"How?"

"Marauders. At the ranch. They hurt mamá too."

"And Tío?"

"So you did run."

"What do you mean?"

"You didn't stay by his side, did you? Or you would have known he died on that field."

"I didn't see nothing like that," he whispered. His head was buried between his knees.

"I expect not."

"Ifi and Rusty?"

"Gone too." I looked away so he wouldn't see my tears.

"Who?"

"Well now, this you ought to know." I cleared my throat. "It was your gambling buddies. Rove and his boys."

He drew a look so harsh that I didn't think he had that kind of wickedness in him and I was glad he showed a tough streak that riled him up. His face screwed up and he shut his eyes as if to close off what he was imagining.

"Can't be. It wasn't them. Not those boys."

I paused and thought he was joking but when I saw him swallow some knot in his throat, I knew he wasn't joking at all but holding back from howling.

"You know it was."

"Nope. Not Rove. Can't be. Those boys were with me. I know what I'm telling you."

"You're lying, Jed."

"Suit yourself."

"Why you protecting them?"

"I just know what I know. Had to be someone else but not Rove. Not Runner neither. And Sonny's a coward. Won't find him making no trouble."

"You sure do know them pretty good. I guess you got to protect them." My boots had warmed in the sun and their moistness cooled my heels as

I led Lágrimas from the river and into the forest back to the path from where we had come.

"Girl, you better get yourself home," he yelled. "Soon as some ole boys get a whiff of you they're gonna know you're a girl and danged if I'm gonna be able to save you. You can't even guess the kind of trouble boys like that will make for you. And what did happen to your face? Look like you got scratched by a polecat."

I kept walking and mounted Lágrimas.

"Micaela, get back here. Okay, so maybe they did do it. And maybe they weren't with me at all. Maybe I'm trying to protect you from those sonsabitches. Maybe I think it's best you get on home and let me do a man's job. I know where to find them and you got to trust that I will. I swear I'll find them and slice up their throats clean through till their heads fall off. I will. You can count on that."

I jumped down, walked back and stared at him face on so he'd recognize that my earnestness could not be swayed. "You don't get to have the fine pleasure of whacking their heads off without me."

We mounted our ponies and rode through hills and grassland as high as our knees and the grasses brushed against our ponies, tickling their bellies. For comfort we told stories about papi and the twins as though the memories would conjure them and bring them close and although they were dead each story brought them back whole and living. Jedidiah told about the time he and papi caught the twins stacking pellets of rabbit dung and when asked why they were making so many piles, Ifi told them straight out, "cuz we aim to build a house with the pellets."

"A house? You cain't make you no house with rabbit pellets," Jed said to them.

"Sure we can," said Rusty. "You'll see."

And they did what they set out to do. "Built themselves a tiny house fit for a bird or rodent." Jed shook his head and laughed. "Just got to wonder, where did those two get such crazy ideas? I mean, who thinks to make a house of dung?"

"It's cuz they saw us making adobe," I said.

"But adobe ain't dung. It's mud. And water."

"Well, they were experimenting, I guess."

"Still. Sure is a strange thing to do. Thing is, that little house was sweet. I mean, it stank but it was a nice little home for insects, I guess, and those two acted like they'd built the Taj Mahal or some such thing."

"Taj Mahal? What in the heck is that?" I asked.

"Now see. That's why you should have stayed in school longer."

"I thought you always said schooling ain't what makes you smart."

"I ain't talking about being smart. I'm just talking about book learning."

"I got plenty of that. Don't you worry none."

We began to play as we always had, bickering and chiding each other, needing to forget the cruel loss we each had a hand in. I suspect talk of our familial ties kept us close for now.

The sun's bloodred descent persuaded us to set up camp a few feet from the river, where we built a fire to avert mosquitoes that were already buzzing and gnawing at flesh. Jed slapped his neck and looked down at his palm where a squashed smudge lay dead and then he slapped again at the welts reddening his neck. He glanced at my unblemished skin while I spread a blanket on the ground and buried branches for a pillow beneath the cover.

"Mosquitoes don't like you," he said.

"I'm lucky that way." I set up my bed and plucked out my red leather-bound book from my saddlebag and placed it on the makeshift pillow. I set a vial of indigo tincture on top of the book and paced around the campsite until I found a duck feather and shaved back the quill with the bowie knife I had recovered from my father's body.

"Where'd you get that?"

"Found it."

"I swear I've been looking for that knife."

"You've been looking for it? You want to tell me why it was cutting clear through my father's insides?" I gave him a hard stare and his face turned blank either from hiding fear or hiding something about papi's death.

"That wasn't me. You don't think that was me?"

He spoke so fast I got even more suspicious.

"It's your knife."

"Maybe Tío took it."

"Why would he take it?"

"I don't know. Maybe I dropped it and he picked it up, thinking he'd give it back to me."

Jed studied the knife I held across from him on his bedroll. "It was what killed Tío? Are you sure?"

"Well now. I saw it with my own eyes. Ain't that sure enough for you?"

"But when I left, I saw him standing. And fighting."

"You're a coward, Jedidiah Jones."

"And you're no better."

"I was there. Where were you?"

"I was there. Where I should have been while some folks were supposed to be back on the farm."

I whipped up my bedroll and placed it a good distance from Jed but he turned over and fell asleep. I studied the stars popping in the sky but Jed's snores got so loud I had to get up and shake him until he stopped. He turned over on his side and I went back to studying the sky when I suddenly saw shadows inside the forest. The oak trees swayed with the breeze and I squinted trying to discern what was out there and as the shadows got closer I ran to Jed and roused him again.

"What? What?"

"I heard something, Jed."

"Heard something?"

"Saw something too."

"You still afraid of the dark, you big baby."

"That's not it, Jed. I swear I saw something. I heard it too."

"Fine." He rose and picked up the rifle that lay by his side and walked into the forest. "Yoo-hoo. Anybody out here? Come on now, cuz my scaredy-cat cousin won't let me sleep till you come on out." He walked back to his bedroll. "See, nobody's out there. Now, get some sleep." He slapped his ear and a mosquito stopped buzzing.

I slipped into my blanket fully dressed and placed my hand over my chest and inhaled deep breaths. I swear I had seen shadows running through the forest. I decided to gaze up at the stars and their constellations instead and that's when I concentrated hard on the big dipper and the little dipper until they distracted me from what could have been made-up fears. I thought about papi when he would point out constellation shapes and I always pretended to see but could never make out the scoops filled with sparkles of light. I fell asleep dreaming of my father pointing toward the night sky.

The fire's embers crackled and woke me at dawn. Darkness and light mingled at this hour but as the sun's light grew stronger, the darkness fell off. I picked up my leather-bound book and opened to an empty page, dipped the quill into ink and scratched out a scene of the oak forest on the other side of the river's edge. I sketched Jed's face hovering above the campfire. He leaned back on an elbow, legs stretched, and kindled thin branches that burned long enough to brew coffee and heat up tortillas as tough as my book's leather cover.

"Here." He handed me a tin cup.

I took a sip and made a face. "Sure is bitter."

"Next time you make it."

"Don't get all thin-skinned on me. It's just a little bitter, that's all."

"I said, next time you can make it."

"All right. All right. We'll take turns, then. What else you got there?"

He handed me a tortilla. I bit into it and frowned.

"Now what?"

"Delicious." When he looked away, I spit into my hand and buried a chunk under my blanket.

"What are you writing there?"

"Not writing. Drawing."

"You an artist now?"

"Just drawing."

"Drawing what?"

"The trees, the river, that hill, your ugly face."

"Let me see."

"Nope."

"Fine. Come on. We got to go before sunup."

We rode on and soon enough the sun roasted our hands and the back of our necks. Following the path between the forest and the river, we reached a bend with a path into a tangle of trees and I held back my pony's reins.

"I heard something," I said.

"No, you didn't."

"I mean it, Jed. I heard something."

"Nope. Nothing out there to hear."

"I've been hearing it. It's like somebody or something is following. Inside there." I nodded toward the woods and hoped I could convince him this time without him thinking I was acting weak-willed, as members of my sex were so often accused.

"I swear." He spit and his horse also spit as if to mock me.

"Listen."

But all we heard anymore was my horse sniffling and his mesteño scratching his hooves on the ground, impatient to set out.

"See. Ain't nothing but Lágrimas and Moreno here, ready to get going and thinking you ain't nothing but a scaredy-cat. Right, Moreno?" He patted the mesteño's shoulder and the horse nodded.

We rode into the tangle of trees where the sun disappeared and darkness grinned from the borders of the path causing me to cover my chest with my hand and breath deep into my lungs. I picked up Lágrimas's reins, pulled back and held tight. We galloped ahead of Jed and Moreno, pushing harder, and when sun twinkled through branches above I slowed Lágrimas to a steady pace. Jed caught up to my side and kept quiet. We rode out of that gloom and into a path of light and I insisted again that I heard footsteps lagging behind us but Jed ignored me and rode silent letting me talk myself into fright and knowing he would have to calm me when we settled into camp again.

At night, it happened as he had predicted and I woke him as I had the night before and he rose again with his rifle, which was not even cocked or ready to fire, he simply held it to reassure me as he strode into the trees and yelled out for someone or something to show its eyes. Again, he neither saw nor heard any kind of creature except for a rabbit that had probably been the baby to the mother we had skewered and roasted for dinner. He stretched out on his blanket and set the rifle at his side and its length extended from his head to his ankles.

I shivered not from cold but from sounds I'd heard all day. It was not like me to be afraid and I had to wonder why I had become fearful after Jedidiah and I had joined up in our travels and I had no answer except that I might have felt insecure to rely on someone else and not my own daring for a change. The blanket covered my head and I shut my eyes so I would not have to see shadows the fire cast on trees but when footsteps sounded louder, I shut my eyes into wrinkled half-slits. A figure loomed over the fire and a hand reached for remnants of burnt rabbit meat on a spit.

"Wait just a danged minute." Jed grabbed the wrist of a girl who was pulling away but he tugged until she fell over and he held her down.

I flung off my blanket and saw Juana struggling beneath Jed who grinned as he straddled her body and pressed her arms against the ground.

"Let her go, Jed."

"Why should I? She was stealing from us."

"I said let her go."

"Oh, all right." He got up from straddling her legs and Juana ran to me. "I reckon you two are acquainted," he said.

"This is Juana." I wrapped my arms around her skinny waist.

"Juana?"

He reached down and pulled back the girl's snarled black hair. She flinched.

"You're scaring her."

"So sorry, little miss." He bowed his head to her.

"I told you I heard something. Didn't I tell you?"

"Yeah, yeah. You told me. How long she been trailing us?"

"Cariño, how long have you been following us?"

Juana whispered into my ear.

"She says she's not sure."

"Where's her horse?"

We whispered into each other's ears and I reported to Jed that there was no horse and that the girl had walked and run behind us smelling my trail and tracking my pony's hooves on the ground.

"Ain't no way a girl can run that fast much less track us," Jed said. "How old is she?"

"I don't know. I faced her and asked, "How old are you, mija?"

She shrugged her shoulders.

"She's a tiny thing," said Jed.

"I know."

"What you aim to do with her?"

"Bring her with us, what else?"

"No sir. She ain't coming with us. She found us, she can find her way home."

"We can't send her home."

"Micaela, she's going home."

"You don't want her to go back there, Jed. You got to believe me."

"Believe you? Why should I be believing the likes of you?"

"Because I'm your cousin and you got to believe me on this one thing. She can't go back to Walker's farm. Believe me. She's better off with you and me."

"Walker's farm?"

"Walker's farm."

"She got family there?"

"Sort of."

"Well then, it's settled. They'll be looking for her."

"They won't."

"What makes you so sure?"

"I just know. I told you, you got to believe me on this."

He threw his head back and gazed at the night sky. "Damn, damn, damn."

"She's hungry."

"Yeah, yeah. All right then. Give her some of that stringy ole rabbit and let me get some sleep. We're heading out early."

While Juana slept I cuddled her tiny body under the blanket and she wrapped her arms around my neck and I saw she had that same silly smile on her face. I couldn't help but think of Ifigenia and the missing of my baby sister made me melancholic but I was happy that the girl Juana had found me and that she had left a place that was nothing but damage to her spirit. Fish crackling in a tin pan over fire finally woke her and we got up to eat, then washed in the river, where I scrubbed dirt from the girl's face and hair until she screeched and giggled. After Jed packed up, he leaned against a tree and laughed at the sight of us.

When we headed out the sun was already hot and steamy on our backs and I was sweltering that much more with Juana pressed against my back, holding on tight with skinny arms wrapped around my waist. I told Jed the story of Juana and how her great-grandfather had been Comanche, like papi's grandmother, and that as far as I knew they might be from different tribes but still related in Indian ways.

"We might even be blood relations," I said. "Maybe my great-grandmother and her great-grandfather were cousins. Like me and you."

"Yeah. And maybe they was blood enemies 'cause the one wouldn't let the other live in peace," he said.

"Blood enemies but still kin."

When the winds picked up and the gusts blew leaves and twigs that scratched our faces, we approached gray clouds with caution knowing we could not turn back because there was nowhere to turn back to. We rode into rain and wind through a cloudburst and only our hats protected our heads from the downpour; that is, until I gave my hat to Juana and was left bareheaded and Jed gave his hat to me and he was left bareheaded. We rode through sludge that slowed us down and found a path that led straight to a passageway with a steeple towering above as if to guide us. We abided by the path until we reached the steeple and the town of Columbia.

We saw a man standing beneath a roof's overhang protected from the rain and I sensed that he scrutinized us. Jed ran across the muddy road and spoke to this man who pointed toward a barnlike building and then Jed ran back and we guided Lágrimas and Moreno to the stable. We hitched them up, fed them and patted them down with dry rags the stable hand gave us. Jed asked him a question and the man pointed back down the same muddy road to where the other man had been standing and watching and then my cousin ordered us to stay in the stable where it was dry and warm and for once I didn't argue with him and he was glad for that one moment that Juana was along to appease me.

Jedidiah passed with ease through those double doors and it was not until long after that night that he recounted what happened in that saloon. After he hopped in and brushed off the rain from his sleeves and shoulders, Jed leaned into the bar and removed his hat, placing it on the oak top. When the bartender raised his hand and shook his index finger from side to side, Jed set the hat back on his head, pushing it back to sit on the crown of his head and pretending he was equipped to take on what was before him.

"Got any good games going on in here?" Jed knocked back a shot of bitter whiskey that tasted like ammonia.

"Not for the likes of you," said the bartender.

"My money's as good as anybody's."

"You traveling with them meskins?"

"What?"

"Let me handle this, Mat." A tall, potbellied man stood next to Jed. "And give us another round of this cheap shit you call whiskey." The man rubbed his stub nose. "Well now. If it ain't my gambling buddy."

Jed fumbled with the whiskey glass, spinning it in his palms as if to warm the whiskey or his hands. "Well hey, Rove. How you been?"

"How I been? How you been?"

"All right, I guess."

"Heard you had some trouble."

"Huh?"

"Back at your uncle's ranch. Heard some boys did some nasty things to your family. That's too bad. Just too bad. I don't know why them kind of boys take to that kind of life. Making trouble for innocent folks."

Jed drank his whiskey and kept silent.

"I might be able to get you into a game."

Jed shook his head and pursed his lips but the grin wouldn't come. "Not interested," he said.

"Boy, I thought you said you was looking for a game."

"I guess I'm kinda tired."

"Tired? Tired? For a game? Since when?"

"I been riding all day. This whiskey's made me tired."

"I tell you what. I can get you into all the games you want. One or two or two hundred if you want. Come on with me and I'll set you up with the Colonel. We're riding out tomorrow. Going south. You'll get all the poker games and blackjack games you've ever hankered for. Course you might have to do a little bit of rough riding and rough dealings but hell, you up to that, ain't you, son?"

My cousin said he continued to shake his head, emphatic and righteous as if enough protesting would make Rove disappear into darkness or mist. "Not interested," and my cousin pushed his hat forward to gesture good day and walked out into the downpour.

When he came back to the stable, Juana and I were huddled at the far end in a stall with hay piled up high for our beds. He handed me a piece of stale bread with a chunk of hard yellow cheese that he pulled from his coat pocket. Juana and I bit down on old cheese and nearly choked on dry bread.

"Soon as the rain lets up, we got to go," he said.

"Recognize anybody in there?"

"Nope. Ain't nothing here."

"You sure?"

"Come on. Get some sleep. We got to go before sunrise. It ain't safe here."

It happened so suddenly that I thought I was asleep or in a trance but the day had not been that fortunate nor would the night be. I was fully alert when I witnessed that which would haunt me so long as I was awake and alive. They must have entered the stable after I dozed off although I had not planned to sleep at all but my eyelids weighed heavy and my chin fell to my chest for no more than a second it seemed. Grunting and sputtering woke me and I saw a man on top of Juana with his hand covering her mouth and nose and as she fought for breath, he grunted louder rocking up and down and that's when I felt another man, as big and as coarse, twisting my arms behind my back and my throat choked silent. I saw Jed reach for a rifle that wasn't there and he tried to stand but tripped since his ankles were bound by twine.

It was over fast. The one coarse man stood and his pink stub hollow of a nose shined in the moonlight as he buttoned his pants and the other man with an ear half gone hurled me down and said, "Help your little meskin whore." I crawled to Juana's side and lifted her body hugging her close but the body was limp and when I placed her face to mine, there was no breath. I tried to scream but no sound came from my mouth, wide open to the sky, silent and fraught with a pain that would lump in my throat, then pass to my lungs until my voice became a whisper. I cradled Juana and pressed my cheek to hers, still warm and flushed. Jed stumbled and crawled on his knees, his arms flailing and grabbing at air until he made fists and punched at his stomach and chest, bent over and wept.

We buried Juana far from that sorry town beneath a red oak in the same forest from which she had trailed us. The morning after we buried her, I woke to a deserted campsite and I stamped out the fire's embers, cursing Jed, cursing the men from the new republic, packed my saddlebag and rode on unplanned as to where I would go. The only favor my cousin did me at that time was to leave a bottle of whiskey, three-quarters full.

CHAPTER 10

Trusting family when deceit is in their blood is as complicated as not trusting them because their blood is in your own. Jed's deceptions were what I had come to expect and I decided, whether or not he intended, he had led his gambling buddies back to the stable. I was so sure about it that the reality of it became fresh on my skin and malice seeped up from my blood but being weighed down with thoughts of Juana complicated my certainty, making me unsure of what to do next. The horror of war and a world man-made of war caused me to hate everyone and everything. I was so gripped by hate that only whiskey gave me reprieve. More than once I thanked my cousin out loud, holding the bottle up to the sky and toasting all that was in sight. I toasted the oak and cottonwood trees, I toasted rabbits hopping by, I toasted Lágrimas, who ignored me mostly.

"Brindis a ti, mi cielo, y brindis a ti, mis árboles y también les brindo, animalitos del bosque." I began to sing songs I'd known when I was a kid and the twins were not walking yet so singing became one of the ways I entertained them. They giggled because I was loud and off key and like today, no one was nearby so I belted out hymns from church and ditties from cantinas and jumbled them up forgetting which belonged to which society. I was particularly pleased with myself for one of my inventions: "Amazing grace, how sweet her bosom that saved a wretch like me." For the first time in my life I felt freedom and I realized it was whiskey that had banished all troubles brewing inside my head. As I rode I drank until I was unconscious and fell flat on my back unable to come to. Not even Lágrimas's nudging could wake me. When I finally came to, a man hovered over my face and I heard someone yell to him, "¿Es niño?" The man who hung over me had a leathery face and a cigarette dangled from the corner of his mouth.

"Romundo, ¿quién es?"

I heard the same voice from a distance and I hoped Romundo was not in possession of information about me to reveal my real identity. Since he had come upon me when I was knocked out, I couldn't be sure what he may or may not have seen beneath my rumpled shirt. He squinted his eyes and gazed straight into mine.

"Sí, es un joven. Help me get him back on his horse, Octavio."

Romundo pulled on my arms and I sat up and stood on my feet. "I can get on my horse, gracias." My legs went weak as the sky and trees swirled out of control dizzying me and I landed on my butt. The two men hoisted me up and shoved me on Lágrimas and Romundo pulled my horse's reins and followed his friend with me in the rear singing.

That was the moment in my life when I stumbled into ranch work and the ritual of daily labor and evening whiskey kept my mind from all I had witnessed in my young, short life.

Weeks came and went and one morning when I rose from my hay tick I heard a sparrow chirping as sapphire light became visible on the horizon. Beyond the barn doors and along the pasture, I watched criollos roaming and chewing on mesquite grass. I had been cowpunching on a ranch called El Paraíso and I have to admit after all I'd been through, the place did seem like paradise. The ranch hands were nice enough and I told them to call me Lorenzo making sure to hide my face as much as I could behind my uncle's hat but after a while even if they stared right at me, the occasional pus still oozing from my cheek was enough to distract them from any suspicion of my sex.

"¿Bonito, verdad?"

I nodded my approval at one of the ranch hands who pointed out a black mustang with a mane so long and elegant the horse swung around in a gesture as prideful as any man's. I reassured the horse and patted him, then I joined the vaqueros to round up calves. In late spring we rounded up newborns out on the range and we branded them before rustlers faked their own markings. I cinched up my saddle, hopped on my horse and rode into outlying acres as far as twenty-five miles away.

I rode a mile out on my own and spotted criollos grazing at mesquite trees and chomping on pods weighted down and tapping their mouths. A skinny newborn bawled and wobbled next to its mother, unable to feed, bobbing its nose at its mother's udders and bawling some more. I slid from my saddle and caught up to the calf and tugged open its jaw to finger the tongue. It was split as I suspected. I shook my head and petted the frightened creature, then picked it up and whistled to my horse to follow. I walked nearly a mile and felt my arms tired but continued until I reached the corral where a few of the men had stayed back preparing the fire and irons.

"Ya ain't supposed to carry them dogies," said Octavio. He slapped his hat against his thigh and dust spread into an orb. "You're supposed to round it up and let it run with the others."

"You're going to break your back," said Romundo.

I staggered closer struggling to keep the calf from jumping out of my arms. "This baby's been handled by rustlers," I said. Putting the calf down, I hugged its neck to my hip.

"No puede ser," said Octavio.

"Look in her mouth."

The calf bawled and fell on wobbly legs. Romundo opened the calf's mouth and saw the tongue had been split. "Take her in the barn. Ask La India to give you some mush. You're going to have to feed her yourself."

"Looks like she ain't been weaned yet," said Octavio.

"I guess I figured that," I said.

They all called the cook La India for her cinnamon color and although she had only been on El Paraíso for less than a week, I had peeked in on her more than once. Before I reached the kitchen, she placed a bucket of mush outside and disappeared. I picked up the bucket and steered the calf to the barn tending to it as it bawled for its mother. "You can't suckle with that tongue, sweetheart. Might as well settle in and settle down." I fed mush to the newborn, putting the soft feed in its mouth and the calf swallowed and dropped down in a corner to sleep.

The roundup brought in twenty-five to thirty calves and I wondered if we'd find more with split tongues but whether we did or didn't, we'd hear about it from the hacendado anyway. One hurt calf meant others might have been taken but we had no way of knowing and I didn't care. It wasn't my ranch and they weren't my criollos.

We penned them all up in two separate corrals, one for the mothers and the other for the babies. I brought in around five more on my own and stood studying the little ones wondering how many would make it to maturity and as I prepared to rope them for branding I thought back on Juana and her innocence but that led me to thoughts of Ifi and Rusty so I expelled the rumination as quickly as I could because I didn't have the time to conjure sweet memories right then.

I mounted Lágrimas and with a rope's end tucked inside my belt, swung the six-foot lariat above my head at least twice, then tossed a smooth loop over a calf's head. I yanked on the rope and slid down my saddle gripping tightly until I advanced on the calf and with my shoulder shoved it down on its side. I snatched a string attached to the rope from between my teeth and tied the front leg, then swung its two back legs forward, tying all three feet in two fast wraps and knotting the rope. Octavio ran over and with the branding iron burned a pictograph of a rabbit with long ears in the shape of curlicues on the animal's left hip. The work of branding went late into the night and I was weary and hungry by the time we delivered the last baby to its mother. Mothers and babies quieted after a long day of separation and the ranch itself was peaceful, the sun having set and the moon hanging over the trees.

I joined the vaqueros at a long table under a cypress tree set with candles to light the feast of roasted cabrito, frijoles, warm tortillas and chile peppers so hot that they competed with each other to see who could eat the most.

"Romundo, ask La India if she wants hot chile," said Octavio.

We had not seen her standing in the dim silhouette of the cypress and when she heard Octavio's voice she stepped forward so that the moonlight shone on her black hair and her eyes like copper pools glistened.

"Romundo, tell your friend that I've had enough old chile to last me a lifetime." She turned and strolled back to la casa grande and I thought I saw her glance at me and raise an eyebrow.

"Ya ves, she doesn't want any of your old chile, Octavio." The men laughed and ribbed Octavio.

"Pues, it's her chile," said Octavio.

It was barely dawn and stars glittered in the sky and the moon sparkled on the path to la casa grande when I saw La India alert at the kitchen door as if she had been waiting.

"You're up early," said La India.

I took a pail of mush from her hand and her finger lightly grazed mine and when I looked up at her eyes I saw again her eyebrow arched in some sort of recognition or message.

"Gracias." I tipped my hat's brim and walked away side-glancing, tripping on myself but recovered before I fell.

La India's apron flew up with the breeze and I saw her legs, solid and unreserved, and she promptly gathered her skirt and fanned the width stretching it out with both hands and bowed to me like a dancer I had seen in Bexar during fiestas.

I fed the calf, then rode out on Lágrimas searching for clues of cattle rustlers. That I found none had as much to do with being absentminded as with my indifference to clues or tracks. I plunked down near the riverbank and chewed on a blade of grass unable to chase away images of La India's skirt fanning red and orange print. The sight of her legs raced through my mind so I shook my head to wipe those images away and my hat toppled. I pulled on my hair and spoke out loud as if the pronouncement would prevent a need that had already rooted itself in my body. I grabbed Lágrimas's reins and he waggled along beside me as I patted his neck.

I strolled for a while then mounted Lágrimas and rode slow and easy back to the ranch. Octavio and Romundo sat under a row of cottonwoods smoking cigarillos.

"Te buscaban," said Romundo.

"¿Quiénes?" I said.

"That sweet young creature," said Octavio.

"Heck, you could have fed her," I said.

"You'd like that, ¿verdad, Romundo?" said Octavio.

"Shut up, old man," said Romundo. "La India. She's looking for you."

"Me? What for?"

"Quién sabe. Go ask her."

I walked the path to la casa grande and when I saw her pouring water from an urn onto red and violet flowers, my heart fluttered in an unrecognizable manner. La India spoke to the flowers as water cascaded through her fingertips. I felt myself spying. Right then, I returned to the barn where I busied myself sweeping loose hay and gathering eggs hidden in nooks and cracks, often covered by hay or nesting in sight. After I collected all the eggs I could find, I placed them aside in a pail and decided to repair the barn's loose boards that were sure to flap when the northers blew through and although northers were not expected until fall, I thought it was as good a time as any to repair rotting planks. On the back wall of the barn, I kicked two decayed timbers and squeezed through to stand outside, then picked up a two-by-four. I tossed it through the crevice and nailed it down against steady boards, hammering hard and deliberate until they were secure against the bottom plank. Just as I felt content with my occupied self was when I peeked through a notch in the wood to see her legs. La India stood in the barn and set a plate of chile relleno on a small table that rested next to my bedtick.

"I've brought you supper."

I was silent.

"Aren't you hungry?"

I squeezed through the crevice and felt a nail rip the back of my shirt, severing flesh from my shoulder. Blood trickled down my back.

La India approached me and touched the cut through the torn shirt.

"Come to the house. I'll put yerba mansa on the wound."

"I'm fine."

She glared at me. "That's a rusty nail."

I twisted my neck to see blood soak through the cloth. "It's a scratch. I'm fine."

"Take off your shirt. It's getting bloodstains."

She started to unfasten the top button but I backed away to steer clear of her. I could see she was confused.

"It's fine."

"You're stubborn," she said.

"I guess."

"Let me have the shirt. I'll mend it for you."

I backed off farther and clutched my collar.

She scanned my chest then pointed to the plate of food on the side table.

"Are you going to eat?"

"Looks good."

She raised an eyebrow, then turned and walked out of the barn and I heard myself shouting after her and although I wanted her to stay instead I thanked her for the food. I sat on my bedtick and with the plate on my lap ate the chile relleno and mopped up sauce with corn tortillas. I patted my cut and felt the wound sting. As I started to unbutton my shirt I heard footsteps and saw her enter.

She returned with a poultice of yerba mansa and sat on the bedtick next to me and ripped the shirt at my shoulder, making me panicky for so many reasons I couldn't count them all. She pressed a warm dressing against the cut and held it tight as she wrapped a bandage over my arm and when she twisted the bandage under my arm's crook she brushed against the binding at my breast. I tried to pull away.

"I'm done," she said.

"What's this for?" I sniffed at the poultice.

"Yerba mansa will heal the cut. It cures a few extra things."

"Like what?"

"Like a weak heart."

She raised her black eyebrow and picked up the empty plate and disappeared so fast I didn't have time to think on how I could have been less prickly but I knew I was only protecting myself from someone I had only just met.

I touched the poultice and lay down on the uninjured shoulder and stared out through the hole in the barn that was like a window to the back pasture where darkness descended upon weeping willows, their leaves spreading shadows. I slumbered and woke to tranquility but the nearly full moon that shone on my face through my makeshift window made me twitchy and sweaty. I sat up and when I saw my bare arm I remembered the poultice and felt the fever in my body inching down from my wound to my chest and my stomach. My waist and legs were drenched in sweat and beneath my tattered shirt my breasts were bound so tight I removed the shirt and the sheath against my breasts, put on another shirt and finding Lágrimas awake, whispered to him to follow. We strolled to the far end of the stream where a waterfall was covered by brush and created a hidden alcove. I bathed here often late in the night when the vaqueros were asleep in their own bunker beside the barn. At the waterfall I removed my clothes and hung them on a rosemary bush, then slipped into the water easy, waiting for coolness to calm my skin.

I hadn't expected to see her. La India bathed in the moon's shadows, her hair falling down her shoulders and back and beads of water fell from the tips of her hair to the arch in her buttocks. I took a hushed breath, released it like a whisper and stood in moonlight. I was aware of that which I could no longer wrestle. Her cinnamon skin glistened and I was done for. In the icy stream, I paused when she turned and stared at me. I feared she might circle back to herself but instead she inched toward me, placed her lips on my shoulder and with the flank of her hand grazed my breast, touched my injured cheek, then cupped my shoulder's wound. I pulled her close until no cleft of air divided us and we caressed beneath water. I dared not move beyond the shallow center of the stream.

"Does it hurt?" She tapped the cut on my shoulder.

"No." I answered without thinking and wondered why I had said what wasn't true.

We stayed like that until she paused and I was sad to feel her pull away but when she tucked her arm inside mine, she led us to the water's edge where we lay upon soggy grass and kissed until my mouth ached and her loins stung, she said. I breathed in the moonlight's air feeling warm and secure from her nearness. I sat up and took a long deep breath and filled my lungs with something unknown to me. Something that was not sorrow. I did not recognize all I felt.

"You're running," she said.

"Running?"

She looked at me with that same raised eyebrow. I felt as if the eyebrow was linked to my gut in some way because every time she raised it, my gut jolted nervous and happy. She had that way about her. Making me feel opposite things at once and the confusion of it all made me forget who I was and what I was doing.

"Someone disguised the way you are has got to be running from something," she said.

"This is how I dress."

"Like a boy?"

"Yeah."

"But you're not."

"I guess I know that."

"I still think you're running."

"Maybe."

"Am I going to get any straight answers out of you?"

"I been giving you straight answers, darlin."

"Okay then. What's your real name?"

"Who wants to know?" I laughed because I was deliberately annoying her.

"My real name is Clara. Now tell me yours."

"Just Clara?"

"For now. Just Clara."

"What are you hiding, Clara?"

"Who said I was hiding anything?"

I shook my head and grinned from the bottom of my soles all the way to the top of my head's crown. Someone like Clara had never walked into my life before but here she was. An apparition. Lying delicate and simple with long hair spread behind her head like she was in the air. Flying. She smiled up at me and a sharp twinge went through me.

"Well then, tell me your name."

"Micaela Campos. See, I'm not afraid to give my full name."

"Anyone else know?"

"Just you."

"Just me." She touched my hand and yanked on my arm.

"¿Qué?"

"Don't you think they'll find out?"

"Find out what?"

"That you're a woman."

"Who's going to find out? I'm not telling. Unless you plan to?"

"Why would I tell?"

"I don't know. I hardly know you."

"You hardly know me?" She sat up fast.

"I mean, we barely met."

She tapped my arm. "Come closer and get to know me better."

I kissed her cheek and we lay back down on the damp grass and its chill soothed me from the night's humid air. I held her so near that sweat dripped between our bodies.

"I want children," she said. "Lots of children. Running around, laughing, playing jokes on each other, eating the food I make them. All happy and fat."

"Children? Why?" The mention of children caused dread within me. I could not stomach the pain of losing them to a vile world.

"To see them all running around giggly and messy, that's why. You got something against children?"

"No, no. Course not." I studied her cheekbones, smooth and golden brown. "How you plan on having them?"

"Same way as always."

I had only met her and already I felt like I was drowning.

"You plan on getting married?" I asked.

"Why would I do that?"

"To have children. And a family."

Clara tossed her hair back, laughed and grabbed my face between both her hands. "Preciosa, eres bien preciosa." She kissed my lips so kindly that I felt tears swallow up my face. Suddenly, all the treachery and blood that had come before me and that would come after today swept through me in that kind, tender kiss and I sensed that Clara was fierce enough for someone wounded, inside and out, like I was. She understood things before I did. And she purged me of the hurt I had been carrying for so long. The thing was, I wasn't sure I could do the same for her. I wanted to try.

"It's hard out there," she whispered. "I know."

Her forehead touched mine and she wiped away my tears with her thumbs and kissed my eyes. That's when I cried with so much force that I almost became embarrassed of myself but the way she cooed and pacified me made me feel like I could be anything with her and she wouldn't mind. We both got up to dress and as I stared at her naked body I felt such solace that I thought, maybe we can have a family together. Maybe that's what she meant. But I didn't have the courage to ask her. I'll ask her later. For sure I'll ask her later.

In the morning I saw Clara at the breakfast table under the giant cypress tree and I sat silent eating frijoles con huevos with the vaqueros who were so loud slurping on their coffee and joking as they always did that I wanted to scream at them to shut up.

"I need to go to town." When Clara spoke they quieted.

"Take the buggy," said Romundo.

"I need someone to help me. I can't load so many pounds of frijoles and flour by myself."

"Ya ves, Romundo. Let one of us go with her," said Octavio.

"Tú," Romundo tipped his chin up at me, "round up a couple of them lady-broke geldings and hitch them up."

The men laughed and ribbed each other as I tripped on my own two feet rushing to the corral.

As we rode, I felt myself grinning and got embarrassed of my transparent emotions but to have Clara by my side was enough to make me forget grief that had come before today. My impulses stretched across all divides and boundaries and suddenly I was so happy I began to talk about Ifigenia and Aristus.

"You'd love my baby sister and baby brother," I said without thinking how I'd said it.

"How old are they?"

"You mean, like right now?"

She looked at me funny after I asked that question and I realized that was the moment to tell her they were gone. I don't know why I couldn't.

"They would be about eight years old."

"Both of them."

"Son gemelos."

"Can you tell them apart?"

"One's a boy, the other's a girl."

"But can you tell them apart?" she repeated and I guess I understood why she was asking.

"Rusty dresses like a boy and Ifi dresses like a girl."

Clara grinned and that's when I saw how plump her lips were. I'd felt her lips but had not seen them in clear daylight so close to me.

"When they were really little, like about two years old, maybe smaller, I'd sing to them and they'd giggle and giggle and imitate me. I decided to make them this stage, you know, a platform with a tiny roof over it and a big ole space between the floor and the roof. All open. They loved that little stage. They used to sing and dance on it and play with these puppets that our mother made for them."

"Don't they still use it?"

"Huh?"

"They're not that old. They must still use it, right?"

"No. I mean, I don't really know."

We sat in silence for a moment and although I wanted to say more about the twins, I couldn't. Everything I'd said was a lie.

"How'd you know about stages and puppets and things?"

"Bexar. Every summer dancers would have some kind of show. Family would go to the extravaganzas. The twins loved it." That part was not a lie.

"Seems to me you're good with the raising of children."

"I guess. Never really thought about it."

"Seems you'd be pretty handy to have around if a woman had a few children that needed raising."

"I guess so."

"Why don't you go back home? To see them."

"I can't."

"Why not?"

"I just can't, that's all."

"Why?"

Clara's insistence annoyed me especially because I could not tell the truth of what happened that day at the ranch. That I was the reason for the murder of the twins. I got quiet and she took my hand and squeezed.

We reached town soon after and she purchased food at the mercantile and I loaded the wagon with twenty-pound bags of beans and flour and as I paused to kick manure from my boot I looked up at a man who blocked Clara's path from the store to the wagon.

"Looks to me like we got ourselves a nigger lady in town," he said.

Clara sidestepped to avoid him.

"Boys, take a look. I betcha she's running. Ain't ya, nigger lady? You running from your master?"

I flew up to the walkway and stood between the man and Clara. His breath smelled sour from morning whiskey.

"That's enough, mister," I said.

"Enough? Hell, boy, I aim to make some money off her hide."

"I don't think so," I said.

"Who the hell are you? Look like some greaser is all. Didn't we get rid of the likes of you at San Jacinto? You ain't no better than this nigger." He reached around me and grabbed hold of Clara's arm.

I gave a swift chop to his arm, then drew back and punched him square on the nose. He tumbled into the horses' water trough and staggered to find his footing as he held his bloody nose.

"You dirty greaser!"

I hopped onto the wagon and pulled Clara up beside me and although we rode away fast, we could still hear him howling.

"You ain't seen the end of me!" he shouted.

We drove back to the ranch without speaking. The expression on her face told me she was not in any kind of humor to tell me what had just happened and I thought best to leave her discomfort alone unless she brought it up herself. After arriving, I held out my hand to assist Clara but she refused and stepped off the wagon and strolled to la casa grande, entering the patio and withdrawing to her hovel off the kitchen.

"¿Qué pasa con La India?" asked Romundo.

"Nada," I answered and walked back to my corner of the barn wondering what to do. Already I missed her.

I guess I wasn't too surprised when the white man I knocked around in town appeared at El Paraíso the next morning. I hid behind a cottonwood tree, smoking un cigarrillo with Romundo.

"Gringo," said Romundo.

"What does he want?" I said.

"Work."

"I thought Octavio didn't hire gringos."

"Sure he does."

"This one's trouble."

"Friend of yours?"

"Saw him in town yesterday. He's trouble."

I got up and called to Octavio, who stood talking to the troublemaker. Octavio listened to me and went back and told him what I hoped he'd say. When the man saw me he started yelling.

"Hey, where's that nigger lady? Keeping that brown sugar all for yourself? Come on now, where is she?"

I lunged towards him and the look on my face must have said it all because Octavio and Romundo held me back and ordered the troublemaker to leave.

"Y'all a bunch of nigger lovers here? Is that it? A decent white man can't get no job from a bunch of nigger lovers? If that don't beat all." He peered at me, his eyes bloodshot from too much whiskey. "How old are you? You ain't no man."

When he stared clear into me and said I was not a man, I got panicky. What was even more telltale was the way Romundo squinted at me, then looked away real quick as if he knew something too.

"You ain't nothing but a boy," said the troublemaker. "Just a little ole boy. Look at you. You about as short as a tall hold on a bear."

That didn't sound so short to me but I didn't really grasp the man's meaning anyway. I was just glad he focused on my height and not my sex, which I thought for sure he would be revealing.

"All right. Time for you to go," said Octavio. "I told you we don't need no help on the ranch right now."

The troublemaker got back on his horse and only then did I see Clara at the kitchen door. I tipped my hat to her and she shut the door. That's when I saw Romundo gawking at the both of us as if he was reckoning something. He stared at me and wouldn't let up. I didn't like his eyes fixed on me that way. Not one bit. It was as if he was wanting to do something to me. Something a man would want to do to a woman. I didn't like it but I didn't feel like I could tell him to stop without calling attention to my awkward self. I told him anyway.

"Why you looking at me like that, Romundo?"

He was quiet and bit down on his cigarrillo. In his eyes I saw wheels turning as if he was figuring something out. I turned away from him, afraid my shirt might be open or worse, well, there really was no worse. Things felt all twisted up for me so I walked away without letting Octavio or Romundo see my face 'cause suddenly I felt self-conscious. My wound was healing and my cheeks probably looked too soft 'cause even a boy would have had a bit of peach fuzz, of which I did not.

My thoughts were mostly on Clara and how she had shut that door so eagerly without so much as a wink or wave to me. Had I known that was the last time I would see her for a while, I might have done something different but then again, I was too young to know when real love was upon me. What I did know is that the little speck of happiness I had on El Paraíso was gone. She must have run out in the night because the next morning the ranch hands were already frying eggs as if she'd never even been there. I ate my breakfast, packed up and mounted Lágrimas without bothering to say good-bye. Was I going to look for her? I was too mixed up in my head to consider what it meant to go looking for a woman I barely knew. And yet still I hoped I'd see her again. I prayed I'd see her again. I longed with every piece of me that was still breathing that I'd see her again even if I didn't know what I'd do if I saw her.

CHAPTER 11

I had been riding for weeks when a fierce rainstorm forced me to stop and look for cover beneath a cypress tree on the bank of the San Jacinto River and as I scanned the surroundings I saw I was near the muddy battlefield where my father had died. The branches broke the vigor of the rain and droplets plummeted in a cascade plopping onto the ground before me, deepening a puddle I could not sidestep. It swelled larger and deeper as the rainstorm lingered and refused to move out and away from me. I hung back beneath the tree, my hat drenched around the brim and when I dipped my chin I cupped my hands to catch the rainwater. I drank and it tasted like the farm and it tasted like the smell of the twins when they were babies. I could see them kicking up rainwater, getting so wet and grubby that mamá would have a fit on me for letting them get so filthy but I saw no wrong in consenting to their amusement in pools of muddy water. Such a little thing brought them so much joy and I cherished seeing their baby legs waddle in and out of the puddles, giggling as if this playtime was all that mattered in the world. An ache in my heart reacquainted me with the reason I had left home at all, reminding me that I could not return until my purpose was fulfilled. I could not allow those sonovabitch marauders to get away with the fact that the twins would never play in rainwater again. For some reason, I felt stronger in ways I'd never known before and I was unaware of how I came to newfound courage. That's when I found myself speaking Clara's name over and over, out loud and in a whisper.

I hadn't eaten a real meal in days and so I searched in my pockets for the last of a few pecans and cracked a nut between my teeth that tasted like the sandy bitterness of the shell. I peeled and pricked my fingers with the shell's sharp edges and when I had peeled a small mound of pecans I placed them in the palm of my hand and offered them to Lágrimas, saving half of a pecan for myself. I patted Lágrimas's nose and he nodded and seemed content momentarily.

"I know, I know. It's time for some real food," I whispered into his eyes and scratched behind his ears. He drew his head back and stepped away from my touch.

"You're a moody thing." I laughed and Lágrimas murmured as if to apologize. "Stay here and rest. I see a peach tree over there. How'd you like some juicy peaches?"

In a light mist, I meandered through grass that rose up to my breast as I scoured for a trail through the pasture, with arms out, swinging at my sides. The weeds struck my cheeks and they tingled and itched but I moved forward toward the peach tree resolute that I would find fruit ripe enough to eat. I arrived at the tree and reached up to the branches to pick fruit that was diseased with bugs or worms or something I didn't recognize. I hurled a bug-ridden peach to the ground and it plunked on a carcass. An animal's carcass. I bent down and poked at decaying flesh with a stick and decided the carcass was a field mouse. Plump and long, it had been. I kicked it and when it turned over I saw maggots scrambling on moist earth, alive and thriving. The field mouse's skeleton was starting to poke through dried flesh and through its eye sockets more maggots swirled searching for spongy flesh. I prodded at it again and it fell apart. I gazed out at the prairie and thought about my father and where he had fallen. I didn't even dig a grave deep enough and wide enough to protect him from bugs and things that devoured human flesh. I had left him there and for that I was surely a coward.

Staring out into the prairie I said a silent prayer but my lips moved and there were S's in the sound of moving lips and suddenly someone called out and startled me. A boy of fourteen or fifteen stomped toward me lifting his boots high, one hand pulling on straps flat against his chest and the other pulling along a mule with a bundle on its back. The straps on the boy held down a day sack that formed a mound on his shoulders and a rifle rested across the middle of the day sack poking out like thin arms of a plump scarecrow across his back. A scarecrow with a sheet covering its head. As he came toward me, his legs parted the grass and weeds that slapped at his waist and chest. Broad-shouldered and round-bellied with buttons popping his shirt open, he plunged the sack down onto the ground.

"Bet you're hungry," he said. He pulled out flat sticks of dried meat and handed them to me. "I got more. If you come on over to that riverbank, I can fish you out some good catfish. Even got some cornmeal to fry it in."

I followed him and his mule back along the trail I had forged where the grasslands bent sideways and we joined Lágrimas, who greeted us impatiently, waggling and spitting.

"Here. Give him this." The young boy pulled out a sack of ripe peaches he'd found somewhere and handed them to me. I opened them one by one to tear out the pit and flat-handed the fruit to Lágrimas. He chomped on the peaches and the juice dripped down my arm where my long sleeves had been pushed back to my elbows. I unfastened two top buttons of my shirt and brushed with my thumb the yard of gauze strapped tight around my breasts.

"Name's Pete. Well, Pedro. Around here they call me Pete."

He took out a knife from his pocket and whittled away at a long, thin branch, tied a string to it and then tied a piece of peach to the string and it hung onto the end of his makeshift pole. He flung the pole into the water and concentrated on the circles that pushed out from the center disappearing. He jerked back on the pole fighting the river's pull.

"You got a name, don't you?" He turned his head to look at me. "I reckon you'll tell me one of these days."

I looked up at the sky and felt my head and stomach swirling. Dropping to my knees, I sat on my legs, steadying myself by putting my head down.

"Heck, you're just hungry," Pete said. "Just give me a minute and you'll have the best supper this side of the Pecos River."

I tipped over on my side with legs scrunched to my belly and an arm over my eyes and fell asleep.

"Everybody has dreams, Micaela." It was mamá.

"Not everybody." I heard papi clearing his throat and saw him sneaking up on mamá to pinch her from behind. She laughed and slapped him with her dish towel.

In my sleep I giggled and when I awoke my cheeks were wet with tears.

"Hey, time to eat." Pete was crouched beside me and he shook my arm. He had kept his promise and fried what seemed like a school of catfish. On a blanket spread on the ground, he had set plates made of tin and forks and knives made of silver. The fried fish was piled high in a frying pan oozing with oil. Cornmeal lumps had fallen onto the blanket and I plucked them and put them in my mouth.

"There's plenty here," he said. "You don't got to eat them crumbs."

He handed me a plate and watched me eat as he picked apart the meat of the fish selecting the bones, transparent and thin.

"Careful. Lots of fish bones. You could choke and I sure as heck don't need to bury no more folks. Buried enough of my own kin."

After I had eaten two full plates of fish, I reached for the peaches he had placed on the blanket lining its border. I stood and fed the peaches to Lágrimas and returned to sit on the blanket facing the prairie with my back to Pete.

"You was crying in your sleep."

"Yeah," I said without turning to face him.

"I won't tell nobody. Don't matter to me if a man's got to cry. I figure he's got himself a damn good reason if he breaks down in front of another man."

I removed my hat and my hair stuck to my skull sweaty and oily. I brushed strands back and then studied the boy's features. He stared back as he ate, spitting out bones from the side of his mouth.

"How old are you?" I said.

"How old are you?" He squinted at me.

"Older than you." I smiled.

"I reckon you are." He placed his plate on the blanket, then wiped his mouth with the inside of his shirt smearing oil on the tail. His shirt was open and his stomach was chocolate brown with mounds of flesh creased and round. He dumped more fish on my empty plate and handed it to me.

"I don't want to eat all your food."

"Plenty more where that come from," he said.

I took the food and ate with my fingers, swallowing spiny needles whole with the meat.

He shook his head and spit out of the side of his mouth. "Where you going?"

"Just rambling, I guess."

"Rambling? You best be careful. Lots of evil men out here these days."

I ignored him and I guess that gave him enough reason to tell me a story that might warn me but I already knew the dangers and didn't care.

Pete put down his plate and scanned the field beyond our reach, waving his arm across the prairie. "My brother was here. On the side of Houston." He pointed to one side of the prairie, then to the other side. Months had passed since that infamous battle and although corpses were scattered on the battleground, we were too far from the center of that past commotion. "My uncle too. With Santa Anna. Both dead." He picked up his plate and bit into another piece of catfish. "Heck, I know this old gal up the road got mad and said a bunch of dirty stinking dead Mexicans were on her land and she wanted Mr. Sam Houston to get them on out of here."

"I fought beside my papi. Right here," I said. "That's how I got this." I pointed to my injured cheek.

His eyes bugged out. "You did? Lemme see." The boy inched closer to my face and tried to touch me but I pulled back.

"Oh. Sorry. Didn't mean nothing. Just wanted to see how it felt."

"It feels fine."

"How'd it happen?"

"Some ole rascal came at me with a bowie knife. This one right here." From my buckskin jacket, I plucked out my knife and handed it to him.

He examined the blade and gave it back to me.

"Did you shoot him?" he asked.

"Sure did. With this right here." I patted my rifle.

"That's a beaut. Can I see?"

He grabbed it before I had a chance to say yes or no.

"What's the initials stand for?"

"Agustín Campos. My papi."

"You miss him, don't you?" He put the rifle down by his side.

"Yeah."

"I miss my papi too. And my mamá. We had a farm. Squatters took it. Right from underneath us. But I'm getting it back. Soon as I make enough to buy it."

Pete nodded toward his mule. "Ole Petra there helps me. I'm in the trading business."

"What do you trade?"

"All kinds of things, pots, dishes, knives both dull and sharp, even got some jackets and pants in there if you're needing to outfit yourself and I got plenty of firearms too. Petra carries it all for me. You got any need for a new rifle? I just traded for some new ones over in the town of Harrisburg."

"I like the one I got, thanks."

He eyed my papi's rifle again.

"That's some fine work." He brushed his hand across the silver filigree. "I'll trade you two rifles for it."

"No thanks."

"You could sell the one and make yourself some money and still have one left for your travels."

"No thanks."

I sat silent for a while and watched him smooth his palm across the barrel.

"You believe in ghosts?" I said hoping to change his perspective.

"Don't you?" He quit coveting my rifle and reclined onto his back using his day sack for a headrest.

"I don't know."

"You mean to tell me you don't talk to your papi? I bet you seen him too. I bet you seen him right now. When you was asleep."

"Maybe." My eyes moistened and he looked straight at me, held up a rag and when I didn't take it, he shook my leg back and forth.

"That's all right. Go on ahead and cry all you want. It's good for the soul. That's what my abuelita says." He wiped tears from his face with the cuff of his sleeve.

I stretched my legs out on the blanket and felt a cool breeze rise and blow off my hat. It rolled but I grabbed it before it rolled too far and I placed it over my eyes.

"Sure miss my abuelita. Skin like chocolate and smells as sweet. I was with her down south when it all happened. When them damn squatters come and squatted on our little piece of land. Over near Trinity River. East of here."

The way Pete told it, he said it was a known fact that squatters had been crossing the Sabine River coming through Louisiana seeking land and cotton fields with slaves in tow. They came from the Carolinas or Tennessee where they had dried out the soil and they brought slaves often treating them worse than the mules. Slaves and mules were weighed down with pans for cooking and blankets for sleeping. They brought cornhusks and dried pork, flour and sugar, whiskey and tobacco leaves and it was all heaved on the backs of mules and slaves but their provisions ran out quickly enough.

"Toe-heads," Pete said. "That's what my mamá heard the squatters call their children. 'Thems our little toe-heads.' Mamá gave this one family a big ole basket full of eggs, fresh from our barn 'cause she felt sorry for them and she told my papi, 'a few eggs won't break us.' The squatters set up tents not far from our main house and even acted friendly the first few months. My papi let them eat corn and fruit from our farm 'cause we had plenty and my mamá gave them eggs, worried for the children who ran around the cornfields barefoot kicking up dust and wearing underwear caked with dirt at the seat. She said their stomachs were concaved with ribs sticking out and she never liked to see children starving.

"One day, mamá saw a plank pulled back and hanging loose at the back of the barn. Well, she thought an animal had forced it loose and crawled inside at night to steal the eggs. But any animal would have eaten the chickens too. Another morning she saw that the tan chicken was missing and the plank was pulled, crisscrossed against the other planks, leaving a gap open wide. It had rained a few nights before so the earth was still moist near the shade of the barn. She bent down and saw footprints, tiny footprints, leading from the back of the barn through to the field where the squatters had pitched by the river under a cypress tree. She said she could smell the aroma of firewood and chicken fat. Mamá looked in the black pot filled with water and saw a chicken, plucked and cut up in pieces, rolling in the boiling water. Tan feathers were lying on the ground and the children had feathers on their heads, standing straight up, and they circled the boiling pot, running and screaming with their palms patting their lips. The woman stirred the pot and threw in ears of corn. A few drops of water sprayed the children, who screamed and then broke into high-pitched laughter.

"My mamá asked her straight out, 'Where'd you get the chicken?' And all the squatter woman could say was, 'Shouldn't sneak up on God's children like that.' Mamá said she stood close to the woman's face and saw how she was wrinkled and pale. Brown strands of hair stuck to her forehead and to the back of her neck. Her dress was thin cotton ripped at the sides and anyone who cared to look could see her breasts sagging through the rip beneath her armpits.

"Mamá asked her again and the squatter woman called out to a slave named Lucius who came out of the woods right then and answered her real polite saying 'Yes ma'am?'

"'This here neighbor lady wants to know where you done got this chicken,' the squatter woman said to Lucius.

"'What chicken, ma'am?'

"'Why the one I'm fixing over these coals. Don't you remember nothing? You told me some farmer done give it to you last night. For helping him chop down some old oak. I swear you better be telling the truth. I ain't going to put up with liars and thieves.' She stirred the broth and chicken flesh fell off the bones.

"Mamá said Lucius looked at the squatter woman and sighed. 'Yes ma'am. I helped some old farmer. That's what he give me. A chicken.'

"My mamá swung around and walked away.

"Poor Lucius," Pete said. "He weren't no thief and if he lied it's 'cause they made him lie. He told me his real name was Agamemnon. Funny, huh? Seems his white papi read about them Greeks in battle. Wanted to call him Agamemnon and I guess he did but seeing as he wasn't around to tend to him, his mamá called him Lucius. Me and Aggie—that's what he told me to call him, he got kind of shy if anybody said his other name out loud—anyway, me and Aggie used to go swimming in the river at night. Beneath a rustler's moon so nobody would see him. They kept after him. Him being their only slave. He finally run off and I'm proud to say I helped him. Showed him the trail down south to my abuelita's. I took him there. To Monclova. Years back when things started brewing around here. I shouldn't have left them alone. Wished I'd been here. I could have done something. Them squatters live on my farm now. They took it. Just up and took it. Some of them white men did what they wanted to my mamá and it broke my papi's heart. He died soon after and she kept going. Working the farm but there weren't much to work right then. The cotton got eat up by the boll weevil and the corn got all dried up. Didn't have nothing to trade or sell to nobody. For miles it was that way for all the farmers. The chickens got all eat up by those dang squatters so we didn't even have eggs no more. I guess my mamá got too sad or something. She used to look out to the back pasture where I buried papi and I swear she used to say to him real quiet so's I wouldn't hear, she'd say, 'I'm going to be with you soon, Pedro. Sure as I'm standing here, I'm going to be with you.' And then she died. That's when I dug up my papi. He'd been rolled up in an old blanket and buried that way. Let me tell you that dead body stunk to high heaven. It did. It weren't my papi no more. It was just some stinking hide. You know fingernails and hair keep growing on a dead body? Anyways, I couldn't leave them at the farm cause them squatters had taken over. Soon as my mamá died they was in the house, in my mamá's kitchen ransacking the flour bins and tearing open anything they could find like they was looking for gold or something. They ran straight to her bedroom and tore open her jewelry box. The one my papi give her for her birthday one year. Their little girl Millie was the only one that gave me some of the trinkets her sisters dropped on the floor and claimed as their own. I guess she must have stole them from her sisters and so I kept them little silver earrings and brooches hoping to find my sisters 'cause my mamá would of wanted them to have her things but I finally traded them off. Wasn't worth much. Anyway after mamá died there was too many of them and only one of me and they thought I had something to do with their Lucius being gone and all. 'Agamemnon is a warrior,' I said to them. 'Who?' was all they could say. Not like they knew how to read or cared, for that matter. So I put both the bodies on the rickety old wagon. Let me tell you dead bodies is heavy. I used a plank. Set it at the end of the wagon and pushed up with a big old piece of timber. Did all this in the night so's they wouldn't see me taking the wagon. It's a wonder nobody heard all my racket. Rode night and day. Didn't stop. I brought the bodies here and buried them so's they could be with my uncle and brother."

Pete stood and pointed to an oak. "That's where they are. Sad story, ain't it?"

"And your sisters?" I said.

"Oh, they run off. Probably working at some whorehouse. Who knows? Alls I know is they run off. My mama wanted me to go find them but soon as my papi died, well, she needed me on the farm. I sure miss them. Maybe I'll run into them one of these days. Heck, maybe they're lying in a field like this. I don't really know nothing no more. Not that I ever did."

The sun set in rose hues and we sat quiet and watched for a long time until the sun tucked away behind the horizon. Pete rested his head against his day sack and looked up at the sky's dome then pointed. "See that? That's the first star coming up over there. Venus. The goddess of love," he said. "What do you think about that?"

I dozed, comforted by Pete's droning voice.

"Aggie used to tell me stories about all them stars. My favorite was about Orion. See that? Here it comes. You can see the belt lighting up over the sky. Sure is pretty."

"Orion," he repeated. "I'm going to be as good as you one day. A warrior for everyone to see. They're all going to remember me. You wait and see."

Although I slumbered, I heard his pledge out on that prairie where we had blood relations mingling with the earth, perhaps even rising at night as ghosts. One day, the ghosts would come alive and never let me rest or let anyone rest for that matter but there was nothing I could do about that and even if they awakened they could do nothing except maybe inflict ghost desire.

CHAPTER 12

At dawn I poked around for my boots and when I reached for my saddlebag, it was gone. So was my father's rifle. A cool breeze flapped and rustled the pages of my journal which was creased open to a page with scribbling that was not my own. It was Pete's hand and all it said was "a faire trayde." Peaches, dried meat and other foodstuffs were scattered on a blanket but I had no need for so much food and without my papi's rifle I was what would be considered a dead man. "Thieving scum." I packed up, grabbed Lágrimas's reins and we rode on.

Into the late afternoon I traveled east then north on the Trinity River to Liberty, a town unknown to me and with so many white folk I felt uneasy. In a saloon, I horned in on a poker game thinking I could make enough to buy myself a firearm especially since I had nothing left to trade except Lágrimas and that was not to be an option. I approached three scrawny men and a dealer who shuffled cards and dealt out bad hands in a game of five-card draw. I could see by their faces not a one had a good hand except the dealer, who always had a pair or better yet a set of triplets.

Sizing me up, the dealer nodded as he shuffled and the men at the table chuckled. Only one of them spoke and he spoke for them all when he said, "Ain't you a little young to be playing poker, son?" But it was youth that encouraged them hoping to win off of me, thinking their luck would change. I sat down, beer mug in hand, picked up five cards and discarded one. The dealer raised his eyebrows at the men, dealt another card facedown and I picked it up to see the jack of spades to link up with a queen of diamonds and king and ace of clubs. Those four with a ten of spades gave me a flush but it was too early in the game to win and from the look of the pot there was nothing to win so I folded.

The dealer saw me and guffawed, then adjusted his crotch and smoothed his thumb under the left suspender while he studied his hand, laid it out and won the sorry pot with four queens and that confirmed my suspicions. As he dealt another hand, his beard nearly caught fire from the cigarette dangling from the corner of his mouth but he must have known because he tossed the butt on the floor and stepped on it with the toe of his boot quite delicately. His name was Oscar. At least that's what I heard someone call him. Four or five men hung back listening and watching and a few others were seated behind him. All listened while he continued some tale he had been telling before I horned in on the game so I listened too while I studied my cards, peeking over at the sorry men to see their faces fall each time they picked up a new card.

"Yep, the Colonel is looking to change this territory," Oscar said. "He don't like Indians and he sure don't like meskins." He glanced at me. "Unless he can make a little bit of money off of them, then he's likely to sign you up to ride with him. You in?"

"Sure," I said. I took some dried meat from my jacket and threw it down on the table.

"We bet with money around here. Son." Oscar called me son in a way that made me think he suspected my sex so I made sure to make my voice gruff when I spoke.

One of the other men picked up the strips of meat and chomped down. "It's all right. Let him be." He looked Mexican like me. As he chomped on a dried stick of meat, he reached in his pocket for a coin that he hurled in the pile. "I'm in," he said, "and here's for the boy." I was relieved when he called me boy and even eased myself into the game but when he threw in another coin pulling back on his coat pocket, I saw my rifle leaning on the chair, half hidden by the coat.

"Where'd you get that?" I said.

He saw me pointing at the rifle and ignored me.

"I said where did you get that rifle?"

"From my abuelito," he said.

"Can't be. It belonged to my papi."

"You're lying."

"That's my rifle. A boy named Pete stole it from me. I swear."

"Well now, how can that be if my abuelito gave it to me?"

"It's got my papi's initials right there. See?" I pointed to the filigree that curved into an A and a C.

"Now, boys, no need to fight. Let's just put it in the pile here and see who wins that fine firearm," said Oscar.

"Hell no. It's mine," said the Mexican gambler.

Oscar cocked his pistol. "I said put it in the pile."

"All right, all right. Here it is."

I had no choice but to play. I counted on their sorry hands to help me, that is, if Oscar didn't take to cheating—but the pot was too good now for him not to.

I laid down my hand of three sevens. Oscar had three eights.

"You didn't win that hand," I said.

Oscar fingered his suspenders up and down and gave me the kind of look that should have scared me but I was too mad or too senseless to back down.

"Now, son, you don't want to get mixed up with the likes of my temper. You best leave well enough alone."

"I want my rifle." I stood up and my fists were tight.

"Sit yourself down, son. Tell us how you got that scar of yours."

"Some ole rascal come at me. At San Jacinto." I was pleased with myself since I had practiced the story.

"That so? You mean to tell me you fought with General Houston?"

"I did."

"Well that deserves a drink. Don't it, boys? Let's hold up our glasses for this young hero."

Oscar waved to the bartender to bring me a drink and he brought a whole bottle, then he cleared his throat like a muted message to two scrawny men, who pushed me down on a chair, held my head back and I felt spiny fingers holding my nose. I opened my mouth and they spilled whiskey that tasted like fusel oil down my throat. I tried to toss my head around but somebody held it firm and I choked and spit but the fingers around my nose stayed fixed and the sting of cheap drink slid down my throat with ease once I stopped fighting. They emptied at least half the bottle into my belly and I felt woozy and sick and when they let go of my head I banged it down on the table and they all laughed.

"Like I was saying, Colonel made sure we all got paid in pure gold for them Indian scalps." He gathered his winnings, my rifle included, and pocketed about forty dollars of paper script. "Damn script," he mumbled, then looked up at us. "Things are about to change. Not right away but it's going to happen, boys. The lone star's going to join up with the U.S. flag. Mark my words. Better get yourself some land. Steal it if you got to. Much obliged for the card game. I got to catch up to the Colonel now. This rifle is gunning down Apache scalps for gold."

He hovered over me and slapped me on the back. "Good day to you, son. And thank you kindly for my rifle."

They all laughed.

Oscar nodded to the man who had first claimed my rifle then strode away, head high, through the swinging doors and out to the street.

My head ached and my mouth was dry like cotton. I pushed up on my elbows and tried to balance on my boots but I crumpled to the floor and hard as I tried to stay awake, I fell unconscious. Despite my condition I sensed a loathsomeness around me and I knew for the first time on my journey, since I'd left the criollo ranch, that danger was upon me in a different way from the time Jed and I rode together and buried Juana. Fists wound tight on my arms and legs and the tightness cut off blood that churned and boiled inside me and I smelled cowhide dank and stale and rags were all around as flies batted about crashing into curtains that leaked light into the corner where I lay. Even in my sleep I sensed close by something unidentifiable. Voices hummed outside but I was too far gone to make out what was being said. The lull of motion woke me into a disturbed consciousness and when I heard a braggart loud among the others, I recognized Oscar's voice. I didn't know at the time he was not the one to fear. Instead, the one who would prove to be the devil spoke in restrained whispers.

When I met the Colonel, my wrists were tied with rope and I had been tossed from a wagon covered in cowhide. I was filled with worry over Lágrimas since he was probably left behind. I was one of three; the other two were Mexican boys, well, I guess we all were. With tied wrists we stumbled from the ground to our feet and we were ordered to stand upright before the Colonel. He was a short sprite of a man with a thick waist. The camp of men he led called him Colonel and I was to learn they hated him and revered him but most feared him, making fear their real reverence. And even though no one liked the Colonel, they believed in his spite. He himself spurned anyone brown or black or red, anyone whose skin was not gray with pale ruddiness like his and as Oscar had informed me, the Colonel was resolute to rid my home of those who had known the region for centuries through ancestors of countless origins.

Nobody talked to the Colonel since the Colonel talked to no one. Instead he whispered orders while he rubbed his crotch with one hand and pointed with the other holding a long ten-inch bowie knife jabbing at air and pointing the blade's tip at his men's heads telling them all to do this and to do that. "Set up the tents far enough from the riverbank, close enough, but far enough," he'd mumble and almost no one could discern the Colonel's mumbles. "Walk the steps from the bank and count ten paces, ten exactly" and he'd come and measure and if it wasn't ten, he'd have a field day with whoever he thought pitched the tent. It didn't matter if you had or hadn't. If you were close enough to him after he measured the paces to the river, he'd throw you into the water and hold your head down until he felt your body go limp, then shove you on the muddy bank and someone would run and blow air into the lungs of the poor culprit. It was a kind of baptism. The Colonel baptizing his men. He had his ways.

I looked past the Colonel to an open prairie with no paths or rivers that I recognized and I was so disoriented I wasn't sure how long I'd been traveling on the back of that wagon but what I was sure of was that I saw my cousin. Jedidiah Jones leaned against a cottonwood tree and the tree's white feathery sprouts blew around his head like a silhouette or halo of cotton balls with spears stabbing at the sun's yellow light shining on him. When I saw him I thought I would be protected but he gazed into my eyes and acted alien as if I was the stranger. He looked away, walked to the riverbank and brought out a fishing pole, indifferent to the scene before him.

What I witnessed next confirmed for me that Jed himself did not know what he was up against and that was when the Colonel grabbed him by the scruff and shoved him in the water. My poor cousin thrashed about so steadfast that he and the Colonel toppled and disappeared beneath the murky river. When they surfaced, the Colonel splattered about like a wet, mangy dog and lunged at Jed, plunging his head down and battling its muscle until bubbles of air were all we could see circling the Colonel's thick gray fist. I was to learn that no one had ever brought the Colonel down like that, sunken into water with his chosen victim. Jedidiah's head bobbed but he couldn't get air and the Colonel now dunked him steady with both hands.

No one dared jump in to save my cousin and since my hands were tied I too stood by listening to the silence throughout the camp that was so soft and real it announced itself like a prayer on the men's lips. When Jedidiah's head went limp and no longer wrestled for air, the Colonel released his grip and waded back to the bank, dropped and gasped, wiping his face with a wet shirt, showing a fat belly that had once been gutted by a man who, it was said, despised the Colonel for doing to him what he had just done to my cousin. The scar on his belly was as fat and long as a fat earthworm and it wound around to the tip of his spine. It was an old scar, but that wasn't the way the Colonel told it. The Colonel muttered he'd been a war hero and no one dared challenge his lies whether they heard him or not. It was Oscar who splashed into the river pulling at Jed's limp body floating facedown with his arms spread-eagled. Oscar threw my cousin down on the ground and breathed life back into him and Jed spit and spattered, coughing up gray water, then sat up leaning on his elbow. He stared at the Colonel, who laughed quietly.

"Bet you thought you was about to meet your maker," he said to Jedidiah, who did not move from the ground but kept observing the Colonel, who fell to his back, hands splayed on his scarred belly, and exhaled.

For dinner I ate some cold beans that tasted sour and the Mexican boys spat out the beans and left them in a mound for the ants to climb. The camp slumbered, or at least the Colonel did and Jed finally verified he was my family relation when he came to my tent.

"What the heck are you doing, Jed? That evil menace of a man almost killed you."

"It's just his way."

"Just his way? Walker never even treated you like that."

The mere mention of Walker had always infuriated my cousin but he ignored what I said and handed me a piece of cheese and did the same for the other two captives.

"Micaela, I swear," he shook his head. "I told you to go home."

He explained we were headed south to Chihuahua and that the Colonel intended to sell us as slaves to plantations in Mexico where young boys were often sold to work all their lives and no one, not their families or friends, heard from them again.

"Next town, I'll set you free," he said.

"You're coming with me."

"I can't."

"You can and you will."

"I know what I'm doing. Just leave me be."

"You're acting dim-witted, Jed."

"You don't know nothing. Now leave me be."

He snuck out of the tent and his shadow appeared like a coyote as he slipped away.

In the morning the Colonel kicked the sleeping men, shoving his boots at their stomachs, and hissed for them to rise before the sun beat them to it. The wagon traveled behind, following south to the Río Bravo until we pulled into an Apache encampment near a silver mine and I was concerned that we had not found a town yet and questioned whether Jedidiah intended to free us.

Then the Colonel's actions confounded me. He offered the Apache whiskey and meat from deer his men had slaughtered that afternoon and the Apache offered their home and the Colonel agreed. The men set up camp and as captives we were allowed to roam untied and no one had any concern that we'd run since we were so far from any township. We were at that feast for days and late into the night all the men, the marauders and the Apache, drank and danced and women danced too as did the children and even Jedidiah pranced around drunker than I'd ever seen him. Making conversation with him futile. It was a fiesta and all were happy to celebrate with what they considered heathen but the Colonel called them God's children. "All are God's children," the Colonel repeated, mocking the men and women and winking at his militia of maniacs. Most knew why we were there at all, some suspected and others anticipated but I had no inkling of the massacre that was to come. Not until a quiet peace came over the camp did the Colonel pick up his Wesson rifle and begin the slaughter, slow and methodical. They were asleep, the women with the men and the children. All asleep.

I staggered to my feet, rubbed my eyes and witnessed what I thought I could not be seeing. Blood spattered on my face and arms. I thought I was asleep and in a nightmare and then I thought I saw Jed but the moonlight was dim and the blood in my eyes muddled my reasoning even though the man appeared to be my cousin. The Colonel stood beside Jed and ordered him to fire but my cousin froze, then shook his head. That was when the

Colonel drew his pistol and patted the barrel against Jed's temple but my cousin kept shaking his head until the Colonel whacked the butt of his gun against Jed's skull. I saw him topple and I thought to myself I was glad he was the right kind of coward but then he got up, snatched the Colonel's pistol and shot at someone sleeping. The Colonel grinned, picked up his rifle and aimed at a woman with a baby folded into her breast. She gazed up at him as he rested the firearm on his hip, shot her, then pointed at the crying child and shot again. I could not fathom what I saw; Jed could not be butchering with the Colonel. Oscar handed me a rifle, my rifle, and ordered me to shoot but I couldn't and he egged me on and called me coward and without any thought I blasted him in the chest at such close range that more blood sprayed on my face and the rifle butt punched my cheek knocking me a few steps backwards. Shocked at my triumph, I stood over his body without speculating what to do next. With my father's rifle in my hand I cowered, stunned at the massacre. When it was over, when bodies were heaped upon each other, I crawled and hid behind an oak but couldn't stop myself from looking and so I gazed upon the encampment and heard the Colonel barking orders in a way I'd never heard him bark. He bellowed to his men to start the scalping. Their bowie knives glinted in faint moonlight and the men sliced from foreheads to earlobes to the crook of the neck pulling at long hair sleek and slippery from blood that drenched the hair and drenched their hands trickling down their arms to drip off their elbows. I ran from fear and dread and I ran so fast and so fierce I didn't even know when I stopped and collapsed into sleep until I awoke and ran again, the rifle heavy at my side.

Not for months did I hear that such a massacre occurred at all and that was in a saloon in some unknown settlement where I heard about Apache scalps and their worth. Some man pointed at sketches in a broadside and explained to those who hovered over him, "These here are worth one hundred pesos. The men's. Women are only worth fifty but that's still good and the babies only bring twenty-five pesos but heck that's better than nothing and anyway, means they won't grow up if we kill 'em now. Before they get too big. Before they get to be men and women who make more dang Apaches."

That night I escaped through the southern desert and my single survival was foremost on my mind. I was a fugitive who had shot a man and although he was the worst kind of man, his compatriots frightened me enough to keep me running. Firearm or no firearm, I was a woman alone. And Jed, well, I couldn't trust my cousin. My blood relation had been christened into the Colonel's graces.

With a tight grip on my rifle I ran following the trail of a dry riverbed for what seemed like miles until I collapsed. When I gazed up at Pete riding like a prince on Lágrimas I was neither stunned nor displeased.

"You was crying in your sleep again," said Pete.

I sat up and searched the campsite and felt consoled when I saw Lágrimas tied to a creosote bush nearby.

"He's all right. I been taking care of him for you."

Although I opened my mouth to argue with him, no sounds came out and I realized that shock still trembled through my body. I was so exhausted and shaken that I didn't know if I could pull myself together again and on that day I didn't care who I was or where I was. I buried my face in my hands and sobbed.

Pete shook my leg to comfort me and although I had planned to punch him once I met up with him again, I forsook that plan. I sat and let him feed me as he had done before.

"You can wash off that blood over yonder," he said. He pointed to a hole in a stream that was no more than a puddle.

I crawled to the water hole and stripped off my clothes without appraisal of my deed and waded into the pond to rub from my arms and breasts blood that I could not forget. I sensed Pete's gaze on my naked, woman's body but I didn't care; he was only a boy and I was someone who had beheld and survived butchery. I finished washing and walked upright and naked to the blanket where he had strewn fresh clothes and I dressed in front of Pete and neither of us spoke.

For longer than a week, we both rode Lágrimas with Pete's old mule Petra pulled behind and I was curious how Pete transformed into a gentleman while nursing me to sanity that seeped back slowly into me. We passed rivers and streams until we were far enough east of the Pecos River for me to reason again and when Pete passed out one night from too much whiskey, I seized the opportunity to take his plump bag of coins and leave him behind. I mounted Lágrimas and we headed as far away from the memory of that slaughter as I could go.

CHAPTER 13

Fugitives are plentiful on a frontier with nameless roads and settlements and I became as ghostly as any fugitive who did not want to be seen or heard but still yearned to live a life beyond contemptible existence. I became so unsure of myself that I no longer had a resolve that mattered. I took to wandering through towns without any cause except to run from men who may or may not have been chasing me. I became my own accuser, judging that which I had not executed but convinced that I was as blameworthy as my cousin and although Jedidiah Jones had pulled the trigger, as his witness I believed I was as accountable. Nothing could hinder my crazed point of view and I did the only thing I knew to do and that was drift from town to town, drinking more whiskey than I should and hoping something or someone would finally bring me back to life because I was numb.

"Girl like you got no business in a town like this."

A husky man stood brushing a horse and with his back to me, I saw how his legs stretched wide apart showing he was taller than he appeared. Markings on his back were wide with protrusions of bumps and knobs that shaped thick lines like a map with rivers going nowhere and everywhere. I wanted to reach out with my fingers and smooth the lines but the man turned around and stopped brushing and scrutinized me up and down and then resumed his chore. I stood staring and he stood brushing until finally I spoke.

"I'm no girl," I said.

"Yeah, you're no girl and I'm no slave and this world is paradise for us both. The Republic of Texas ain't slave country and you and me, why we're free to come and go. Course, dressed like that you're pretty free, I'd say. So many damn fools around here they don't know to look into a face and eyes to see what's really there. I bet you nobody ever guessed it. That you're a girl running."

He put down the brush and picked up a shovel that leaned against a wall. He scooped horse dung, separated it from straw and dumped dried lumps the size of his foot into a bucket, then stopped to stare at my face.

"That's a mighty fine scar."

"I got it fighting. With my papi at San Jacinto battle."

He chuckled. "Sure you did."

"Some ole rascal come at me with this knife." I held out my six-inch blade.

He smiled and resumed his activity.

"Don't just stand there. Come on over here and help me," he said.

I stood for minutes, maybe longer, examining the wounds on his back.

"I can't believe your mother brought you up to be so rude, girl. You just going to stand there and stare like you've never seen a man shoveling shit?"

I moved closer and touched the bucket and he slipped the handle in my hands. He tossed me a shovel and I helped clean the floor that looked as if it had not been cleaned in days. I shoveled the dung into the bucket, then emptied it into a large mound heaped at the back of the stables. He said it was manure for farmers who fertilized peach and cane land that barely needed fertilizing because the land itself was rich and black, full of minerals and ready for planting cotton and corn, melons and peaches, but these migrant farmers didn't know the soil and underestimated its purpose and worth.

"Where you headed?" he said.

"I don't know." I scooped wet and dry mounds of dung until I filled the bucket and emptied it only to begin again.

"You best be going somewhere. Not going to catch me with the likes of a girl in my stable." He swept and as his arms swayed with the broom, the muscles flexed and pumped up and plumped out.

"None of your business what I do," I said.

"You're right about that. I mean, why would I care about some ornery little Mexican girl running around in a getup that's likely to get her killed. Any of these good ole boys find out, well, the killing will come after they do with that pretty little body of yours what pleases them and let me tell you I've seen it plenty of times. What can be done to a girl like you. You best be careful, that's all I've got to say about the matter. Mostly, I'm just hoping you'll ride out of here before morning. I'll even groom your horse for you. You don't even got to pay nothing. I'll say you took it out in trade. Worked it off."

He stood beside Lágrimas and dangled the horse's reins.

"I've seen what evil men do," I said. "I still see it. Every night before I fall asleep I see it so clear that I wish I could pluck out that vision from inside my head but I can't." I pointed to my temple, then pulled out a bottle of whiskey from the inside pocket of my buckskin coat and swigged long and hard.

He bowed his head again. Gray hair peppered his reddish temples and his cheekbones were high and bony. "What's your name?"

"Lorenzo."

"That's not your name."

"What's your name?" I sounded like I was accusing him when I was the one guilty.

"They call me Lucius."

I squinted. "Is that your real name?"

"It's what they call me."

"Agamemnon," I whispered.

"What did you say?"

"Agamemnon."

He grabbed a blue shirt hanging from a nail and as he buttoned, he gazed down at the floor. "I reckon you ran into a young boy named Pete."

"I did."

"I reckon he told you all kinds of stories about a slave named Lucius who comes from a family of warriors. In Africa. Long line of warriors."

"He did."

"I reckon he told you stories about taking me to Mexico?"

"He did."

"That poor boy is nothing but a liar and a thief. Don't go picking up his habits."

"I ain't no thief." I offered him my bottle but he waved it away.

"But you're a liar."

I stood silent.

He straightened his back and legs and I saw him tower high above me. With his fists on his hips he looked me up and down again as if he was curious about who I really was and where I came from.

"Texas. Sure is a hellhole. Ain't it?"

"It's Coahuila y Tejas to me. And to my family." I didn't know why I was defending what I felt so estranged from right then.

"Look here, you better wake on up to what's coming. You might as well get yourself on back to Mexico and leave this place to ole whitey because, darlin, it's slave lynching country and it's Mexican killing country and it's Indian scalping country and it's going to be that for a mighty long time."

I stared at cleanly swept dirt. My eyes almost watered but I fought the impulse by brushing back my hair, wet from sweat. "He told me he took you to Monclova. To his grandmother's. A few years back."

"All Pete did was bring me here. Sold me." He laughed. "So Pete went and told you he took me to Mexico. So I could be free?" Lucius laughed again. "Hell, least I'm not around them squatters breaking my back on farmland."

I scanned the stable and he saw I judged the piles of manure and rotting wood beams that held up stalls that wobbled if you bumped them.

"It don't look much better but in some ways it is. I got some thick-headed master who spends his days over at that saloon drinking and he leaves me here to clean up after the horses and take the money from those that keep their horses here. Nobody asks me questions. Nobody bothers me. I'm just old Lucius doing my job."

Suddenly, a squeaky loud voice boomed from the entrance of the stable and a scrawny man staggered in and bumped the pails strewn across the dirt floor. He could not have been more than twenty-five, but his head was already bald.

"Lucius, where you at?"

"Yeah." Lucius's voice dropped down low.

"I been looking for you, you ole darky." The bald man stopped and leaned into the stall's beam. He looked at me and I looked away. "It's the meskin boy. I seen that face before." He traced a line on his own cheek to match the scar on mine. "Ain't I seen you before? You was playing cards with me and some ole boys. And Oscar! That's right. Oscar won your daddy's rifle. How is ole Oscar? You seen him? He ain't come through town lately. Sure miss that ole boy. You seen him?" His mouth opened so that the gaps between his teeth looked wide and then he toppled over, landed on horse dung and dozed off pointing a finger at me.

"Looks like you got yourself a friend," said Lucius.

"I don't know him," I lied.

"Well he knows you."

"He from around here?"

"Nope. From the Carolinas. Wealthy family. He went and fell in love with a slave girl. Can you beat that? His papa packed him up and sent him to Texas with a bundle of money and told him not to come back ever because he was ashamed of him. Now he just drinks himself to sleep. Lucky for me." His hands rested on his waist as he looked down at the bald white man. "Help me move him. When he wakes up, he'll be asking after you. He may be a drunkard but this ole boy ain't likely to forget anything. He still talks about that slave girl like it was yesterday."

I slept for an hour, maybe two, tossing about uneasy and restless. I'd been recognized and I had no idea what this sorry drunkard planned to do but I was not going to give him an opportunity to think up a design against me even though I was too tired to ride out yet. Lucius must have taken pity on me because he hid me in a corner of the stable and said he'd rouse me before his drunkard master awoke to ask after me. I guess Lucius suspected I'd lied about not knowing his wretched boss man but I wasn't ready to confess my life to someone I'd only just met.

Lucius sat beside me as I lay on a mound of hay with more hay piled on top of me covering me like a blanket with only my head poking out of the heap. In that dark night, he talked about his wife's slaughter with a voice throaty and cavernous. He soothed me in a rhythm that echoed like an angel or some spirit that rose up to comfort me but I suppose that in the telling of his story, he comforted himself as well.

"Only woman I ever loved was Indian. Comanche. A warrior, she was." He smiled but the smile quickly disappeared. "She died like a warrior. Fearless. Ready for death. I saw her die. Right in front of me. These ole boys held me down. Wouldn't even let me shut my eyes to the sight of what they did to her."

He told how men sat on his legs and yanked on each arm then pinched open his eyelids so the whites of his eyeballs shined as he watched them rape and butcher his wife. Her face remained unchanged, he said. Facing him, she lay on the ground beneath the harsh heaviness of each stinking marauder and she lay peacefully unafraid of death and looked to Lucius to calm him but he was dry-eyed and uncontainable. When her body was limp and he was out cold, the marauders rode away supposing they were dead. Lucius finally woke and crawled to his wife, her pink scalp exposed to the sun like a raw peach peeling and wrinkling from the heat. He caressed the body and wrapped her in a blanket she had woven years before, then tied the rolled blanket to a makeshift wooden ladder that he fixed to his saddle and he rode with this peculiar open coffin dragging behind him until he came to rest with his wife's Honey-eater band. He didn't speak a word to her mother and father. They had warned them, told them it wasn't safe to venture out alone without their tribal kin. Too many white men invading and marauding, they had said. Too many white men had already arrived and there were more to come. So many more to come. Although her family warned them, his wife was fearless and so they rode searching for her sister's home with the Antelope band. They found her in the northern plains near the Llano Estacado, then returned following the Red River to the Brazos but when they hit on the Colorado, they crossed paths with the marauders.

Studying his profile I saw he was a handsome man and he looked Mexican, or could be Mexican, and I told him that but he said, "Sure, I guess I could be. But I'm not." Braids fell down his back and they were tied with a string.

At the end of his account, I sat up and drank from my bottle, then squeezed my head between my hands leaning on elbows and knees until the whiskey burned my insides and freed my tongue.

"My papi died in a battle that my mamá said he had no business fighting, my baby sister and brother got killed by the same men who raped my mamá and a poor little Mexican girl got raped and killed by those same men. My damn cousin is running with the likes of men I never thought I would see him running with. I killed one of those men. Oscar was his name. Friend to your boss man lying over there." I paused and wiped my eyes and took a drink. "I left home so sure of myself. I was gonna find those men who killed my brother and sister and I was gonna shoot them dead and let the vultures feast on their livers after I pierced their hearts with this blade." I tossed my bowie knife on the ground. "But when I saw the slaughter and scalping being done to babies, I don't know, it's like I lost my will to be. Just to be."

I wiped more tears, swilled from the bottle and watched Lucius set it aside and pick up my knife.

"I can't remember time anymore," he said. "I can't remember how or why or when it passes. Seems like the same day to me. All the time, the same day. Not much changes except that I'm still a slave and I reckon I will be till the day I die."

He leaned back against the wall, sitting on the stable floor where the hay was piled evenly beneath him. One leg was stretched out in front of him and the other was crooked. His elbow rested on the bent knee and in his hand he twisted and turned the bowie knife as if it was a baton and he was directing an orchestra. It was as if he heard music in his head. Fine music. With drums beating a backbeat to a heart that had stopped wanting because it had been told that it had no right to want anymore but it kept on beating a rhythm for everyone else, reminding everyone else that life went on.

"Texas is a hellhole. So long as men like those ole murdering whiteys run this place, Texas is gonna be a hell hole." He handed back the knife and the pearl handle took on a different sensation to me. "Ain't nothing you can do about that. Except go home. Just go home and save yourself from more heartache."

"I can't go home. I got to find them." I startled myself when I said this out loud.

"Them murdering butchers?" He whistled through his teeth softly. "Child, all you got to do is get yourself home. Ain't no way you can beat the likes of them butchers."

"I got to find them. I set out to find them and I got to find them." My heart raced and sped through my body, stirring conviction. "They killed my baby brother and baby sister. I can't let that be. I got to do something. I don't care if I die anymore. I got no reason to live."

"Ain't you got a sweetheart? A sweetheart is a reason to live." Lucius was sketching lines on the dirt floor with a twig.

"Used to. She's gone."

He didn't blink when I specified my sweetheart was a she.

"Dead?" he asked.

"No. Just gone."

"Child if she ain't dead, she ain't gone." He looked me straight on. "You got yourself all turned around, don't you? Looking for murdering men who will kill you and not looking for the one thing that could make you forget all this. All 'cause you're too proud. Revenge is pride and that's what you got right now. Vengeful pride. All that amounts to is more death. Don't need that. Nope. Don't need that. You got to go home. That's all there is to it. Find that sweetheart of yours and go on home."

What I didn't tell Lucius was the thing I had yet to admit to myself. The night of Juana's death, they had done to me what they had done to her and for too long now I had denied it. Acted like it didn't happen or even if it did happen, it didn't matter because I was alive and Juana was dead. For too long I had reasoned that I had no right to be alive and yet here I was thinking back on a savage memory I had put aside as if that could make it not so. But what I had tried to forget surfaced again. And what those men had done to me hit me hard. At long last, it hit me hard. But I put the memory away quickly. Maybe I didn't feel prepared to contend with that pain right then in the dark without Clara to hold me, clutch my hand, or just be at my side. The missing of Clara was not something I wanted to dwell upon since the act of longing would not bring her to me. Suddenly I felt a rage come over me and I wanted to scream the way I did not scream the night they took Juana, the night I became crazed and useless to myself. That is, until I met Clara.

CHAPTER 14

At the first sight of daylight I snuck out of that stable. I rode Lágrimas along the river's edge for miles trailing bends and curves as my head bobbed exhausted from the night's talk. I reflected on Lucius and his advice to go home but it was advice I could not abide. Revenge filled my body each time I thought back on that night those men did to me what I had refused to speak. Still, I felt indebted to Lucius, who, without intention, reminded me that memories were a breathing thing and mine had come alive when he and I summoned the horrors of our past.

I searched towns where gambling was plentiful and each time I thought I had caught up to those murdering defilers the vengeance in my gut erupted. I resolved that I had more to gain than I had to lose once I found them. Self-respect, for one. And if they killed me first it didn't matter because since I had already slayed a man, my place in Hades was secured.

Everyone knew that Galveston was a gamblers' den and I was glad I was finally upon the town by the bay. I peeked into the distance where the shoreline became the horizon, blue upon blue with sunlight glossy on the waves, far and beyond my scope. The gulf waters warmed from that distance and the breezes made me glad I had arrived at the port of Galveston by early dusk. Swathed in sweat from the day's ride, I must have reeked of the buckskin jacket festooned on my body that had gotten drenched and dried and drenched again. I unsaddled Lágrimas and fed him a peach, ripe with dark red fruit at its center, and he snorted while I brushed down his back to the wide girth of his belly, then up his sturdy quarters to pat his rump. In the town stable I wound his reins around a wooden pillar so he wouldn't wander in his sleep. He was prone to sleepwalking. Once, he walked into a stream and woke frightened and cold, unaware of how he had come to be in this predicament. Since then, I tied him to a tree or a pillar depending on whether we were on a prairie or in a town. After I set Lágrimas in the stable, I walked through the town aspiring to be close to the whiskey that placated my nerves.

In a muddy town square across from a newly built church, I heard the din of betting men. I entered a saloon and glanced about the room, smoky and crowded with voices clamoring above the piano's clinking rhythm. Someone in a corner of a makeshift stage, which was a box turned over on its end, sang a sad ballad but no one listened because no one could hear above laughter and slapping on thighs and backs. I felt less conspicuous there since they all seemed entertained with amusement of their own making. A card game at the center of the room was so raucous that I was surprised when I saw only four men betting but when I saw each focused on the dealer, I appreciated why the men were rowdy.

It was Clara. She was the dealer and the gaming men each attempted to impress her, more interested in impressing her than winning since winning her attention was their real game. I ambled toward the table and nodded in a gesture that asked if I could sit and since it was her table, no one would object to Clara's choices. The game was monte, a game unfamiliar to the region and more likely to the recreation in Santa Fe, I'd been told. No one knew how to bluff or much less win and the one who racked up our money was clearly the dealer but just as we began to lose everything, we all began to win enough to stay in the game. By the end of the evening I garnered more than five hundred dollars and I thanked Pete in my head for not hiding his stash of coins, which gave me an opportunity to win at Clara's table. No one suspected the dealer had been assisting me and I kept quiet about my small fortune.

When the saloon quieted and only I and Clara and the bartender were left in the room now tiny and dank in its emptiness, I wrinkled my brow and lifted my chin as if to say, "Now what?" She clutched my hand and led me up a flight of stairs adorned with floral, red frayed carpet. At the end of a narrow passage, she shoved me into a room against a wall and as she bit my lips and tongue, she removed my jacket and pushed me on the bed unfastening my trousers. I darted up securing the buttons she loosened but she was persuasive and her yearning was as fanatical as mine and although I wrangled with her for a moment, more for fun than anything, I finally gave up and gave in. I let myself be pulled back down and I did not rise from that bed or leave her room for days. To be with her meant my inner turmoil subsided momentarily and I was hopeful again about some kind of future for me but only if she was in the future I envisioned. I must have been fooling myself thinking she would want what I wanted but at the time I fell under her spell even if she may have told me lies. In her bed and in her arms, nothing she said to me was a lie. I believed Clara's words and I believed her body when she came unto me. It was bliss I had not known and it was one I yearned to feed forever, even if forever is a foolish prospect, I wanted to crave that possibility. The thing is, I hadn't given up on my quest to find those who had murdered the twins and sometimes I think I fell upon bad luck because my love for Clara distracted me from my plan.

During those days alone with her, she confided secrets that she had not confessed in El Paraíso. I suspected that being close to her real home brought up things she had a need to remember because remembering what we miss makes it all real again. That's when I realized my love for Clara was as bound up in her past as what we had right then in her tiny room in Galveston. When she told me her mother's people were Karankawa, a coastal tribe that had mostly vanished seeking sanctuary that was not to be, I decided not to reveal that my mother's ancestry was Tonkawa, bitter enemies of her mother's tribe. What did she and I have to do with those past crimes anyway? I made up my mind that we had to start our own family just to prove long-standing stories wrong. Of course, I didn't tell my new conviction but I was sure in time we would blend our families and no one would remember or care that our tribes had once been rivals.

For centuries Clara's people had lived along the gulf shores and for centuries they had been chased from their home into missions and other desolate federations by men like Austin and such colonialists. Her grandfather was French and his daughter, Clara's mother, coupled with a black man to spite another colonizer's whim.

"Most folks don't know what to make of me," she said. "Some think I'm white like my grandfather, and others, they see my papa's blackness shining through me. It's mostly Mexicans who call me India. They wanna see my mother's blood."

"People see what they wanna see," I said.

"Or what we want them to see."

"Why'd you leave the ranch that night? Without telling me?"

"What do you think?" She raised an eyebrow as if to call me stupid without saying it. She picked up my hat from the bed and put it on. "Call me Lorenzo," she said.

"Give me that."

"Not till you call me Lorenzo."

"I'm not calling you by my tío's name."

"Your tío?"

"Yeah, tío. I fought next to him at the battle of San Jacinto. With my papi. Both died. But I got my revenge. I killed off a few of them damn soldiers."

"You killed Mexicans?"

"Huh?"

"Mexicans?"

"Of course. Who else would I be killing?"

She sat up in bed and leaned against the headboard.

"I don't understand you," she said.

"What do you mean?"

"Why would you kill your own people?"

"Tejanos?"

"Hmm," was all she responded.

She squinted her eyes at me as if she was examining my story, which was nothing but a story. I needed to be a hero in her eyes and instead I was sounding like a mixed-up murderer. I was afraid she was going to question me more but instead she sighed and gazed out the small window of her room.

"I don't know why I came back here. Don't know why I stay. Nowhere else to go, I guess."

It was my moment. To ask what Lucius had advised. But I let the moment pass.

Clara slid to the center of the bed and lying back, reached for my fingers and held them. She closed her eyes and rested and I wanted the image to last but knew it wouldn't. Her breath slowed and deepened and I gleaned her breasts rising and falling through her gown. When I placed my head on her soft bump of a belly, she twirled a strand of my hair and I whiffed the scent of lavender and rose petals from her skin. She gripped my hand and turned to face a wall of books piled high and strewn across the floor, dog-eared and marked from her self-schooling.

For days we neither slept nor paused from our duty to each other and instead would lie awake, light-headed and steamy in sheets damp and perfumed with our sex scent. Clara read to me from her books, Dante's *Inferno* being among her favorites and I came to relish the sound of her voice

announcing each new quest into misery. That she had so much book learning surprised me but she claimed it was the only good thing her grandfather had passed on to her mother, who passed it on to Clara. That was
the first time I was glad that my mother had insisted I study the books in
my papi's library. I kept thinking that her little library would help us with
the raising of our own children. Maybe I was getting ahead of myself. At
the time, I didn't think so. I was counting on our lives together as she had
planned in El Paraíso. Well, not exactly planned but it seemed to me she
had thought about it just as I was thinking about it.

When I finally got to my feet, my knees wobbled queasy and guilt-ridden
from the pleasure I had found and my prayers were only to sustain pleasure with a woman I had thought I would never see again. And here
she was.

I sought out Lágrimas and fed him personally and when I saw he was
fine, I did what I had not done in those days in Clara's room and retrieved
whiskey and my red leather-bound journal from inside my jacket. I sat
with Lágrimas in the stable and I drank and sketched from memory
Clara's face. The eyes were almond shaped and the lips were round and
plump; her chin protruded slightly forward as if to point the way before
her. As I sketched I decided to buy Clara flowers. I would pluck the petals one by one and let them fall upon the bed, then wait for her to rush
through the door to admire the candlelit room with rose petals strewn
across the sheets. But I drank so much I forgot that plan and instead I tottered up the stairs to her room and waited. The candle burned to the wick
and I neglected to light another, preferring to sit in a stiff chair, assessing
shadows that took shape then disappeared.

When Clara climbed the stairs to her room, she was tired and cranky
from dealing cards all night to men who pawed at her with coarse, scratchy
hands. Nights like this wore her out to fight them off when all she really wanted was to slap them across the face and knee them in the groin.
She walked through the door smelling like cigars and whiskey that had
stained her dress and she slid the dress from her hips and sat naked on my
lap. Clara kissed my cheek and wrapped her arms around my neck and I
sensed she could smell drink on my breath but she said nothing of it.

On a squeaky bed, we swayed and rocked through the night and at
midnight while Clara slept I stirred tired and hungry, attempting to en-

dure a craving that would not let me rest. My whiskey bottle emptied, I dressed and descended the stairs to the saloon, where quiet engulfed the room now insignificant except for the cheap rye lining the shelf behind the bar. I grabbed a bottle and sat alone in that dank drinking hole and the only light was a flicker of the moon shining from the street and through the doors.

"She's a beauty, ain't she?"

I heard the whisper in the dark and decided it was my imaginings but when I turned around there stood an outline of a man I thought I recognized but I put that thinking aside and took another drink.

"I mean, if you like women with a little bit of darky in 'em."

I looked up and saw his face. It was Oscar. He laughed out loud as any devil would who believed in his own providence. He sat beside me and swigged long from my bottle, then waggled his head as an animal would and wiped his mouth on his sleeve.

"Left me for dead, didn't you, son?" He laughed again, louder than before, and the bellows of his cheer alarmed me as an evil spirit one encounters past midnight would alarm. "I tell you what, son. Seeing as how you're a betting man, I bet you can't make it up them stairs fast enough to save your slave girl from the fun she's about to have."

I darted up the stairs and flung the door open. Clara slept tranquil and the room was empty of any other soulless man and so I ran back down the stairs and only a half-empty bottle rested at that same table but two chairs were pulled out opposite each other in a looming confrontation. I plucked my bottle and swigged some more, bewildered of a ghost I might have seen. Back in the room, Clara awoke and pulled me close. Her breath was sweet and hot and that heat goaded me into her arms and I ripped her lacy underclothes and bore my mouth down upon her until we fell sleep.

When we woke in the early afternoon, my temples throbbed and I grabbed my bottle from the floor and sipped. The throbbing dissipated and I got up from bed and thought back to the night when I'd seen a ghost or thought I had but the sight of Clara in her shredded garments took my mind from ghosts and things. I felt my guilty pleasure once again but had no way of wrestling with its presence in my body. I pulled on my pants and washed in the hand basin, then slicked my wet hair back and tugged at my suspenders over my shirt.

"You look like you're getting ready for your own wedding," said Clara. She leaned back against the bed's headboard.

"Maybe I am," I said. I sat on the bed next to her and slipped on my boots.

"Where do you think you're going? So early in the day?"

"Thought I'd take a walk."

"A walk?"

"Yeah. A walk. On the water. I've been here almost a week and still ain't seen that ocean."

"It's not an ocean. It's a gulf leading to the ocean."

"Same thing to me. Come on. Let's go for a walk on the water. Just me and you."

"It's too hot and I've got to work, Micaela."

"Not till later. It's early yet." I shoved my shoulder into hers. "Ain't it time you took a little break?"

"If you make me a promise."

"What's that?"

"Let me buy you a new jacket. That buckskin stinks."

"Darlin, I stink."

She raised an eyebrow in that judging manner women have.

"Tell you what. Put on one of your pretty dresses and come hang on my arm for a spell and if I get the notion I might try on a fancy jacket or two."

She raised the same eyebrow and smiled. Her skin glistened in the afternoon light and when she rose from bed, I felt my knees go weak from the way she dabbed her neck with a towel. She dressed in a rare color of orange or pink, I wasn't sure, never having seen such a color, and against her skin the color's luster surfaced vivid and receptive to the daylight. In her left hand she held a parasol and with her right she grasped my arm and we stepped out of her room together. I was content when no one gazed at me but instead at her and the stares did not indict or suspect.

On the street she hauled me into a tailor's shop and he welcomed our business having glimpsed her style and grace but once he saw me he stepped back in visible contempt. Clara removed my heavy buckskin jacket that smelled as bad as any carcass and she set it aside as the bald-headed tailor held up fancy waistcoats with his spiny fingers, willing my arms to slip inside. I felt outnumbered and anyway, there was a part of me savoring notice from Clara and so I indulged her and was fitted for the waistcoat of her choosing along with a blue shirt of my own choosing. She had insisted on a white one with ruffles and when I refused she insisted again but my stubborn fortitude made her give up and settle as I did on a blue shirt with a fancy wide collar. The tailor nagged that I try on the shirt before making my purchase and when he yanked on the buttons of my tattered stained chemise, I nearly socked him but Clara elbowed between us and the man was saved and so was I. She distracted him and asked him for the latest fashion in pants and he produced a pair with buttons up both sides like a bib over one's private parts. When Clara whispered in his ear, he raised his eyebrows and nodded, pointing to a curtain. She led me back behind the curtain and appealed to me to remove my pants and since I felt secure behind that drape I humored her. She stood outside and I heard whispers once again but this time louder as if not to mind if I heard.

"He's stubborn, your son," he said.

I balanced on a naked leg and peeked out of the curtain to see Clara smiling.

"I'm not her son," I yelled for them to hear.

The tailor flushed red and Clara smiled again and I wondered how he could think I was her son since she was barely three years older. I realized her fashion made her appear older and had I not been so thick-skulled I might have understood she was attempting to age me with a wardrobe that would help me look less conspicuous at her side. We left the tailor, who grinned delighted with our purchases and I assumed he was unsuspecting of my sex. In my new attire, I transpired into someone respectable for a woman so fine as Clara and the tailor understood this truth before I did.

We walked out into the late afternoon but the sun's heat had not yet subsided. I felt like a dandy in my new costume and did not object to the sensation so long as Clara was beside me. Along the boardwalk of crumbling planks, we sauntered as a married couple would and the sea breeze cooled my face as waves burst forth and christened us. I was overjoyed and blissful and when I saw two children strolling with their mother, I stopped before they passed us. One was a girl and the other a boy and they looked so much alike they had to be twins. The baby girl smiled up at me and gave me a piece of hard, sweet ginger and I took the candy, holding her hand for a long minute, maybe more. I couldn't let go. Her mother touched me gently and that gesture brought me back to the present but by then guilt and sorrow had already latched on to my body and whispered in my ear to jump into the sea and forget the life I thought could be with Clara. Self-reproach surpassed any contentment I had come to know these last few days. Suddenly I was desperate to return to our room since I had no drink with me. Clara saw my desperation but said nothing of it and led us back down the boardwalk to the town's center. We entered through a back door leading to dingy stairs, then to her room, and I tossed my black waistcoat wrinkled from my sweat on a chair and swallowed the last bit of rye in my bottle.

"It's hot," I said.

Opening the wooden shutters to the lone window in the room, I let the cool evening breeze blow in and I rested on the bed and kicked off boots, muddy and worn, reminding me of things still common to my body. I picked up a boot and placed it on my lap and tipped the empty bottle on my tongue for the last drops. When I was done, I put on both boots, tore off my fancy shirt and replaced it with my old chemise and buckskin jacket and slipped out of Clara's room.

It was early evening but already a rowdy bunch sat at the center table and gambled at a game I identified as straight-laced poker. Five-card draw. Nothing fancy. I was about to intervene when Clara strolled down the stairs and all in that saloon gazed up and whistled catcalls that irritated me. I suppose I became conscious then that I was the jealous type and this character flaw would humiliate me throughout my life during moments when I was not vigilant of that emotion crawling inside my skin. Clara dismissed the dealer and set up her box of cards for monte and no one left the table except for the dealer, who went back to tending bar.

I sat back and watched and what I saw was men who stared at my Clara with an ugly longing. I signaled to the barkeep for another bottle and he slapped it down on my corner table and held out his grimy hand for payment. I nodded toward Clara and he saw her nod at him and then he went back behind the counter of his miserable post. The glass he had left was too small but out of decorum I poured and drank leisurely and peered at the men who sweet-talked Clara as they lost money undisturbed by their losses and continuing to play. One of the boys, neither handsome nor ugly, pawed at her waist until the evening wore into the night and then he fondled her ass and each time he did she laughed and warned him, tossing his hand off her buttocks. I could see from my corner he had a persistent temperament and that was when my jealousy did the things I did not think I was capable of doing. Up to that moment I thought only fear and revenge had provoked me and brought me to the time and place where I now found myself but something else erupted from inside me and I had no acquaintance with this sadistic reaction.

At first I was polite. I stood and inched to the center table and locked his neck with my arm and choked the unfortunate slug until he spit. Then I knocked his head over and over against the table and blood poured out of his nose and he spit saliva mixed with blood onto the other boys, who got up and scattered. I didn't care if they defended him or not. I was lunatic enough for the lot of them and I think they saw that I was crazy and that my lunacy came out of nowhere and none of them cared to test its sincerity. I shoved him on the floor and kicked from his head to his groin and I kicked over and over and couldn't stop and I have to say I was not inclined to stop. There was something freeing and wondrous in this state I was in and I reveled in a pleasure I'd not known till now. I even thought that this bliss equaled what I had with Clara during our most secret moments and I was surprised that a part of my logic was still in place as I kicked in the poor slug's head until he lay unconscious and bloody on the floor in a pool of his own urine. The unfortunate menace had pissed in his pants and I was glad.

Clara inched away from me and when I saw her eyes I knew I was done for. What she did next I didn't think I could ever forgive but when you fall in love the way I fell in love with Clara you learn to put away emotions that only drive you mad each time you think on what women like her are capable of doing without a thought to your own humiliation. She knelt and hovered over the beaten man and the other men followed her orders and placed him on top of the bar and someone skipped out for the town doctor.

Watching, I felt like the half-wit I had become. She had not even thanked me. Instead, she whispered in my ear to go to our room and that she'd follow shortly but shortly turned into an hour and then two and by then I was nearly passed out from having drink after drink in my own peaceful celebration. Maybe I was more like my cousin Jedidiah Jones than I had thought was possible. Maybe I was nothing but a fool.

"Micaela! Wake up. Come on, wake up."

Clara's smell aroused me as she poked my arm and chest to wake me and once she roused me her skin's scent put me in a trance and I wanted to sleep and dream of her instead.

"Micaela." She slapped my cheek, almost cruel, and I opened my eyes.

"Get up. We've got to pack and leave."

I stared at her puzzled.

"Don't you know what you did?"

"I was protecting your honor."

She shook her head. "That boy is hanging on by a thread."

"He'll be all right."

"He may make it, he may not and we're not going to stay around here to wait one way or the other." She gathered clothes from a chest of drawers and tossed them into a trunk.

"He's some stupid sonovabitch who deserved what he got," I said.

Clara snatched my collar and tightened her grasp around my throat. "He's the sheriff's son, Micaela. The sheriff's son!"

"So? Everybody saw how he was pawing at you."

She let go of my collar and then spoke softly, as softly and kindly as she ever had or I'd ever known her to. It was as if she took pity on me and realized that if she coddled me I might come to some sense of clarity about our predicament.

"Micaela, sweet thing, drink this coffee." She handed me a cup that came out of nowhere. "Now, get up, wash and pack."

I can't explain how my heart fluttered when I heard her speak my real name with such consideration. At that moment, Clara was all that mattered to me. That some slug was about to die was as insignificant to me as my own life had been up to then and I didn't care if he lived or died. All that mattered was that Clara and I were on our way somewhere together.

We left before daybreak, one step ahead of a sheriff no one had bothered to notify since he was gone trailing who knows who and I guess I was glad for that not so trivial fate. A waning moon peeked through willows as I lurched to the pier dragging Clara's trunk forward in clumsy strides of stop and go. My saddlebag and my rifle were wrapped across my shoulder and Clara led Lágrimas by the reins but he poked along as if unwilling, as if to warn us that the better life we sought was an imaginary tale that would be my ruination.

CHAPTER 15

It was July and rain fell on and off during our brief, afflicted voyage. The cargo ship sailed as stars vanished and the sun's faint light shimmered on waves that lapped against the hull. Outside standing at the bow I breathed erratically, feeling somewhat troubled as I gazed at a horizon of a vast gray ocean blending with the sky. With Clara at my side, I strived to forget what I had witnessed and what I had become—a loner and a killer who was in love but doubted the possibility of a forgiving love. Something had changed in me and I guess I needed Clara as my only family to anchor me. I fixed my arms to the railing and rocked back on my boot heels as I watched the drizzle scare away all but a few passengers. I thrashed my head about in the rain and bumped Clara repeatedly in a gesture that begged for her attention. Her skin shined golden in an emerald velvet dress and her breasts burst full in a V-shaped bodice that hugged her body. Her hips swayed with the rhythm of the ship and her body pulsed against my own, distracting me until I looked up and spotted a man who stared at my Clara much too long for my satisfaction. She saw me staring back at him.

"Micaela," she whispered.

I kissed her cheek to reassure her, then looked again at the man who faced the sea.

Clara nuzzled closer, her bonnet hiding lips upon my neck but when I saw that she thought I was diverted, she peeked through her bonnet's cap at the stranger in a black beaver top hat. His double-breasted waistcoat was fastened high with gold buttons and as he coughed into a handkerchief, a scaly knob of an Adam's apple bobbled over his collar. He stuffed the handkerchief in a wide flap pocket, glanced up and met my stare, then tipped his hat so I nodded quickly and placed my arm around Clara's waist.

We stood in the drizzle leaning shoulders and hips into torsos warm from each other's heat speaking loud and in whispers depending on what we said and what we preferred to remain secret and I liked how the whispers made us co-conspirators. We became accustomed to rain that neither drenched nor irritated until evening when a storm came in and we squeezed into a cabin so small I felt ill at ease. I rummaged through my saddlebag for a flask of whiskey I had stolen in Galveston and I drank long and hard to calm a fear that had caught up with me again. I felt guilty of so many things I couldn't get my mind commonsensical. I poked a hand outside the porthole and felt relieved at rain pelting on my skin but when the ship rocked from waves high and erratic, my stomach turned queasy and disordered. I laid my head on Clara's lap and the lavender scent of her skin through her dress sated me until the next swell teetered the ship and we swayed in the tiny berth back and forth. I hung my head outside the porthole, upchucked, and my face chilled with shame and although the breeze and raindrops pacified, the unrelenting swaying soured my insides for the duration of that voyage.

If she was angry with me for what had occurred in Galveston, she hadn't let on but I had an eerie sense she was holding back. I decided not to probe the topic of my stormy temperament and mostly I was grateful she was treating me so graciously but on the other hand it was like waiting for the goddess Hera to rear her torrent of fury, even though I doubted that Clara was so heartless or wicked as that. After all, she had protected me by getting me out of that town and I was the one who had created circumstances that forced her to leave. Clara smoothed my hair back, kissed my nose and bore fingers down on my cheek's scar.

"Where do you think he's from?" I said.

"Who?"

I nodded toward the ship's bow.

"When do you plan on growing up?"

"I'm grown up."

"I mean in here." She pointed her index finger over my heart. "When you plan on letting go of childish jealousy?"

"It's not so childish." Here it comes, I thought. She's about to lecture me, I know it.

"I can't have myself a family with someone who hasn't learned to control her emotions in public settings."

I smiled. "You want a family with me, Clara?"

"I want a family with someone who knows better than to lose her temper every time someone rubs her the wrong way."

"I can do that. I promise. I can. You got to trust me, Clara." I lifted my head up and kissed her cheek and made my way slowly to her lips. When she returned the kiss I was satisfied because that kiss was a most certain yes.

Without warning, the whirling room accosted me and I pushed my head out of the porthole and threw up into the sea again. My head dangled through the hole and bobbed up and down so that from a distance I must have looked like a single round ball bouncing on the water. I squeezed my skull back through the porthole and dropped back on Clara's lap.

"You're ruining my dress."

I reached beneath the berth for my buckskin jacket to line Clara's lap, then dropped my head down again and closed my eyes to avoid the ceiling falling in on me.

Clara pulled the jacket out from under my head and threw it out the porthole into the sea. She placed her hands over my ears to warm them.

"Feel better?"

"That was my papi's jacket." I sat up confounded.

"And I gave it a decent burial." She shoved my head back down to her lap and the softness of her flesh triumphed over any objection I had about that buckskin.

"Are you hungry?" she said.

"Not really."

"You need to eat something."

She took my head from her lap, got up and opened her parasol. My head began to ache again.

"Don't be opening that in here. It's bad luck."

"You need to eat."

"I'm fine."

"You're not," said Clara. She climbed up steep narrow steps though a trapdoor leading to the deck and yelled back down, "I'll find some food."

I lay on the berth with my head still throbbing and realized that I couldn't rest without her so I rose and climbed the stairs hoping sea mist on my face would soothe me but instead of feeling soothed, I was overtaken by rage when I saw Clara with the stranger. His gold-buttoned waistcoat was less shiny in the dusk and as he leaned against the railing and tipped his hat, she dipped her chin. He approached her and when he was a foot within reach, a wave slapped against the hull and she stumbled but he grabbed her arm and held firm as she lunged against his chest laughing. She told me later that his breath smelled rancid and that she had only laughed to calm her nerves. His teeth were yellowed from brown spit that curled in his mouth from some illness but despite the odor, she said, he had a handsome face in a craggy sort of way. I had already sensed her interest in him. My gut sank and I was immediately agitated from the sight of Clara laughing with this bungling man who couldn't know how to amuse a woman like her. His smile through those yellow teeth perturbed me and the way he held her arm firm further provoked my sensibility, so what I did next was not surprising having just done something comparable in the town we were running from. I ran so fast I still amaze myself with my speed that day and I grabbed his arms behind his back and kicked with my knee over and over until he tumbled facedown on slippery planks and standing over him I shoved my boot in his stomach, repeating my task until I heard a hymn in my head that reassured me in the same way I'd been reassured when I beat the man who pawed at Clara in Galveston. Mr. Gold-buttoned Waistcoat coughed and spit like someone who was ill because the coughs resounded deep and hoarse as an ailing man might sound. From my periphery I saw two boatmen charge behind me. They clutched each of my arms and shoved me to my knees and when I looked up searching for Clara, I saw her kneeling before her fancy stranger, then helping him to his feet. I yelled to her but she ignored me as the boatmen yanked my arms and I slid on my knees until my legs fell behind me and they dragged me across the sodden planks to a hole in the floor and thrust me down into its darkness and closed the hole and left me there for a day or maybe two.

With bumps on my head and bruises on my arms, I should have been fuming or at the least forlorn with my new dilemma. Instead I took the time alone to think about where I was and what I had done to bring me to this part of my journey. Here I was on a ship with a woman I prized but each time I saw a man entertain a thought of wanting her the way I did, I went fanatical in ways I never had before. I didn't understand what I was becoming. Was I to be possessed by these demons so long as I was near her? I didn't know. Had I already killed a man for her? Or had I killed him to temper jealous streaks that had become so powerful I had no control over their authority? I wasn't sure if I had killed that boy in Galveston. Maybe I should have stayed to make it right but she had persuaded me to run and here I was. Already, I could hear Clara's voice saying to me,

"Grow up, Micaela. I won't be with someone so hot-tempered." My disappointment over what I had just done to that fancy stranger swept over me. I looked around and when my eyes focused from the light that shown through the cracks in the ceiling, I realized I was in a storage room and in the corner of the room was an oak barrel with the word "rum" scribbled on the sides. I thanked the ghosts of my ancestors and crawled to the keg and cracked open a spigot that drained straight and neat into my mouth.

When I awoke either the next day or a few hours later, the ship rocked unsteady and above me I heard voices.

"I say we go for the reward now," said one voice. It was low and gruff and I decided I was listening to one of the boatmen who had tossed me in this den.

"Reward's not enough to turn back now. Best we stay on course and when it's time to return, we find our captive," said another voice lower and gruffer than the first.

"You willing to take that chance?"

"We cain't keep captives here."

"Well, somebody's got to mind our reward."

"You saying we oughta follow that little creature?"

"That's what I'm saying."

"You fed them horses yet?"

"Nope."

"Well, get to it."

I heard a rumbling of chairs and footsteps above me and with no sense of time I wondered if they had plans to feed me. When I looked around the dark den for a semblance of nourishment, the rum keg announced itself and so I drank some more. I didn't want to face what was coming and I didn't know how to escape my latest predicament. Maybe I had no need to escape. Maybe these men had not been speaking about me at all and I was only imagining the worst of prospects. They could not have known about a reward on my head since we had left before anyone had news of my wrongdoing. I sat back and decided not to worry about a conversation that may or may not have been about me. The ship doddered faintly now that the storm had passed and the planks creaked from the heavy cargo of rum kegs that had been brought from islands far beyond my knowledge.

For the second time since in that hole I dozed and with my hands clasped above my forehead as if in prayer, I fell into a dream of my own imagining and the sweetness of the vision brought the twins but they were not babies. They were full-grown and dressed fancy as if today was their marrying day. Behind Ifi and Rusty stood Clara, smoothing the shoulders of Rusty's suit and placing a white, lacy veil on Ifi's head. I hung back and observed the happy scene until Clara called to me and said, "They're ready." I opened two heavy double doors and held out my arm for Ifi to take and we marched forward with Clara and Rusty behind us. In the pews of the church were our family and friends, from Miss Elsie and Byron to la curandera and papi sitting with mamá. Juana and her mother and father with Tomasa and her husband were also present. The smiles on everyone's faces made me cry from the joy of such unity.

"Where's Jedidiah?" I whispered to Clara but she didn't hear me. I repeated my question over and over until I awoke with the same words on my lips.

CHAPTER 16

Through sapphire fog and mist, the port of New Orleans hung above a murky ocean in a cloud puffy and fat like a satin curtain fluttering open. I'd never seen a sight so beautiful except for Clara. Down below, the streets were narrow and cobbled, lined with carriages elegant and profuse transporting women in fashion gowns and men in top hats and velvet double-breasted overcoats.

It was late evening by the time my captors permitted me to disembark but I was not to be at Clara's side. From the deck I watched embittered as she walked beside her fancy stranger, who had paid a footman to carry the same trunk I had helped transport a few days back. My heart twisted and turned upside down or at least I felt it mangled and contorted in my chest as Clara clutched this stranger's arm not once turning back to the ship, proving she was traveling onward with him, stopping only briefly before a black coach that may not have been as elegant as the ones that passed them by but nonetheless it was the one that took her from me. He seized her arm as if she was in his possession, helping her to climb up, and as the door closed behind them my knees buckled and my hands froze to the railing. I buried my face in the crook of my arm to resist howling out to her. All I knew was that she possessed my heart. I was young enough to believe that I would rather die than live without her but in retrospect I have realized that my young woman's heart had already suffered so much more than that moment presented and that it was really the culmination of my life's drama overwhelming me with a death wish. Every family that I'd had or made I had lost to circumstances beyond my influence but with Clara I was convinced a godly power might protect us from losing one another and yet here she was, abandoning me. It was more than I could accept. First the twins, my father and Juana, then Jedidiah and now Clara had all been lost to me either through death or condemnation. It's odd how at that time I had no thoughts of my mother, as if she wasn't worth the reflection and instead I erased her from my memory, relegating her to a life of comfort and bliss with Venustiano. Right then, on that cargo ship in a place that looked like paradise, I felt the torment of a wrecked heart and I asked how much was I to endure before I found my peace. But there was to be no peace, at least not yet.

I ambled down a plank to dry land with Lágrimas beside me and I was reasonably aware that my captors watched me stroll through milling crowds. Lágrimas nodded and grunted and wobbled his head. I patted his mane and said, "I know. I feel the same way." As I held on to his reins, he toddled beside me, his gait long and slow, and I came upon a stable with rooms to let above it and decided this was good enough but mostly I just didn't care, so I handed the proprietor a couple of silver coins for the week's fee and was glad I had come away with more than sufficient winnings in Galveston. I settled Lágrimas in with enough hay to last him a few days, then I laid down on a feather bed with sheets perfumed and silky. But the perfume was from a gardenia tree's blossoms wafting in through an open transom and the silk sheets weren't silk at all but worn-out cotton. I fell into a sound sleep for the first time since I had discovered Clara in Galveston.

I woke early and anxious with no plan in mind so I washed and dressed in my fancy clothes hoping some strategy for dodging the boatmen while searching for Clara would come to me soon. I took the stairs to the stable, where I found the liveryman hammering wrought iron to turn its shape into something other than a long, straight iron rod. He did not look up when I greeted him and I decided the banging and hammering must have kept him from hearing what I had to say so I gestured with my hands to my mouth and soon enough he understood and pointed out in front of him to a street that led to shops and food. With my black waistcoat across my arm, I felt the sea breeze on my back flapping my shirt as I sauntered along peeking into shops through open doors. The smell of unusual spices drifted through the avenues and I grew hungrier and stopped to breakfast at a public house that was more like a tavern where light-skinned and dark races congregated and spoke in a language so unrecognizable, it resonated guttural and lyrical at once. I listened while I ate rice spiced with garlic and chile peppers covered with syrupy beans red and smoky from plump sausage bits. There were other spices that I had never tasted but they were agreeable and I had a second bowl to savor the flavors in my mouth a little longer. Filling my mug from a spout of earthenware crockery, I swallowed and spit as soon as I had the initial sampling. It was a vile, muddy drink, bitter like no rotgut I had ever drank. The watered-down whiskey at Miss Elsie's tasted like champagne compared to the concoction in my mug diluted with something as foul as turpentine or creosote and spiced with cayenne or chile peppers. I had seen Miss Elsie water down whiskey before but she only added a bit of oatmeal and molasses to thicken and darken it and some snakeroot from time to time to give it a kick, she said. She had warned me. "See this here," she said. "It's turpentine and creosote. Some old fellows like to spike their whiskey that way. Say it goes further. Take a swallow. Come on now, take a swallow so you know never to drink it again. I say it just rots your gut and then you ain't got customers no more cuz they're all belly-up on you. Stick to natural bits and pieces, I say. Little bit of oatmeal gives the boys a bit of something in their bellies, especially those who cling to the bottle and won't eat nothin, not even chicken soup and you know how good that recipe of Byron's is. And the molasses. Well, that just sweetens the brew. That's why my customers come back for my whiskey. It's my special blend."

Thoughts of Miss Elsie made me homesick but not enough to get me caught and sent back to Tejas, if that was my fate. I left that tavern and strolled in the heat and felt the sun burn my neck and felt drowsy from too much food eaten too fast, causing me to fret in that excessive state about my captors who could have been near. I chose a less-traveled path that led to a square and beyond into a quarter where I heard foreign languages intermingle. I soaked up the sounds and gazed at light-skinned brown women who returned surreptitious gazes, escorted by white men speaking loud about balls and festivities, mothers and currency. The couples spilled out from houses with balconies ornate from iron carvings of butterflies or flowers. Two-story houses lined the lane and I glimpsed curtains stirring not from wind but from hands and heads that poked through cracks from above on the second floor looking down upon the passing couples as if in need of someone's arm but too young or too dowdy or too white to be permitted or desired. There was a strict protocol among these inhabitants and although there was a guise of freedom between and among their society, I learned that a rigid, disciplined hierarchy ranged from dark- to light-skinned, from colored to white. My tanned skin did not rouse the passersby as I meandered with my coat draped across an arm and since I had no cause to abide by laws or codes of conduct I continued on my walk. Beads of sweat gathered on my neck and when I unbuttoned my collar a few stately women stared as if to recognize something familiar about me and when I dipped my chin they looked away and their escorts peered at me as if I was a rival. For a moment I felt the pleasure of women gazing upon me and for that moment I allowed myself to forget Clara and any scheme to find her.

The smell of baked bread interrupted my stroll and I paused and poked my nose through a door. I spied upon couples sitting at tables where women fingered squares of puffed bread doused in white sugar and the men drank chicory-scented coffee. I entered and sat and waited until the puffy pastries were placed before me and asking for more I ate until I felt dizzy and sated from sweetness and coffee. I wondered if Clara had ever tasted anything like this and if she might learn to fry the delicate squares in hot oil, toasted brown and coated in white sugar. And then missing her put me in a gloomy misery.

Someone stood above me and set another platter of the pastries called beignets at my table. I looked up at a woman in a head turban, her skin light and dark at once and its darkness was as rich as cinnamon. She adjusted the tignon on her head and the colorful scarf of orange and red lay bare against her skin.

"You are far from home, mon cher." A strip of the scarf fell on her naked shoulder and the cloth fluttered from a slight breeze wafting through the door.

"No. Not really."

"Ah. We have only met and already you are lying to me. Are you accustomed to lying to women, mon cher?"

"It's not a lie." I looked up at her.

"Ah. You lie again?"

I smiled. "I've got no need to lie to strangers."

"And now you insult me and call me a stranger." She clucked her tongue against her palate and a smile grew in the corner of her mouth.

"To me you are a stranger." I chose to play along.

"And so, will you answer this stranger's question?"

"I'll try."

"You are far from home, no?"

"I have no home."

"Ah, mon cher, you are full of the self-pity." She clucked again. "You are too young to be so full of the self-pity."

"I'm not young."

"But you are. And one day soon, very soon, you will feel young again. Perhaps this afternoon?" Her eyebrow turned up.

"That's too soon, I think." My insides fluttered and the flutter was unmistakable.

"Perhaps you will find a home here? In New Orleans? There are many young beautiful women who could assist your broken heart, no?"

"No." I gazed at the woman's face and saw crow's-feet around her eyes and I realized she was older and far more lovely than I had initially noticed.

"You are not from here? Yes? Of course you are not. No, do not answer. I have the answers. Right here." She pointed to my chest and grazed my shirt with a long, slender finger and grinned slyly at what she might have discovered but probably already knew. Then she grazed my cheek outlining the scar, as Clara often would. I trembled and she grinned again. Quickly, I focused on her headdress fastened with a ruby brooch to keep myself from staring at her breasts.

"Come." The woman named Miss Celestine took my hand and I felt spongy softness and became embarrassed of my calloused fingers. Walking behind her I attempted to avert my gaze but the pleated skirt swung back and forth as if beckoning with each forward step and although I felt timid, I turned myself over to her persistence which could not hurt me any more than I already felt.

"Sit." She pointed to a bench in the corner of a garden overgrown with vines and flowers.

I stood and looked around the open garden at crimson roses, which had unusual violet petals at their core. A goat wandered about nibbling leaves from flowers and vines, then sat under a shaded tree, rested its head and closed its eyes while half a dozen chickens roamed the garden and scribbled hieroglyphics on the earth.

"Sit." She shoved me down onto the bench and began to shuffle cards. These were not playing cards but instead had images of queens and kings and swords and cups upside down and right side up.

"You must tell her."

"Tell who?"

"The woman."

"What woman?"

"Ah, mon cher, there is always a woman. You must tell her you love her."

"She knows."

"Ah, she knows, yes, in her heart she knows, but not from you. She doubts, you see."

"She doubts? How can she doubt?"

"You are bitter. You should not be bitter when it is you who have abandoned her."

"Me? She's the one who walked off with Mr. Fancy Pants."

"Ah. You do not understand women, mon cher."

"I understand."

"Believe me, you do not understand. You only think you understand and what you think you understand you only imagine as correct when all you have done is invent falsehoods, cher. That pleases you, no?"

"I'm not pleased."

"Ah, you are pleased." She shuffled cards, placed the pile in front of me and ordered me to cut.

I examined the pile, repositioned the cards into two stacks and piled them back into one as she instructed. She spread the cards and pointed to one with an indigo background of sea and sky and beneath the water a crab made slow progress to the shore while above in the sky a full moon shone.

"There, you see. You are crawling on an ocean floor, disillusioned and alone when all along the moon shines above you. And see? See this?" She pointed to another card. Two children, a boy and a girl, twins, stood caressing each other beneath a bright, shining sun. "This is your paradise but it is not easily won. You are in pursuit of your paradise, yes?"

Tears like welts reddened my eyes.

The woman reached across the table and touched my scarred face. Her kindness distracted me and I got angry at the distraction and pulled away but she was indifferent to my bad humor.

"Yes. You have cried. You have cried and felt it would never end. This crying. But it will, cher. I promise it will end. See?" She took a card from the table and held it up for me. "You see? Victory." A chariot pulled by two horses with someone at the reins was the picture. "You are victorious, mon cher. You will win. In the end you will win. But you must continue on your journey. Yes? Of course, there will be sadness, there is always sadness but the sadness comes and goes and you'll find your own happiness. And the woman, well, you will see."

"How do you know?"

"Ah, because I know. It is my gift."

"I see nothing," I mumbled into cupped hands and bowed my head to study cards that foretold lies and trickery as far as I was concerned. Tears fell inside my palms.

"And these?" I pointed to two cards that lay side by side. One had a young man holding a pentacle, a coin perhaps, while the other was stamped with a man who dangled upside down from a tree limb, tied to a knotted rope. His blue hair flopped down from his head as he dangled, suspended with one leg bent or crossed, parallel and beneath the other.

The woman in the headdress brushed aside the cards I pointed out.

"Those? Those are warnings, mon cher. Warnings that you must abide by your heart and not let your head rule your heart or you will end up like this. Upside down and ruled by money." She swept her hand across the table. "That is not the way to live, cher. Money is only money. It is around every corner, but love, that is another tale, altogether another tale. It is not around every corner and if you find it, when you find it, you must cherish it. And fight for it. Yes?"

"Fight? For what isn't mine?"

"Love belongs to all, mon cher. It is people we do not own and no, you do not own her. No one can possess her. She will not allow such possession but she will allow love and it is your love she waits for, but you, ah, you think you are like him."

She pointed to the hanged man.

"I feel like him." A card had fallen from her pile and I stared at a ghostly character with horns on his head.

She rolled her eyes up to the sky and raised an eyebrow, then stared at me.

"That is the devil, mon cher. We all know the devil. And as you suspect, evil is following you and you can either fear it or tame it."

Fear rose up in my gut but I crammed it back down.

"Be a nobleman, mon cher." She winked and inched her face so close to mine I could feel her breath on my lips. "Self-pity, mon cher, self-pity is the tool of evil. You must muster courage and forget yourself. You see, you are the crab under water, crawling slowly to the shore. Sometimes sideways, sometimes faster, but you are nearing your destination. You are nearing your fate. You see? Here." She displayed the card with the chariot and handed it to me. "Study," she said. "Study and you will learn."

I searched the images for answers or hints about my future but nothing came to me. I studied this victor on his chariot wearing a crown and wielding a baton, then my eyes shifted to the figures of the twins in blue underpants, the sun pouring multicolored drops upon them.

"I'm sorry," I whispered as if they might hear me and prayed to some god or goddess that the angels of absolution might take my prayers of guilt and sorrow and end my life so that I would never have to feel their loss again. "I'm so sorry."

"Look inside. In here." The woman placed her hand on my heart.

I held her hand and pressed it tighter to my chest and bowed my head to kiss her hand. "That's no answer," I said. "That's not an answer."

"Ah, cher, but it is. It's an answer you are not yet prepared to hear but it is an answer. And see this? You will find him too. As you thought. As you suspected." She aimed her finger at the card with the young man or boy who wore a floppy hat and held up a coin proudly. Another coin was tossed on the ground at his feet.

"Here." She handed me a card. "This is my gift to you. Keep it safe and pressed inside your coat pocket. It will be your amulet against the evil that will come upon you."

"What does it mean?"

"You know what it means. It is as clear as the heavens on a day like today when the blue sky covers us and protects us from harm."

I took the card with two cups and hid it in my pocket and rose from the table heading to the door that led from the garden to the streets.

"Cher, where are you going? Wait—wait a minute."

I turned and reaching for coins in my trousers offered her a handful.

"I don't want your money, mon cher. I don't need your money. Look around. I am a wealthy woman. I am inviting you to the ball this evening."

"The ball?"

"The quadroon ball."

"Why would I want to go to a ball?" I fingered the card in my breast pocket.

"Because I, Miss Celestine, know all and you must accompany me tonight. It is an order."

CHAPTER 17

I entered a fairy tale or paradise not my own replete with treasures, novelties and chattel, although those who crossed that threshold did not recognize their treasures as chattel necessarily. If they had, they would have had a conscience of sorts and men like this had no need for a conscience when the world lay before them, spread out like a platter of pastries, sweet to the tongue and amusing to the eye. After wandering through the streets I came upon Miss Celestine in front of a building resembling a palace in former days but the years had weathered the palace and it stood more like a mausoleum with its occupants reenacting an indefensible past each time they entered.

"You cannot enter through the front door, mon cher. Come."

We squeezed through rows of well-dressed white men whose pistols and knives protruded from their pockets as if prepared for any incident that might confront them inside the quadroon ball. Street urchins and other beggars lined the alleyway that led us to a service entrance and as we made our way through the back door of that crumbling palace now a saloon, Miss Celestine handed me two items, a wooden flute and a mask, having already donned her own mask of a gold and silver eyepiece, festooned with ostrich feathers and rubies. With my face covered, I stepped through gowns that stretched out balloon-like and inflated. I didn't know what the flute was for until Miss Celestine shoved me onto a bandstand where men in masks held violins and flutes and played a waltz or at least I thought it was a waltz.

"You want to stay in here, you better start blowing on that thing," someone said to me but with masks hiding mouths and reed instruments at lips, I didn't know who spoke. I put the mouthpiece to my lips and slid my fingers up and down imitating the man I thought had spoken. His

brown fingers were finely manicured and they pressed on holes that released the buttons of a flute until he set it down, picked up a violin and
slid fingers along the neck. I paused to watch but for no more than a moment because again he ordered, "Play, or act like you're playing, or you'll
be thrown out and you'll have the rest of us in trouble." I saw someone else
and copied his fingers' movements and pursed my lips as much as I could.
The mask tied around my head with a ribbon fit snugly and I felt myself
grow faint from heat.

And then I saw her. I recognized the red satin dress, the curve of waist
and breasts full and lovely. It was Clara. The mask on her face hid her eyes,
disguising almost nothing. As I gazed upon her body's arcs, I was happy I
had found her even if she was with that same fancy stranger. But it wasn't
him. I recognized this other man easily. His thick eyebrows poked above
a mask thinly covering his eyes. Of course, I thought. He doesn't have to
hide. Not from anyone and not from me. It was Jed. With Clara on his
arm. As he leaned into her neck and murmured in her ear, I caught sight
of her spine straightening either in contempt over what he had said or just
plain contempt over the nearness of his breath. Miss Celestine held her
hand out to Clara and glanced in my direction and Clara followed her
gaze. I don't know why but I hid behind a column fearing she would see
me and when she did, I ran. I felt stupid for running but once I started, I
couldn't stop myself. I was so mad I didn't know what to do and fleeing
from that crowd with Clara on Jedidiah's arm was all that seemed possible
right then. I ran from the stage to the service entrance and out to the alleyway from where I had entered.

When I was six or seven years old, my papi would read to me from Cervantes's *Don Quixote* and like papi I saw myself inside those pages. It was
as if there was no distance between the adventurer and me as he journeyed
through quests I wanted to live one day. As he read I became Quixote
whose guts and wit thrust him through danger because he had a steadfast
belief that no one could soften no matter how much he was belittled. He
abided by his cause and he abided by his love for Dulcinea. That evening
when I saw Clara on Jedidiah's arm, I ached envious for a lover like Dulcinea, wondering if such love was possible. Clara and Jed, I thought. What
was his intention with her? I guess I'll never really know the honest-to-
goodness, uncomplicated truth about Clara and Jedidiah Jones. At this
stage of my life, I have come to recognize that the twists and turns of our
lives brought us to a juncture we never wished for.

After I ran from the quadroon ball, I cowered in the shadows of a street corner where I was alone and full of spite. I lingered for hours assuming Clara and Jedidiah would pass me walking down this main street where the carriages all waited to be hired. A drizzle softened my spite as I thought back to my voyage on the cargo ship when Clara and I endured rain much like this one and I longed for her lips upon my neck as they had been during that voyage and I longed for having been someone other than who I had become when I saw her with the fancy stranger.

And then I saw them. Jedidiah hailed a carriage and they climbed upon it and so I hailed one too and followed closely. When they stopped along the riverfront and climbed down, I waited, then pursued them into a building peopled with dozens of men and women gambling, smoking and drinking with a magnitude and gravity I'd never seen before. I stood with my mouth open and stared at the sight of men and women standing side by side before tables in games new to me. Gathered around a table with a wheel that spun round were speculators shouting out numbers and when the wheel paused, coming to a full stop, they shouted even louder in disappointment or glee. The game of roulette was a world I could happily inhabit, I thought. I approached the table with the spinning wheel and observed carefully to learn its tricks and art. A redheaded woman spun the wheel and when it stopped she gathered the betting coins and sometimes gave a pile to whoever had left money on a favored number. I think she must have liked me because she encouraged me to play and so I joined the crowd around the wheel and immediately won after placing my coins on the number twenty-two. "A lucky number," she said and when I asked why, she responded, "I am twenty-two, cher," and then she winked.

From the corner of my vision, beyond the room's smoke and clamor, I kept a watch on Clara, flanked by Jedidiah and two other men. When I studied their faces I saw one man with a half ear shining in the lamplight. The half-eared man spoke to none other than the fancy stranger and they leaned into each other's faces as familiar friends might do. I studied the scene of Clara and Jed with the two men beside them and felt panic come over me. A sickness beset me and all I could do was hunch over with my arms across my stomach as if to protect myself from some outside evil encroaching upon me. The redheaded woman saw and gestured to a plump dark-haired woman who took over the wheel and I was led to a tiny room behind a curtain. I lay down on a bedtick all the while the redheaded dealer pampered me and toweled my face, then bent to kiss my mouth and although I was ill I returned the kiss but was sorry I had because the curtain flung open and there stood Clara staring down upon us.

"Leave us," said Clara.

"I saw him first."

"You saw nothing. Now leave us."

Clara shoved the red-haired beauty away from my side and she shrugged her shoulders and left the room and a part of me regretted seeing her go.

When we were alone in that tiny hovel with the curtain closed, Clara kissed me and I couldn't catch my breath nor did I want to.

"I don't like who you've become," she said.

"You've got no right to tell me that," I said. I sat up straight and pushed her away. "You know those men?"

"What men?"

"Your fancy stranger. And the other two."

"You've been following me."

"Answer my question. Do you know those men?"

"Why? Do you?"

"Your fancy stranger is named Sonny, the half-eared sonovabitch is his companion, Runner."

"Those are their names. So what?"

"So what? I told you about them."

"Told me what?"

"They killed my brother and sister. On the ranch. That day."

"What day?"

"Why are you doing this, Clara?"

"Micaela, I don't know what you're talking about."

"Those two. Runner and Sonny. They killed my brother and sister. And now you're sweet on them and that's something awful mean."

"You didn't tell me. Why didn't you tell me before?" Her face was red with anger.

"What are you hiding, Clara?"

"I'm not the one hiding anything. What's happened to you?"

I stared at her for a long minute and felt myself go limp inside.

"I'm not the one turning what we had into some kind of hell."

"You're the one friendly with those damn murderers." I attempted to win back some ground in our argument. "And what about my cousin? You two seem like old lovers or something."

"Your cousin?"

"Everything all right in here?" The red-haired beauty peeked in the tiny room where we had been shouting.

"Leave us be a little longer," said Clara, who did not turn her head to address the red-haired beauty but instead stared at me.

"What cousin?"

"Jedidiah Jones."

"He's your cousin?"

"That's what I said."

"I didn't know." She looked down to the floor and her voice got soft.

"I guess he doesn't talk about me much."

"No. He doesn't."

"How long you been knowing him?"

"We met back in Galveston."

I felt my gut go queasy when she said that.

"You like him?" I asked.

"He's a friend to me, Micaela. That's all."

And then she elaborated the details of their first encounter so I decided to believe her since I needed to believe her. It had happened back in Galveston, she said. Jedidiah Jones with the Colonel arrived early one morning and woke the town with gun blasts and sharpshooting long before the sun had winked on the horizon. The moon still shined down upon them and the marauding assassins were hungry for whiskey and noise and women, all the things that could ensure overconfidence and false victories. She had been sleeping upstairs in her room, the same room where I had come to love her, when she heard booming voices downstairs in the saloon and when the piano was pounded in a deafening shrill she and the other women dressed and descended the stairs and discovered the Colonel and his men drinking whiskey and dancing with each other as the Colonel thumped on keys, crafting music only he and his men heard. She spotted Jedidiah immediately because he sat in a corner and shuffled cards and studied them all alone in that rowdy room. The saloon's proprietor had also descended and served up drinks and cooked eggs and steaks for all to eat and seemed quite content with gold coins strewn across the bar in payment for his labor so early in the morning. Clara and the girls observed the mayhem and went back to bed since the men all entertained each other and had no need of women until the next evening when the Colonel and his men appeared from behind closed doors, shaven and bathed and almost handsome, particularly Jedidiah, she said. That observation pinched in my gut.

The younger women stood in line to dance with Jed but Clara only watched and sat with him when he shuffled cards and played solitaire late into the morning and that was how they got to know each other, playing cards and demonstrating the tricks of solitaire for the three days that the Colonel and his men stayed in the town by the bay. She never asked who they were or what they were doing and Jedidiah never volunteered the information but it didn't matter once the two of them climbed the stairs to her room and he stayed through the darkness of the morning, playing solitaire, she said. By sunlight he was gone with the Colonel and his men. She had only just recognized him by sight when they bumped into each other in a gambling house on the riverfront in New Orleans. That was what she told me. What they did in that room remains a secret I do not wish revealed to me. At least, that's what I told myself.

"Why'd he bring you here? To meet up with them?"
  "I don't know, Micaela. You ask him. He's your blood relative."
  "He live here? In New Orleans?"
  "You mean Jed?"
  "Yes. I mean Jed."
  "I just saw him again today. I didn't ask him his life story."
  "Let's go. I don't want him to see me. Not yet."

CHAPTER 18

We abandoned the gambling house for fear of my being recognized by Jed because seeing him before I was prepared to see him did not fit in my plan—not that I really had one. Clara thought to take me back to her hotel room but I reminded her that her newly found friends were bound to search for her and so I hauled her to the only place I thought we would be safe. To Miss Celestine's.

I snuck around to the square called the Vieux Carré leading to Miss Celestine's place, where you could purchase many things including love charms and voodoo spells with your coffee and beignets or brandy and cigars. She was not surprised to see us and I suspected her own intuitive witchery had informed her we would call on her assistance.

Still dressed in her evening gown she reported to us that the quadroon ball had been invaded by two American boatmen who barged through the doors without having paid a cent, believing their Americanness gave them permission to enter and cause a stir. She said they searched the room frantically for someone but were promptly escorted from the ball by self-appointed guards who shoved them into the street. Miss Celestine stared at Clara when she told this story and I was glad she didn't see how uncomfortable I was with news of boatmen on the loose.

After her account of the evening's events, Miss Celestine led Clara and me to a private room and as she shut the door behind us, she winked at me as if to say, you see, mon cher, I told you I would help you find her.

Clara removed her overcoat and sat on the bed. She crossed her legs, leaning on her elbow, and her hair fell down her back. When she held her hand out to me, I tangled her fingers with mine, kneeled before her and rested my head on her lap. She brushed my hair with her fingers and kissed my forehead. It was her tenderness that brought me back to her wholeheartedly, needing no further explanation about my cousin or the men I had seen her with.

We slept into the late morning and as I lay awake I stared at her and couldn't help but wonder how much she and Jed had shored up between them and if they had had anything besides conversation in Galveston. Thinking on those thoughts got me nowhere and it was far better to let that point of view subside but I couldn't. I needed to ask him. When I saw him I would ask him. But I knew I had to get that out of my head. It was clouding my perspective and my main point was to find Rove. Jed, I was sure, would take me to Rove. He had to know where that sonovabitch was hiding, if he was even hiding, 'cause men like Rove like to announce themselves, they've got so much gumption inside their lies and stories. I planned to kill them all and although my cousin was on my list what I was to learn about myself was that blood was as thick as my mother and father had always claimed and my hesitation led me to my own embarrassing demise. I don't mean death, not that kind of demise but the kind that makes you look like a common fool before the woman you love.

Here's what happened.

I was to learn from Miss Celestine who had learned from Jedidiah that the Colonel was miffed at me for having killed Oscar. The boatmen were after me for the same reasons that Runner and my own cousin were after me and that was to return me to the Colonel, who made a poster with my face sketched on it, scar and all, and it read that I had murdered Oscar in cold blood and stolen his rifle to boot. I was done for. Whether I hid with Clara in New Orleans or rode like crazy back to Tejas, I was done for. And even if life had only doled out injustice to me this was no time to cry or whine or fall into self-pity. It was time to take a stand.

I put on a dress. In truth, Clara dressed me in a gown of green satin that pushed my breasts up and out showing me off in ways that I was not accustomed to but she liked my new attire and stroked my waist and breasts, then held my face between her hands and kissed me twice and said, "This Micaela belongs to me, only to me" but I doubted her declaration and thought she was only trying to console me in a costume that itched and felt as awkward as I must have looked.

"Put this hat on," said Clara.

"I won't wear a frilly hat."

"Let me show you how to wear it."

She placed the hat on my head and pushed my hair under the brim to hide short strands. Then she covered my face with a light-colored silk scarf that fell from the top of the hat down to my neck.

"How am I supposed to see with this thing?" I blew air into the scarf and it puffed out.

"You want to hide your scar, don't you?"

"Can't powder hide it?"

"Not that scar. It's too big."

"Oh."

We walked out of Miss Celestine's not knowing what the night held but I was ready to do battle long overdue. When the sky was dark overhead with no moon to shine upon us, Clara and I stumbled through side streets and back alleys on our way to the gambling den. We had only one piece of protection and that was the spitfire pistol inside my dress that Miss Celestine had loaned me. The stench on the riverfront drifted in the air and the wharves were filthy and crowded with cotton bales and coffee beans but that aroma was pleasant compared to the reek that blew in from the graves of yellow-fevered bodies half buried and eaten by rats along the way. We held our noses as we gripped each other's hands through muddy streets and slick cobblestones and when we arrived at the same gambling house where we had met the night before, we entered grandly and felt the stares upon our bodies by the few men who glanced up from green felt gambling tables.

Jedidiah stood in the middle of the room and had not looked up and I was glad of that until I saw the half-eared man, Runner, standing beside him as they placed their bets at the game called roulette, which surprised me since I knew my cousin loved the cards. A wheel with numbers left too much to chance but he played anyway. When he looked up and saw Clara I realized I should have not allowed her to join me this evening but it was too late. He scrutinized her in a familiar, practiced manner and that annoyed me beyond my control but dressed as I was and with a real scheme in mind, I sustained a balanced temperament. Mostly I was glad he didn't recognize me or notice that I was hiding behind Clara.

The only reason two women alone dressed as we were could enter a gambling house was to lure clients to the nearby brothels and Clara was the expert at temptation. I watched her and mimicked her gestures, hoping my decoy would be convincing enough to trick Runner and Sonny out into an alley. Mostly, I knew I had to keep a distance from my cousin because he wasn't so dim-witted that he wouldn't recognize me once he was close enough to see my eyes and face, scarf or no scarf. Our plan proved easier than I had schemed.

"Good evening, Miss Clara." Sonny came up behind Clara and breathed rancid air into her neck and I saw he was smitten but I had already suspected the sonovabitch was after Clara.

"Good evening," she replied.

I stood silent and held back from slamming the wretched beast. I wanted to smack him for a million different reasons that whirled around in my head. Before I had a moment to think on how we would lure him out to the waterfront, I felt an arm around my waist squeeze and pinch in a way that I'm sure was the half-eared man's way of admiring but all I could do was think on how I was going to thrash the swine until he begged for his mamá.

"Got yourself a live one?" Runner, the half-eared man, spoke to Sonny as he squeezed my waist harder.

Sonny must have been the quiet one because he didn't answer and only stood with his hands by his side but he was as close to Clara as a body could get without climbing on top.

"I heard they got some rooms in the back," said Runner. "We can get real comfortable." He breathed into my ear when he said that last thing and I felt rage enter through my gut and rise up to my head and I wondered how flushed my face had become.

"I have a better idea, gentlemen," said Clara. Sonny's eyes sparkled with contentment either at her supposed idea or that she called him a gentleman, which he wasn't.

"'Gentlemen'? Now you is a lady, ain't ya, darlin? Well, come on. Let's hear it," said Runner and he scratched at his half-ear with a bony, filthy finger.

"Have you gentlemen been to the Swamp?"

"Nope, but I heard it's dandy," said Runner.

"It makes a place like this look tame," said Clara. Miss Celestine had told Clara and me about the place, which was known to be the biggest, rowdiest brothel in all of New Orleans.

"Well, what are we waitin on? Show us, little ladies."

I stepped forward and took Clara's hand in mine and said, "Follow us," and as they trailed behind us, I saw Runner shrug his shoulders to Jedidiah asking him to join us but by then my cousin was at a poker table and only nodded with his chin to say, "Go on without me."

I had hoped they would be drunk enough to make my chore effortless but both marauding sonsabitches were full awake and lively when we stepped out of that gambling house. I was too agitated to care about waiting until we reached a darker alley as we had deliberated and for that quick second I could tell no one cared what happened on the waterfront. I reached for my pistol tucked between my breasts and by then Runner was beside me again making it easy to grab his neck, face him head-on and look him in the eyes. First he laughed thinking I was playing and that this was the kind of roughness he had to look forward to at the Swamp but when he saw the fierceness in my eyes he must have reconsidered and just as he was about to call for his friend who was already far beyond us at least by twenty paces where Clara had taken him, I peered into the marauder's eyes and said, "This is for my baby sister," and I shot him in one eye and just as quickly said, "And this is for my baby brother," then shot him in the other and he fell to his knees, his hands covering his face to catch the blood pouring out, then he fell back and his head bounced like a cannonball on the cobblestone walk. He lay there deformed and bloody and the only one who took an interest in the shooting was his friend who came scurrying back and stood over him, then looked at me and never said a thing. I guess he hadn't planned on speaking but I didn't wait much longer cause I shot him in the belly twice and with one more bullet I shot him straight in his chest where a heart might have been. "That one was for Clara," I whispered. "For putting your hands on her." And when he looked up at me all I could see was puzzlement on his sorry face.

Rats scampered from their hiding places and before Clara had a chance to clutch my hand and take me from there, the vermin had already climbed on lifeless arms and faces and started eating at their eyes and sucking up their blood.

"Hurry," said Clara but all I could think was this time I had done it. Killed with intention and malice. But I reasoned men like those two deserved to die. Speculators and gamblers. They were the kind of men who never intended to fight in any battle or war but instead watched from a boundary of their own making while others fought and died and they themselves as scavengers got richer with land not theirs and other things stolen. They were a sorry bunch and I despised them for what they had done to Tejas. And Louisiana.

CHAPTER 19

Miss Celestine told me where to find Jed but before I journeyed out alone, I had to convince Clara to stay behind.

"What if he shoots you?" she said.

"Why would he do that? Jedidiah Jones wouldn't shoot his own cousin." Back in our room, I stripped off the green dress and flung it to the ground.

"Why not?" Clara picked up the dress and rubbed bloodstains that had soaked into the satin.

"He can't. We're blood." I watched her as she rubbed the dress and finally set it down.

"I thought you said he'd changed. Why would he care you're his kin, I mean, if he's changed the way you say?"

"I don't know, Clara. Maybe he'll feel guilty." I searched the room for my pants and shirt and jacket that Miss Celestine's servants had brought from my lone room above the stable. Clara's dresses and finery along with her trunk had also been recovered and piled in a corner.

"Why don't you feel guilty?"

"I do. You know that. I left my brother and sister to die. I can't get over that." Somehow, when I said this now I didn't feel the guilt and sorrow I had before. It seemed to me I had done the right thing and continuing on my journey was also the right thing. My gut told me so.

"Killing those men, did that take away that guilt?"

"Nope. Killing those sonsabitches was just a start. But don't worry. I'm not looking to even any score. I'd have to live my life killing if the score was ever going to be balanced in some way." I slipped on my pants and tucked in my shirt, then put on a simple leather jacket I'd purchased from Miss Celestine's. I had no need for fancy costumes anymore.

"Well, then quit, Micaela. Quit and let's get ourselves a farm nearby. I can come into town and make us some money now and then. You can gamble and bring home the winnings. We'll be left alone."

"I just killed two men."

"In New Orleans. Where men like that die every day."

"Men are probably after me."

"Darlin, all we have to do is keep you in fine dresses and those boys will never find you."

She grabbed my hand and I pulled away.

"I can't. Not yet. Not here."

"Haven't you had enough revenge, Micaela?"

"What's enough?"

"It doesn't matter. It's not bringing back your brother and sister."

"You think I don't know that?"

"Of course you know it. What I want to know is do you plan to do anything about it?"

"I'm doing it now. I'm gonna go find my cousin."

"Why?"

"He knows things."

"He doesn't know anything."

"Why are you so set on me not finding my cousin? Are you sweet on him?" I was only half teasing but a part of my gut felt down deep that something was up.

"Don't start, Micaela."

"Jed knows an ole boy named Rove. That's what I'm after. He's the one who started all this."

"Started what?"

"The murders and massacres and all the goings-on that need to be stopped."

"You're only doing what they do."

"This is different."

"You want to believe it is, but it's not."

"What do you expect, Clara? Turn the other cheek? Is that it? Let that sonovabitch get away with what he did to me? He should rape me again and go free? Is that it?"

"He raped you."

"I told you."

She peered at me, her chin up jutting in the air and eyes squinting.

"I thought I did," I whispered and put on Tío Lorenzo's hat.

She gritted her teeth, then spoke softly. "What am I supposed to do, Micaela? While you're off getting yourself killed? What am I supposed to do? Wait here like a fool? You won't be back. I know you won't."

"I'll be back."

"You won't."

"I will."

"I'm not waiting, Micaela."

"Yes. You will." I kissed her cheek and left her with Miss Celestine.

I rode out on Lágrimas eager to find Jedidiah's farm in Lafayette where he had settled for the time being, I was told, with a slave named Isaiah. Isaiah cooked and cleaned and tended a garden on land once belonging to the Spanish and the French before them but now marauders and foragers from the United States had come to claim what was once a place where Indians blessed the stars and earth and all life-giving things. His slave ancestors had been bought by the French so they mixed with them but then they mixed with the Spanish who wanted a piece of the land themselves and then some of his folk ran off to be with the Indians, then the Anglo men from back east showed up but it didn't matter to Isaiah. His ancestors had stayed put in the same swamps and bayous no matter who came through next running and hiding and looking to get rich.

"Can I hep ya?" asked Isaiah.

"Jedidiah Jones live here?"

"Yes sir."

"You expect him soon?"

"He don't tell me nothin. Just up and goes when he pleases. But I don't ask him neither. I done figure it's none of my bi'ness."

"When did you see him last?"

"Yesterday. Before sundown. He goes into Nawlens. Boy's got to gamble."

"Yeah. I know."

"I tell him, I say, 'That ain't honest work, Mr. Jed. Just ain't honest' and he says, 'It's as honest as a day is long, Isaiah.' 'No sir. No sir, Mr. Jed,' I tell him, 'it ain't honest to take a man's money when he's too foolish to know better. God didn't intend it that way' but he says, 'Sure he did, Isaiah. It was God hisself who created the game of poker. Right up in heaven. Why do you think old Lucifer is so mad? Keeps trying to win back what belonged to him in the first place but God's too smart to lose at a game he created hisself. Knows all the tricks and all the hands. No way Lucifer is ever going to win back heaven. No way.' And I tell him, 'You're talking crazy now, Mr. Jed. Real crazy.'" Isaiah laughed and shook his head.

I saw rolling in the distance something so small I could not discern the shape and as the dust spun closer to the house, a figure in a surrey became visible and Jedidiah Jones came riding up so leisurely it was as if he half expected me.

"Hey, cousin. What took you so long?" said Jedidiah.

His grin made me want to smack him but there was also an impudence that endeared him to me and as I felt that vulnerability come over me I was pleased to see him. I was glad to see he was alive and himself but I felt myself get angry for exhibiting a weak spot for my cousin.

"Where you been?" I said.

"Oh, you know. Here and there. Taking care of things."

"What kind of things?"

"Well now, that would be my business, cousin." He slipped down from the surrey and gave the reins to Isaiah, who took the horse and the carriage to a stable out beyond the field.

"I guess you heard about ole Runner. And poor Sonny too." he said.

"Heard what?"

He stared at me, then poked my arm. "Come on. Let's have ourselves a little drink."

"Fine by me."

We entered his small cabin and he offered me a chair I thought too elegant for his taste and he sat in another equally as stylish and then he reached inside a cabinet and brought out a bottle of French brandy.

"Bet you ain't had this before," he said.

The brandy was smooth and tasted of orange peel and Jedidiah grinned as I downed two short glasses quickly and he poured me another.

"I'll say one thing." He sipped his short glass and tilted his head sideways scrutinizing me. "You sure make a pretty picture in a dress." He slapped his hand down on the cabinet and laughed.

I picked up the brandy bottle and poured another drink, shot it back, poured another and shot that back too.

"Yep. Sure do look pretty in a dress, cousin." He wiped his eyes, having teared from laughter.

"Too bad about Runner and Sonny," I said.

He got serious again. "Yeah. Too bad. You know they weren't as bad as all that, those two. They weren't the boys you wanted. Wasn't them who done what you think they did. At the ranch, I mean."

"You believed those two sonsabitches?"

"I'm just telling you what I think and that is all."

"You telling me I killed two innocent men?"

"Ha! I knew it. I knew you done it. I knew you killed them. I wanted to see if you'd admit it."

"Course I admit it. Why would I hide it? After what they did."

"I'm telling you, I'm not so sure."

"You said that before and you were lying before."

"Well now I know for sure."

"Know what?"

"They weren't alone."

"Course they weren't. Rove was with them."

He shook his head and sipped his brandy. He had not even finished his glass when I was already coddling the bottle and feeling better than fine.

"Clara sure is a fine woman," he said.

"Who was it then?"

"Who was what?"

"You know what I mean."

"Some of the Colonel's boys."

"Aren't they the Colonel's boys?"

"Runner and Sonny? Them boys was too scared to fight. They only liked gambling and pussy. Like Clara's." He grinned.

I jumped him but my cousin knew me well and his gun was already cocked and grazed my temple.

"Sit yourself back down, Micaela. You know you can't beat me. Not at gambling, not at drawing a gun." Then he mumbled under his breath, "And not for a woman neither."

"What did you say?"

He looked straight at me. "I said, you can't beat me out for a woman, that's what."

"You mean Clara?"

"So you're admitting it. Damn, cousin, you do disgust me. You are disgusting."

"Leastways I'm not a murderer." I didn't know why I said that but I did believe it.

"You got yourself another kind of bible? One that says killing ain't murder?"

"Those boys deserved it."

"That same bible tell you that you got a right to bed down a woman? Huh, Miss Smarty-pants? Always thinking you're so smart 'cause you read Tío Agustín's books. I read some of them books too. And not a one said it's agreeable for two women to lay together."

"It's agreeable all right, cousin."

"Ain't you got no shame?" Jed spit on the floor. "Damn, cousin. What is Tía Ursula gonna say about it?"

"What do you care? You're not at home with the rest of us."

"Look to me like you ain't either."

"I'm going home. Just got some business to tend to."

"Do you now?"

I picked up the brandy and guzzled from the bottle.

"That's right, cousin. Have yourself a nice long warm drink. Hell, drink the whole damn bottle. Won't matter 'cause you can't touch me and you know it and what's more you ain't never gonna touch Clara again. I saw her before you did and I know what she likes and it's me she likes. Not some poor excuse like you."

The seething in my insides subsided with the brandy and I guess I was past the place of reasoning or anger. "Clara loves me," I whispered.

"Loves you? Cousin, she pities you and that is all. Feels sorry for your sorry ass. Only reason she come here with you is 'cause she and me, well, we made a pact. All she ever wanted was to be left alone tending a garden of flowers and watermelons and such. On a farm. Just like this one. She said she'd make money in town every now and then and I could bring home my winnings from gambling. She used you, cousin. Used you to make her way here to me."

I gazed down at my hands resting on my lap. "I don't believe you. You wanna trick me is all."

"Trick you? Hell, cousin, you got yourself for that. I ain't the one carrying on dressed in pants one day and a dress the next day, then pants again looking so damn confused I gotta wonder what you see when you look in a mirror."

"You're a bullying bastard, Jed."

"I'm trying to protect you. Don't want you to hurt more than you already do. I saw your sorry face last night when Sonny come up to Clara. When he told me some ole boy beat him senseless on that ship, cousin, I knew it was you. He described that cut on your face and your short, skinny ass and I knew. Hell, I'm just protecting you and that is all. Women like Clara, you can't hold them on a leash, and you, cousin, you think you can control her but you can't. Gotta let her run wild 'cause she's a wild thing." He grinned wider. "She's a real wild thing." He laughed self-satisfied. "I bet she didn't tell you about me."

"She told me."

"Everthing?"

"About Galveston. How you showed up there with the Colonel."

"Did she tell you about our nights in that room of hers upstairs? Did she tell you how she screamed for more, pressing up on my loins? Huh, cousin? And did she tell you how she begged me to give her a baby? Begged me, cousin."

I jumped at him again and I was faster this time. I wrestled him to the floor and held him down with a chokehold on his neck. The pain in my chest wavered from harsh to numb and back again and I was so hollow inside that I wanted to die. But first I wanted to choke him.

"Yeah. I knew she didn't tell you. That was our secret, she said. Me and her." He sputtered when he talked.

"I don't believe you." I pressed down harder on his neck and he grunted.

"You might as well know she's carrying my baby, Micaela. My baby. Not yours, but mine. From my man's loins. Right here."

"No, no, no." I repeated and banged his head up and down on the floor. I spoke but the words didn't come out of my mouth, lingering inside me so that I ached all over and no amount of brandy could deaden the gnawing. I let him go.

He stood up and dusted off his clothes. "Well, thanks for calling on me, cousin. I guess you know the road back to town. And don't go looking for Clara. She's not at Miss Celestine's anymore."

Again I couldn't find my voice but he answered what I wanted to ask, although a full reply was reserved for another time, I was sure.

"Well now, I got to take care of her so I set her up somewhere. She's safe. Safe from you, that is."

"You're lying," I whispered.

"Huh? Speak up, cousin."

"I don't believe you," I whispered.

"Believe what you want, cousin. Don't matter to me one way or the other."

Staring at the ground, I squeezed my head between my hands. "What happened to you, Jed?"

"What happened to me? Why, whatever do you mean, cousin?"

"You got so mean-spirited."

"I am who I am, cousin."

"Running with the Colonel," I said but the words came out muddled 'cause I wanted to weep. "It was running with the Colonel."

"The Colonel," he sighed. "The Colonel," he repeated and walked outside down the porch to Isaiah and I saw them conversing and pointing to plants and fields, Jed giving orders.

I got up and sat down, hung my head on the table and fell asleep on that rickety fancy chair. I must have been asleep for a while because when I awoke, I looked up and saw darkness. For miles around, nobody, not Jedidiah nor Isaiah, was anywhere within my calling reach. My head throbbed from too much brandy and anger woke and seeped through my flesh. The moon hardly shined and I could barely see my own hands in front of me so I crawled down the porch steps and called out to Lágrimas. When he heard me, he sputtered in recognition. He came to me and I mounted and let him lead me through darkness and mist and I wasn't sure where we were headed and I didn't much care, leaving it to Lágrimas to show me the way out of this latest humiliation and grief.

CHAPTER 20

Almost twelve hours passed and the drizzling rain and wet swamplands made me feel as hapless and foolish as my cousin had proclaimed and more than anything I was confused about my location, both geographic and of the psyche. I made camp near a swamp or bayou and I didn't wake until early dawn when chigger bugs ate me alive and Lágrimas also complained since he too was ambushed by bugs that knew no bounds and favored no flesh over another. My whiskey flask half full, I poured drops on my thighs and arms and on Lágrimas's legs to kill the leeching parasites. I thought on how a steamboat at the port of New Orleans would have put us back in Tejas within days but with those boatmen after me I chose the protracted route.

All along the way the Mississippi was lined with so many oak and willow trees I felt lost each time I searched the heavens for the sky. Above me branches loomed high with gray-green moss hovering like a blanket that neither protected nor shielded but instead weighed down in an eeriness I could not define. I rode cautiously through swamps strange and alien to Lágrimas and me since neither of us liked to ride through darkness. Inside the timberline, shade twisted shadows that scurried beside us bullying Lágrimas to lift his front hooves and I held tight to the reins and whispered in his ear to calm him. It did no good but it neither did harm because we continued on our trail until we found the edge of the river and saw the sun shining on the waters and Lágrimas nodded approvingly at light.

Most riders followed a river as I did now but the Mississippi was so long and far and deep, I had no way of knowing where I was going until I climbed aboard a ferry and crossed that wide river. Another ferry named Hickman at the Sabine River a few days later put me at the Tejas border but nowhere near Galveston Island where I hoped I might find Clara but I gave myself a talking-to and reasoned that I didn't need to go hounding disappointment. On the Neches, I jumped on Lewis's ferry, rode south until I reached the Trinity, crossed on Patrick's ferry and rode westward until a fork at the San Jacinto River made me melancholic for days long past and I wasn't sure if I was crying for Clara or for my papi or for remnants of my cousin Jed who had turned into someone I could no longer recognize. I despised my cousin, I did. But a sense of family obligation turned me inside out and back again and I was so twisted up inside I didn't know what to think of Jed anymore. Hitting the Tejas border made me reminisce for that fluky way he had about him and I missed who he used to be, grinning at the stupidest things and making me laugh at nothing. But we would never have that again because the things he'd said to me about Clara were unforgivable.

I can't explain the confused and weary way I felt now that I was back in Tejas and I wasn't sure where I was going since I wasn't sure if I could go home. Thoughts of Clara entered my mind and I dispelled them and went back to thoughts of home and my mother. I missed my mother and maybe I felt forgiving because I missed her.

All this musing occupied me during the weeks that passed on this part of a journey that was all but over. Finally, I sat Lágrimas at the Brazos northeast of Galveston past San Jacinto and the graveyard, past Harrisburg back to where I had been before Clara and New Orleans. In the same saloon in the same sorry town where I had met Oscar, I bowed my head and rested on the bar for hours, dozing in a sleep wakeful and disturbed by the same men from before who played cards at a table in the middle of the room. Their hollers and shrieks were vulgar and they filled an otherwise empty room except for the bartender, who slapped my back so rough I sat up and choked gasping into an empty beer mug.

"This ain't no bedroom, son. Either get yourself a room upstairs or get on out," he said.

I took his advice and climbed the stairs and knocked on a door and when no one answered I slipped inside and dropped upon the bed and fell into an agreeable slumber until I heard a knocking on the wall. I picked my head up to listen with both ears and there it was again, a light tapping on the wall that faced the headboard. I didn't answer thinking that this wasn't my room and whoever was knocking was calling for the rightful occupant so I kept quiet and lay back down.

"Son, now I know you're in there," said the voice.

I picked my head up again.

"Son, how bout a game of poker?"

"With who?" I said.

"With me. Your long lost friend."

"I don't have any friends."

"Come on now, we was poker buddies and we was fighting buddies. How's my rifle doing?"

I scanned the room fast and felt assured when I saw my rifle propped against a corner.

"What rifle?"

"Your daddy's rifle, son. You lent me that rifle and I shot me some Apaches with it. Now don't go acting like you don't remember. You was there." The voice escalated into a high pitch.

"Who are you?"

"I'll come on in there and show you."

I heard footsteps, a door opened and closed and then a hand shuffled with the doorknob to my room. I was sure that I was asleep and dreaming and that none of this meant a thing until the door opened wide and there stood Oscar in the bright daylight but it wasn't daylight at all. A kerosene lamp in the hallway lit the outline of his head in a halo that faded as he came into the room and sat on the bed next to me. I was too frightened to speak.

"Son, I mean, Micaela"—he winked and shoved his shoulder into mine—"you ever read your Shakespeare?"

"What? What are you talking about?"

"Shakespeare. You think a boy like me ain't gonna know about Shakespeare?" His eyes widened and he leaned into me. "I got two names for you, son. Damn, I mean Micaela. Anyway I got two names. Hamlet and Othello. Now that's all I got to say. Hamlet and Othello. You read those two and you'll know everthing you need to know about Jedidiah Jones and the Colonel. It's all right there. Between those pages."

Othello had been one of my papi's favorites so I remembered parts of it. I'd never read Hamlet but I was not about to admit that to some unsightly ghost.

"Jed's not with the Colonel," I said.

"This is a forewarning, son, now don't you know a forewarning when you hear one?" His voice went up in that high pitch again.

"A forewarning?" I was as confused as I was rattled by the phantasm at my side.

"A forewarning. Like in them books of stories you read. And that Clarita reads to you. Dante and such. Lots of forewarnings in Dante. *Don Quixote* too. Ever read them Greek philosophers? Lots to learn from them Greeks, I been knowing some of them boys over on this side too. Anyway, sometimes in a story the main character listens and sometimes he don't. That makes for good tension. When he don't listen. That's not why I think you're not gonna listen to me but I got to try anyway."

"Try? Try what?" The spirit's ponderings about good books distracted me enough to forget I was afraid.

"Ain't you been listening, boy, dangit if I don't mean Micaela. Darlin Micaela, ain't you been listening to your ole friend Oscar?"

"You never were my friend. Never. You stole from me and you kidnapped me and made me see things I never wanted in my memory." I finally responded with a truth he could not contradict.

"Well now. That is only part true. I guess I got to say I'm sorry so I will. I'm sorry. Thing is, son, I got to do me some good deeds or I'm stuck here. I'm tired of wandering. A soul gets tired of wandering. Wandering and wondering when it's ever gonna end. The suffering. So much suffering on this side of things. I guess I caused a lot of suffering." He gazed down at the floor, picked up his bare foot and scratched it. It was full of pus and worms. "I'm here to warn you is all. He's on his way."

"Jedidiah?"

"Jedidiah!" he said impatiently. "The Colonel! What have I been saying? Now listen. The Colonel and his men. I been telling you. They aim to get you, son." He elbowed me. "I mean, Micaela." And he exposed a lopsided grin in the corner of his mouth. "You best be ready. You best be ready cause ain't nothing stopping those boys now, you best be ready, be ready," he repeated over and over.

When I heard glasses tinkling downstairs, I rubbed my eyes and propped myself against the headboard. He was gone. But his visit was so matter-of-fact. I got up and looked out the window searching up and down the street. For what I wasn't sure.

And that's when I saw. A pack of riders, ten or more, coming into town not in single file or pairs to let others pass but all in a horde and crowding the street from one end to the other. The Colonel didn't lead the pack. He rode amid the cluster flanked by men to his left and his right, in front and behind. They dismounted their horses at the saloon and the one who led the pack had greasy hair that hung long on his shoulders and I saw him yell out to someone walking out of the saloon into the street. The one who answered their questions pointed up to my window and I fell back out of sight fast so I wouldn't be seen. It was just as Oscar's ghost had warned. The Colonel had found me.

I pulled on my boots and grabbed my rifle, opened the door to the room and there stood a woman I didn't know.

"Ven con migo," she said.

I followed her out the back way to an unworn path leading to the stable. I saddled Lágrimas faster than I'd ever done and mounted him and as I was about to ride away she pointed me in the opposite direction of my intended route. I was on my way to Galveston but she pointed north and said I'd find peace and safety there among her people and I knew not what she meant but trusted her since I had no other recourse and then something came over me. I jumped down from Lágrimas and swept her up in my arms and kissed her as if I was a soldier off to war and she was my sweetheart. She pushed me away and said, "No seas tonta," and right then I felt stupid since she guessed my sex and then she surprised me and held my head between her palms and kissed me lightly.

"Lárgate," she said.

I did as she ordered and tracked the Brazos River north, racing until I arrived at Groce's ferry, crossed and decided I had escaped the Colonel long enough to rest momentarily. I began to wonder about all the ferries I had crossed on this part of my journey and more and more I yearned for home and reminisced about the river where the twins would swim and scream and the memory of children's laughter gave me peace of mind and well-being. I held their memory close and it felt good even if there was still an ache inside. I was glad for the ache 'cause I needed to be reminded of my love for them. Every day I promised I'd remind myself they had lived on this earth with me and even if that time had been brief, every day I had with them would now come upon me like a celebration. Like the kind of celebration we had when we went to the festivals in Bexar. So much laughing and singing and dancing and eating of chocolaté y dulce de leche that by the time we returned to the ranch after a full day of festivities, Ifi and Rusty were sound asleep. I cherished thinking back on those days and I began to think on them more and more for comfort.

I came to a dog run built of logs with holes as big as a bear cub and

the environs looked abandoned from human habitation. A two-room
cabin was separated by a corridor in the middle where squirrel hides were
stretched and hung from nails. Farming tools were scattered along the
cabin's deck and dogs ran wild even though they were not and the skinny
hounds with flesh hanging from their bones hurtled alongside Lágrimas
and me. There was no herb or fruit garden, no tomatoes or potatoes as
there could have been but instead stumps where trees had once stood. In
the distance I saw rows of corn fluttering like waves that came closer and
closer and I readied my rifle.

"You not gonna shoot me, are ya?" It was a girl, or a woman, depending
on how you looked at her, who popped out of the cornfield. Her cheeks
and forehead were smudged with mud and she wore a dress of burlap with
two holes at the sides for her arms. Her hair fell tangled past her waist and
when she smiled her teeth shone white.

I aimed my rifle toward the ground.

"You a mesikin, ain't you?"

"I'm from Tejas."

"That in Mesiko?"

"It's right here. You're standing on it."

"This ain't Mesiko. My daddy didn't bring us to Mesiko." She laughed
and her teeth twinkled in the sun. "You crazy."

"Where you from?" I smiled because she smiled.

"Alabamy. We come from Alabamy. Me and my daddy. He plays the
banjo. You ever heard one? Oh and my mama and brothers come too only
they all gone. Only me and my daddy left here. Cholera killed my mama.
And my brothers, they done run off. Daddy says they too lazy for this kind
of hard life and so they up and left. I reckon musta gone back to Alabamy
or went lookin for a town with a saloon. Daddy says they loved gettin all
likkered up and fightin. Not none of that here. Just hard work, Daddy says."

"How old are you?" I couldn't guess her age. She talked like a girl yet
moved like a woman with curves at her breast and hips crammed into the
sack dress she wore.

"Old enough to know when a boy is askin after me. My daddy told me
about boys like you. That you be wanting something."

"Wanting what?"

She giggled. "I don't gotta tell. You not gonna make me say it." She
twirled around in her burlap dress.

"What's your name?"

"Sarah. Like in the bible. You know what happens to Sarah in the bible?
"No."

"Oh." She paused and gazed down at the ground then back at me. "Me neither. I was thinkin you could tell me. My daddy won't cuz he says I don't need to know such things."

"Why not?"

"I don't rightly know." She dipped her head to the right and spread the hem of her sack as if it was worth displaying. "He sits reading it ever night and won't read me a thing from it. Says I'm too young to know what's in books like that. Can you read?"

"Yeah."

"You ever read the bible?"

"Sure."

"Can you read the bible to me?"

"I don't think your daddy's gonna let that happen."

"He don't gotta know. I can hide you. In the smokehouse. And give you plenty to eat. You know, if you read to me."

"I'm passing through. That's all."

"Oh. I thought you needed a rest right about now. Just tryin to be friendly."

"Where's your daddy?"

"Fishin. By the stream. He goes fishin every day. Comes home late. Says it's like being close to God out there alone in the stream. I think he misses mama so he goes out there to cry and think about her."

"When did she die?"

"Who?"

"Your mamá."

"Oh. I was a baby. Never did know her but my daddy says she was as beautiful as any lady and that I look like her." She swung around and twirled in circles hoisting up her burlap dress and she whirled until she fell over from dizziness.

I hopped down from Lágrimas and knelt next to this girl who giggled and stared up at the sky.

"She's looking down at us. Right now. From heaven." Sarah smiled and stared at me with crystal blue eyes I'd never seen before.

"You got a scar." The girl touched my cheek with an index finger and traced the healing wound down to the corner of my mouth. "It hurt?"

"Just itchy sometimes."

"Oh." Her eyes sparkled blue and I studied the shade of blue.

"Where can I keep my horse?"

She popped up. "You fixin to stay a spell?"

I reasoned my longing for family tied me to that lean-to log shanty in the back of the dog run but the truth is women have a way of tugging me and by then I had come to realize that I could not resist all that is feminine. I guess I saw no harm in consenting to Sarah's crystal blue eyes sweeping over me like a cool stream. The next day, under wide-open skies, while her father was fishing, I read to Sarah as promised in the guttural language my papi had urged me to learn. We lay on ticks stuffed with cornhusks and stared up at the blue sky and when we were not staring at each other, she mapped out the cut on my face and I gazed in her eyes.

I put down the bible and looked upon Sarah, who lay on her back watching clouds drift by. "Aren't you afraid? Living out here alone?" I asked.

"Look at that." Sarah pointed at a thin strip of white puff floating. "I'm gonna make it disappear." She wrinkled her brow and peered at the cloud.

"What if marauders come here and kill your daddy and take you away?"

"See. See that? I done made it disappear." She smiled and turned to face me, placing arms around my neck bringing our faces closer. "See. Magic. I done some magic."

"What if Indians come and kill your daddy?"

"You crazy. Honey-eaters ain't got no cause to kill my daddy."

"Honey-eaters?"

"Comanche Honey-eaters. Don't you know nothing? Come on and kiss me. I like it when you kiss me."

I kissed her for what seemed like the hundredth time as we lay outside talking and evaluating clouds with no one to stop us or get in our way until nightfall when Sarah's father strolled up the path from fishing and called out to her and she ran to greet him and I hid in the lean-to behind the dog run.

"Sarah. Look what I done brought you. Enough trout here to fill our bellies tonight and then some." I heard his voice soft and his legs moved about as I scrunched down and peeked out from a hole in the wall.

"I done started up a fire, Daddy."

"Good girl." He sat in a rocker and looked out at corn and got up to pick a few ears. "We got to plant us some sweet taters," he said. "Your mama, she loved them sweet taters."

"That's what you done told me," said Sarah.

Through a crack in the lean-to I watched her fry the fish and waited anxiously for a plate of freshwater trout while spying on her father and hoping not to be discovered. Although he was nice enough I wasn't sure how he might react to my kind entertaining his daughter but I guess I was fortunate for the time being. After a few days passed, I was weary of trout and weary of Sarah and I felt myself preparing to leave, mostly 'cause I had no drink and no hopes of any since Sarah's father had no use for whiskey. But I did. Each time I thought I'd leave in the night Sarah pulled at my neck and each time I surrendered to blue eyes that held me down even more than her arms or kisses.

"Come on and kiss me again," said Sarah.

She pecked my cheek as we stretched out on a blanket under the sun.

"You got soft skin. How you get such soft skin?"

I pulled away and gazed up at the clouds so Sarah's eyes would not distract me.

"You ever been to their camp?" I asked.

"What camp?"

"The Honey-eaters."

"I got no need to go to their camp. I live here with my daddy. Come on and kiss me."

"You never been to their camp?"

"I ain't no Cynthia Parker."

"Who?" I asked.

"Cynthia Parker. My daddy done told me about her."

"Who is she?"

"Why you got to ask so many questions?"

"Sorry," I said, hoping my apology would ease her into more talk.

"She's a poor little old white girl. Comanche done took her. I ain't like her, ya hear me?"

She pouted but only to prove a point so I waited before I asked any more of her.

"Has your daddy been to their camp?"

"Sure. But Daddy says they always changing camps. They got summer camps and winter camps."

"Has he been to their summer camp?"

"Sure. It ain't far from here. If you ain't gonna kiss me no more, I'm gonna feed the chickens before Daddy gets back. You askin too many questions and I dunno why you wanna know about the Honey-eaters." Sarah scampered off to the dog run and lifted a pail of dried corn and scattered it about for the chickens.

That night I took the path downstream where Lágrimas had been resting and after I fed him I entered the stream for a calming bath but faint rustling in the woods made me nervous with thoughts of Rove and the Colonel. I dog-paddled to the bank and walked out fully naked prepared to dress but the clothes I had set on a bush were gone and when I looked up I saw a rifle pointed at my breast. The man behind the barrel squinted and I could see he tried to focus in the darkness and when he distinguished me full and entire of body, he dropped the firearm by his side and spun around, his back to me.

"Sorry, ma'am. I'm real sorry. I figured you was someone else."

He picked up my pants and shirt and tossed them to me and as I dressed I realized he was Sarah's father.

"You the one been spending days with my Sarah?"

"Yes sir."

"Well now." He shuffled from one foot to the other as if deciding something. "We got ourselves a problem." He stood on one foot and then the other, shuffling back and forth. "She done told me about a boy who come here and my Sarah says she's in love. So you tell me. What am I gonna do about my Sarah being in love with some boy who looks to me like she's a girl?"

"I don't know, sir." I combed back my wet hair and tried to look presentable as if the father of my probable betrothed stood before me about to give permission for her hand in marriage.

He turned and studied me but his scrutiny was not unpleasant so much as uncomfortable. "Well now, darlin, I got myself a problem." He shook his head and bit down on a blade of grass he held between his thumb and forefinger, suggesting to me he had a proposition that might not be in my favor.

"I can go. I'll go right now."

"And leave me to dry my Sarah's tears? No ma'am. You ain't leaving. Not yet."

I was perplexed by his declaration and was unsure what to do or suggest at this point.

"We ain't telling her."

"What?"

"She ain't gotta know. Just carry on like you been carrying on. No harm in that."

I was mostly stunned and so could not say much.

"Only one thing I ask."

"Yes sir?"

"You best keep your hands to yourself." He squinted when he said that as if to examine me again. "Well, come on. Bring that horse of yours."

I followed behind him with Lágrimas at my side and when we arrived at the dog run, I saw a candle blow out and heard Sarah running. He ignored the whole scene and pointed to the lean-to shanty where I'd been sleeping, making me aware that he had known I had been there all along.

When I awoke in the early morning Sarah was at my side on the bedtick, her head hovering over my face with her legs bent at the knees and her heels up toward the ceiling.

"Daddy says we getting married."

"What?"

"He told me. You askin for me to marry you and he says we could."

She grinned and swung her legs up and down behind her leaning her chin on her arms.

"We gonna be a family. Me, you and my daddy."

I propped up on my elbows and brushed my hair away from my face. Sarah pushed back a single strand from my forehead.

"We can get us some babies too."

"Babies?"

"Don't you like babies?"

"I guess so. Sure, I like babies."

"Good. Cuz I want to get me six. Or twelve. Or twenty." She looked down at the bedtick. "How do you get babies?"

"You're too young to get babies."

"I ain't. Why Daddy says Mama was fifteen when she got my brother. And I'm sixteen. I mean, I could be. I could be fifteen or sixteen, maybe even seventeen. Daddy don't rightly remember."

"Well, that's too young anyway."

"Oh." She stared into me. "Don't you wanna marry me?"

I fumbled with a shred of cornhusk poking out of the bedtick.

"You don't wanna marry me?"

I still would not meet her stare but she grabbed my face and cradled it with her hands and asked again and when she asked I was obliged to gaze into her blue eyes and as I stared I lost myself in silence. She pulled away.

"It's just like my daddy warned me. You boys is all alike. Don't wanna marry or settle down." She rose to her feet and ran out of the shanty and when she returned she held her daddy's rifle and pointed the barrel at me.

"Git."

"What?"

"You git on up and git. I don't wanna see you no more. Just git."

"But." And that was all I could say, realizing that any further conversation or delving into the matter might dig me back into the quandary I had made for myself. I stepped outside as her rifle grazed my back. I mounted Lágrimas and directed him upstream on the Brazos River and as we rode past the dog run I looked back at Sarah, who held the rifle at her side and with her empty hand she waved at me and I was grateful the distance hid blue eyes I would not see again.

CHAPTER 21

The next part of my journey remains unforgivable to me and to those who would come to understand the gravity of the events that ensued. A rifle aimed at my back and the Colonel's men somewhere behind me gave me pause and I reassessed the places I'd been wandering in and out of and decided I wanted to hide from the life I was leading and all I had become through my encounters with people who could not be trusted. Distrust of what Tejas had become is what drew me to the Comanche who felt as much like my family as my papi had always said.

When I came upon their encampment I shivered from an early morning chill and rubbing my hands I cupped them to blow air into the cup and watched the mingling of hot and cold twist into white vapors and vanish. More than twenty tipis were assembled side by side on alluvial plains that led to a stream and already there was movement throughout the campsite. Women flung open flaps of tipis and disappeared inside, then reappeared with hides, stretching them taut on crossbow timber or on the ground and as they scurried from chore to chore they soaked buffalo or deer hides in water and ashes and dried meat in strips as thin as parchment. Dogs barked and children scuttled about in what appeared to be games while men stood in circles talking, faces up toward the sky and fingers waggling at the river as if they planned an expedition.

I sensed they monitored my moves but not with any deliberate cause. I rode in a measured approach so as not to worry them but I was the one to worry since they were as many as one hundred and I was only one and mostly I felt foolish to fret since the Comanche were my father's people, a fact he had neither hidden nor announced since he'd said more than once, "Most born in Tejas have Indian ancestors." The men in a circle fanned out into parallel lines on each side of me and let me pass, then circled around again. A young man patted Lágrimas on the rump and the others laughed and I felt at ease with their amusement.

Across the field, a woman with angles sharp on her cheekbones bent on her knees stretching a green hide and when she saw me, she tilted her chin up in some form of recognition but I knew not who she was although a sense of familiarity kept me staring. Long, gray hair blew back in a breeze as she signaled to the hide, ordering young women about who spread the pelt and held the corners taut, then shoved wooden pins through the borders and fastened it to the ground. The flesh of the hide swirled in crimson and yellow where the blood and fat blended and dribbled down their elbows.

The woman wiped her hands on grass and rose, then stomped toward me. I slid down the side of my horse and when she stood beside me, she took my hand and led me through the center of camp.

"You have kept us waiting," she said.

She used simple words in a language recognizable to me, having heard my father speak his grandmother's tongue.

"Come." She took Lágrimas by the reins and guided me to a tipi and she called upon a young child and said, "Bring this creature food" and the child ran and returned with dried grass and water for Lágrimas who sniffed the child.

Her name was Eagle Mother and although I didn't know her she identified me as a tribal member, lost and frightened. When she held the tipi's flap I hunched over and went inside and settled down on buffalo blankets braced on wooden slats a few inches off the floor and eased into comfort I had not known since childhood when papi would cover me with a thick buffalo robe.

Eagle Mother sat opposite the tipi entrance in her place of honor and pointed to my muddy, worn boots that stank so much I was embarrassed. I crawled outside and removed them and my socks that also reeked. When I crawled back through the entrance, she placed a pelt on her lap and picked through a clay kettle of stew.

"Here. You must eat. You are as skinny as crow's feet."

With her fingers, she took meat from the kettle and placed a large piece in my hands and proceeded to sew her pelt. I watched curiously as I ate tender stew meat. Pulling a filament of fine thread from dried sinew, she moistened the thread in her mouth, rolling it with her tongue, then spit it out between her palms and rolled it back and forth to make it soft and supple.

"You are of the Honey-eaters," she said.

Eagle Mother pierced the small pelt with a thin, sharp awl made of bone. The moistened filament bent as she tried to push it through the hole she had punctured with the awl. After three attempts, she handed the pelt and sinew thread to me and I pushed the thread through on the first attempt, then placed the pelt back on Eagle Mother's lap.

"My eyes are the eyes of an old woman," she said as she pulled the sinew through another puncture. "It is true that blood preserves memory and carries our knowledge through blood vessels from heads to hands and legs and the knowing is passed down to the next generation. But it is not so easy. We are coming to a time when that memory will be robbed and replaced with conquerors' ways and our children's children will be told that their blood memory is weak and that they must learn the ways of white men who have forgotten their own wisdom. They will convince our children that blood memory must fade. From envy. These kind of men want all that is here on this earth. They do not know we are here to share earth's gifts."

She handed me the pelt again and showed me where to pull the thread through holes and wind it around the perimeter of the leather. Eagle Mother observed me and smiled, then took back the pelt and continued to sew what began to take the shape of a moccasin.

"You want to know how I know so much about you? Your father's grandmother, she was the puki of my uncle. My uncle's wife, she died giving birth. My uncle could not be alone and so he took his dead wife's younger sister as his and married her. This younger sister, she was your great-grandmother, your father's grandmother and after she married my uncle, she became my aunt. His puki. She is buried not far from here. She had a long life. A very long life and she saw many massacres of our people. We lost many of our sisters and mothers to such massacres. Those white men came and hunted and at first befriended our people. Some were friends but others came later and they had no goodness in their hearts. Only greed. First for the animals. They trapped the bear and the beaver and sold the pelts and when they thought they could live on the land, they made log homes and invited more white men who did not know how to share the land or honor four-legged creatures. These creatures give to us." She held up the pelt like an offering.

"They give us clothes for warmth and meat for food and we must honor their lives and their deaths. But their deaths mean nothing to white men who do not value any but their own lives. Our deaths mean nothing. You will see. When the summer heat scorches the plains, white men will massacre more than thirty of our band, not far from your father's land, near the river you call Guadalupe."

She paused and I remained silent.

"I offered him wolf medicine but he refused."

"Who?" I asked.

"Your cousin. Jed."

"Jed?"

"What a strange boy," she said. "He played silly games thinking I could read his mind. And he was right, I could read his thoughts. Anyone could. They came like clouds bursting in a rainstorm, thundering and cracking, eager to be heard."

"He was here?"

She looked up at me from her awl and pelt and ignored my question as if I already knew the answer.

"Without the wolf medicine, you will die, I told him but he believes he will die anyway and no medicine will stop death so I had to agree and leave him be. But you, you must not refuse. You must take the medicine. It will protect you from the bullets you cannot keep away.

"Come. You cannot refuse. Not many are strong enough for this medicine and it must come as a vision. At first, it will frighten you, but you will know what to do once the fear has passed from your chest and your head. Fear is of the heart and mind, it is the pictures you create in your mind and heart but the soul knows the truth."

Eagle Mother offered me a bitter broth and I drank and waited. Children's laughter from outside rose like waves above my head and I felt myself topple over on the bedtick, my eyes wide open. I fixed on the flames of a small fire at the center of the tipi, felt weary and closed my eyes. I opened them to see Jed stand before me.

"Well now, cousin, we meet again," he said.

My tongue felt thick and flaccid in my mouth and I could not twist or bend the organ to speak.

"You woulda died if you rode with me. You woulda died but instead, look. Here you are. Making up these pretty dreams."

Again I tried to speak and when I opened my mouth and pushed out my tongue, the head of a rattler lurched from my throat and the split tongue spit at Jed. My mouth widened so that my lips would not touch the scaly head with spitting tongue. Jed pulled a knife from the sleeve of his boot, gripped the rattler and cut off its head. It lay on the ground and as he stomped it with his boot, I put my fingers to my mouth and pulled at my tongue and it was limp and calm but I could not speak and I looked about but Jed was gone.

Eagle Mother shook me lightly. "You have been in the dream world for two nights."

I ate buffalo meat until I could eat no more and when I rose hunched over to step out of the tipi, my legs tottered and I bumped a wolf's head that dangled from a pole at the entrance. Blood had been drained from the carcass and the hide had been fleshed on the skin side but the fur shined a silver luster. Eagle Mother pointed to the hide, instructing me to loosen it from the pole, and the wolf's head and legs hung in my arms stiff and startled. I shoved the hide into a hole and it crackled from the stiffness until I poured water over it and stepped in, barefooted, marching in place until my legs thickened, sore and weary.

The morning chill dispersed and in its place warm winds drifted over the camp and men rode out in an expedition but I was told nothing about where they were going or what they may have been after. When the sun set women gathered at the arbor to sleep for the night and I heard their voices outside in echoes. Families of children with mothers and aunts teased and giggled and I was envious of their play and missed my home and missed the twins and missed Jed yet again.

I fell into deep slumber and was frightened when I was shaken from my rest.

"Come. We have spotted a Tonkawa scout."

I looked into Eagle Mother's eyes and saw that she was calm as if to know what was to come could not be eluded.

"Only one?" I asked.

"We have little time."

A half-moon lit our way as we packed foodstuff and I heard the women at the arbor race about and order children but our timing was off and what happened next remains the thing that I will never forgive because the thing was my selfishness once again and now that I am older I realize that in our youth we endure with an arrogance that destroys the innocents who love us.

Outside I faced the Colonel hoping to divert him but he took no notice of me and I already suspected what he was after. He rode slow and confident and in the distance a band of twenty or more materialized like a veil of haze descending upon us. They came upon us friendly but I knew his trick and I suppose he remembered that I knew because just when I thought we might be all right if they did what I knew them to do and that is wait a day or two while his men ate and drank, we might have a chance but the Colonel was full of tricks and he was not to take a chance.

I fixed my rifle on the Colonel's chest and as he stared exact into my eyes he reached for his gun bracing his elbow on his hip and without aiming shot a boy through the temple and from behind me someone slammed a rifle butt against my head. I collapsed to my knees and passed out.

I awoke to what is not to be described and so I will not say what I saw. I was not to know why the Colonel and his men abandoned the campsite without killing me too but I suspected he wanted to torment me instead as I lay in a mass of death without anyone to honor the necessary obsequies with me. Wiping my face of crimson tears, I rose from my knees in a prayer that I did not believe but what I believed no longer mattered. I needed a god or a spirit to trust but at this moment had none and decided that Eagle Mother had been the closest I had come to any faith but she was gone and I have to say I was grateful I did not come across her body, hopeful that she got away with some of the women and their children. I called out to Lágrimas who had run into the forest and he galloped to me, nudging my face as if to comfort me.

"Here." It was Eagle Mother's voice and although she wasn't present, I heard her voice loud. "Here. For your journey home."

I untied the wolf pelt from where it hung and put on the creature's head like a hat. I covered my shoulders with the hide, tying its legs around my chest and hanging the head down my back like a bundle with teeth ready to strike anyone trailing me. Dazed, I rode shielded by a wolf hide that kept me temperate from the cold gusts rustling orange and golden leaves.

CHAPTER 22

It was the bird chirping that steered me toward the tree. A brown wren chirped loud and troubled and there was no bliss in the twitter that was not a song but a warning or a call for help. The shrill reverberated through the canyon and led me down the river's southeastern path where a grove of black oak trees crowded around the one red oak from which the shrill grew louder.

From a distance I saw limbs hanging low from the weight of strange objects on branches and as I drew nearer the limbs took shapes of appendages dangling and swaying. The nearer I rode the clearer became the apparition of bodies sagging from twine knotted around necks like trunks. I thought of Jed and nudged Lágrimas with my heels and I raced forward and saw two bodies burnt from legs to chest. The eyes had been plucked out and the tongues ripped off by some scavenging birds that feasted on tender meat. I studied the faces and recognized the boy Pete who had fed me catfish on the banks of the San Jacinto. The other face I did not recognize but when I saw that the face was dark brown and the hair curled tight, I guessed that Pete had been deceiving slaves again and had probably been caught by those who despised the darker races wandering through the central plains.

I swung my leg over the saddle's horn, sliding to the ground, and hugging my stomach I upchucked and wiped my mouth with the dry leaves of a black oak. Far above, a brown wren balanced on a branch, overseeing a nest of twigs. I heard the soft cries of baby birds, leaned back to spy upon the nest and felt a lump beneath my boot. A baby wren lay scrunched beneath my heel. I knelt on one knee and brushed the creature with my fingers, spread aside the golden leaves and with a rock scratched a hole and placed the bird inside, covering it with black soil. The wren from above watched me then resumed its shrill screech summoning gusts that swayed the sagging corpses. I lifted the legs of one corpse to loosen its twine necktie and the burnt legs and chest separated from the head that tumbled backwards to the ground. When I boosted the legs of the other corpse, its body also separated where it was burnt and brittle and the head rolled thumping to the ground. I buried the corpses and tossed in the heads, unable to judge from scorched flesh which head belonged to which chest, but the skulls landed where they landed and I guess it didn't matter. I mumbled a prayer to La Virgen and kneeled before the mounds of foliage and boulders that sheltered the corpses. I rode on and realized my fate had been settled and I had nothing but burials and funerals left in my future.

Along the Colorado River, I trailed the southeastern stream until I reached the town of Austin inside Austin's colony not far from home. Weeks had passed and I had spoken to no one since the Comanche camp, that is, no one except beavers, rabbits and other natural world wonders. A bear had walked on its hind legs to wave with genteel paws and then a wolf had yowled at me as if in recognition of kindred long lost to other habits and convention. I arrived in town scruffy and worn out looking like a beardless mountain man with the wolf's skin wrapped around my leather coat. I went unacknowledged by men and women who carried on walking on the dusty main road or loading wagons with sacks of flour or other goods from the general store. I decided on a hot bath now that I was in a town that would expect me to smell like something other than the animals I had befriended along my journey.

I slid from my saddle and tied Lágrimas to a post and entered the saloon and again no one stared and I felt unseen. The bartender wiped glasses and spoke to a group of men at the other side of the bar and when someone standing next to me motioned, the bartender filled the customer's whiskey glass and joined the group at the other side of the bar again.

"Can I get a drink?" Although I heard the words from my mouth, I did not recognize the voice, having not heard myself talk for so many weeks.

"Hey, Mister. Can I get a drink?" I heard my voice louder and beneath my breath I went nervous and shuddered. In the room, men sandy-haired and pasty-skinned stood or sat in groups and no one bothered to mask indifference. A few heads lifted to glimpse at the clatter that had penetrated the room but no one looked at me. They returned to full glasses of ale or whiskey in their own clamor amid the smoke and din. I recognized some of the same pasty pink-faced men or maybe they were not the same men but they mostly looked alike to me. Unkempt and filthy from farm work. The smells of animal urine, soaked into the leather of their boots, drifted through the room.

At the far end of the room, beyond the bar, I saw the back of his neck, a stripe of red above the collar where the skin had burnt from the sun. His hat tipped back on his head and he leaned back in his chair, hovering on its hind legs. Guffaws burst from the corner of the room when he spread a hand of cards on the table. When I approached, I could see that he held a flush. Five clubs. He leaned over and with his arms shoveled the coins in the middle of the table toward him. I kept a short distance between the table and myself knowing he wouldn't turn around.

The group of five men played game after game of five-card draw and although I stood a few feet away, hands shoved in my pockets, they never looked up at me or noticed that I could see their hands from where I stood. And even if I couldn't have seen their cards each time they were dealt, I could see from their faces who held the winning hands and who thought he held the highest rank.

Men were fools at games. The only way they ever won, really won, was by cheating and stealing and believing they had played fair. As if there was such a thing. Games were never fair when there was always someone who pretended he knew more than anyone else and established the rules in his favor at the outset. Then there were those who had tricks of sorts that kept them in the lead. And there was the fool. Pegged by the rest. The born loser. By the end of the first hand, the others knew he would be the one they would all steal from. I'd seen it hundreds of times at Miss Elsie's saloon. Often some fool stumbled in with a month's wages and thought it was that easy to sit and double the twenty or thirty dollars in his pocket. No one cared if he was fool enough to lose it all at the table even when the fool went home empty-handed and was greeted by a wife who slapped him good and hard for his foolishness. He never did that again. But it didn't matter because there was a fool born every day and someone was bound to walk through those doors and sit down at the table and bet a month's salary or a heifer or mule, anything to give him a chance to feel like life might be better, less grueling than it had been since he had come to this godforsaken wilderness. His destiny had manifested into hard labor and no luck. It was no wonder that many chose the fate of theft instead and reasoned that it was not thievery at all but instead their destiny.

"You got to do better than that," Jed's voice hollered.

"Ain't you had enough, bud? Don't go tempting your luck too much."

I couldn't see who spoke to Jed. I glanced at the three men who faced him. The other man who had just spoken sat next to him and his back was broad and his shoulders heaved up and down when he guffawed and he did that often.

"Well now, that's where you're wrong. About the only kind of luck I got is at a table like this with a bunch of fool boys like you," said Jed.

He laid out his hand and someone pounded on the table as their laughter grew louder.

"What did I say? Take a good look, boys."

Jed won another hand with three jacks. He leaned in and gathered the small mound of coins at the center of the table.

"Like I said, I'm one lucky sonovabitch tonight. Look out, boys. Kiss your money good-bye."

"If you're so sure of yourself, let's make this game a little more interesting."

At the sound of my voice his ears grew red but he did not turn around.

"How about it? Are you up to some real gambling? None of that hammered-dollar shit you got on the table."

No one answered and instead they waited for Jed who looked around to stare at me and thumbed his hat farther back on his head so that it toppled to the floor but he did not pick it up. He scratched the back of his neck that must have itched from its burnt redness, then motioned to one of the men sitting across from him. The man rose from his seat and hung back away from the table.

"Well? You need a engraved invitation? Sit on down there and let's see whatcha got."

"All right then. I'm in," I said. I took the empty seat across from my cousin.

"You shore are. Now what you got to play with that's so interesting to the likes of me and my friends here?" He stared into my eyes that matched his in color but not in shape. His glinted gold in the light while mine looked muddy brown in the corner of the room away from any possible illumination, genuine or false. The beady eyes he had inherited from his father had become smaller slits and he wore the guise of evil that befitted him since his travels. A few months before, he had not resembled Walker Stephens even if I teased him so.

"I'll bet you my pony," I said.

"You that sure of yourself?"

"I am."

"What's his name?"

"Lágrimas."

"Lágrimas?"

"It's his name."

"Once I win him I'll change his name to something special. Like Sam Houston. What do you think, boys?"

The man who had been sitting next to Jed, the one whose back was broad and heaved each time he laughed, returned from the bar with a full bottle of whiskey. It was only then that I saw his face. His stub nose was scarred and ugly as ever. He poured Jed's glass full. "There you go, bud." Then he sat and scratched a beard he'd grown down to his chest and blew the cavities of his nose into his fingers and flung the snot on the floor. "We gonna play or what?" he said.

Jed glared at me as if to dare me and I could see clear through to what he was thinking so I stayed quiet. Without taking his eyes from mine he spoke. "Heck yeah. Let's play, boys. We got ourselves a dandy here who's itchin to clean me out in ways you boys can't even guess. And I'm ready. Come on now. I'm about to win me a pony named Sam Houston."

I kept myself from flinching and for the first time since I had learned to play poker I felt unsure, forgetting everything I had learned in the saloons near home or on my travels. I needed a drink to calm my hands and Jed must have seen me shaking cause he passed me his glass of whiskey and I guzzled, held it out and that stub-nosed sonovabitch filled it to the brim without looking at me. I guzzled that too and finally felt an ease come over my body and spirit. I gawked at Rove and Jedidiah saw me gawking and took his empty glass away from me.

"Don't give this stranger any more of our whiskey, Rove."

Rove brushed his beard into a point and placed the bottle on the floor beside him.

"What are you putting up?" I asked.

Surprised at my gall, Jed threw his head back.

"What is it you're going to put up for me to win?" I repeated.

Guffaws burst out and made me flinch from the roar.

"Don't you worry about that. You ain't gonna win."

"That may be, but you got to put something up. Or it's not a real game."

"Fine. Here you go." Jed put a piece of paper at the center of the table.

I picked it up and read and turned it over. My father's handwriting was clear. So was Jed's name. Scribbled on the back of the page were the words "This land belongs to Jedidiah Campos Jones, my nephew and son." It was my papi's signature and right then I became conscious of all my father's shortcomings and cursed him for not trusting me, his daughter.

"What are you doing with that?" I asked.

"It's his land," said Rove.

"I'm not talking to you."

Jed nodded and gazed down into his empty whiskey glass where he caught his reflection and I caught it too, blurred and splintered. "Ain't it good enough for ya?" he said.

"I reckon it's good enough for me. Not for you."

Jedidiah smiled and repositioned the deed faceup in front of me to show off his name and my father's. "Well then. You in or out?"

I grabbed the deed from his hands and tossed the yellowing document to the table's center. Reaching inside my coat, I withdrew the leather-bound journal with drawings of forests and rivers I had sketched on my journey. It opened to an outline of Jed's face, slit eyes beaming, mouth upturned in a smile and I turned the page when I saw Jed glance at my drawing.

"Who's that?" he said.

"Some ole boy I used to know. He's dead now." I ripped out a blank page and scrawled "Lágrimas," folded the page then shoved it next to the deed.

He sat back and we glared at each other with a disdain that escalated from what seemed like years of waiting and the scorn became something uncontrollable.

"We gonna play or what, bud?" It was one of the men.

"Yeah, we're gonna play." Jed waved to the bartender who removed an apron and placed the yoke of the collar around a young boy's head.

"Why you callin him over?" You're dealin is fine with me." One of the other men spoke.

"That's 'cause you boys are my buddies. But I ain't gonna give this stranger any cause to say I was cheatin when I win Sam Houston, fair and square."

The bartender squeezed in another chair at the round table and dealt the first hand. We studied our cards and threw down the ones unwanted and called out the number we wanted to the dealer.

"One," I said.

"I'll take three," said Jed. "And they better be good ones or I'm gonna regret callin you over here, Jake."

We raised and bluffed and finally called and I had a full house and Jed had a pair of deuces and an ace high while the others had nothing at all. I smiled and the scar on my cheek must have been a clownish look as I reached for the deed and my own paper of Lágrimas's ownership.

"Not so fast. That was a practice game. We always play a practice game, don't we, boys?"

"That's right," they said in unison. "A practice game."

"A practice game? What for? Aren't we playing all or nothing?"

"It's all or nothin. Just hold on, we'll get there. You afraid that was the only good hand in the deck for you?" said Jed. "Come on, Jake, deal another. Our friend here is gettin impatient. I guess he's got places to go and seein as how he's gonna be walkin, we need to hurry so he can get goin before the sun comes up."

The next hand followed suit with the last. I asked for one card and Jed asked for three and again I won but this time with a straight starting at five and ending at nine. Jed drew two pair of kings and queens and the others had a pair here and there but since they only bet a few coins each, they folded and sat back to guzzle mugs of ale and bat at flies. I leaned forward to pick up the papers and Jed slapped his hand down first.

"Not so fast. That was another practice game. Boys, didn't we agree that was another practice game?"

They chortled and stomped their boots and slapped each other's backs.

"That's right," they said.

I got up and retrieved the ripped journal page with Lágrimas's name and turned to leave.

"Come on now. Why you gettin so fussy? I expect you ain't got nowhere to go at this hour so you might as well sit. Or maybe you think the next winnin hand has got my name on it?"

"What are you doing with this murdering devil?" I said.

"Who?"

"I think you know." I bobbed my chin toward Rove.

"Boys, anybody here know what this lonesome stranger is talkin about?"

They shook their heads and batted flies. Rove cut cards for the dealer and spoke. "We gonna play or what?"

"Come on now," said Jedidiah. "My friend here is gettin restless. You don't want to get him restless neither 'cause I can't control him and no tellin what he might do if you don't sit yourself back down, right?"

"That's right. I'm a uncontrollable sonovabitch all right." Rove cut the cards again and slapped them down, poured more whiskey into everyone's glasses except for mine and drank his in one swallow.

I sat and kept the hand I drew, four eights and a queen and leaned back waiting for Jedidiah to announce again that it was a practice game.

"All right. All or nothin. Let's see what you got." Jed laid down a full house, the others had pairs and trips. When they saw my hand, they gasped in unison, mocking my fortune.

"Jake here must have taken a likin to you. Never seen him deal so many winnin hands to one customer. Makes me wonder if you ain't in some kind of deal with him. That right, Jake? You taken a likin to this lonesome stranger?"

Jake shook his head.

I got up to leave but not without the paper with Lágrimas's name.

"You forgettin somethin?" Jed picked up the deed. "Let me have that sketchin quill of yours."

I handed him my quill and he scratched out his name and wrote mine in its place, then offered up the document. He winked and turned back to his friends. "Come on, boys, let's play."

After a cleansing bath, I lay in the stable with Lágrimas, listening to his faint snores, and wondered what Jedidiah Jones was scheming. Tapping the document inside my jacket pocket, I took it out, studied it, then placed it back safely in my pocket. The land grant was as tattered and stained as it had been when my father had first promised to pass our land on to me. But he'd chosen Jed. Always Jed. In my wolf-skin, I gazed at the sky through rifts in the ceiling and studied a lone star blinking down at me. When Lágrimas snored louder, I whispered, "We're going home," and kept my eyes on the lone star until it vanished from the ceiling's cracks. I wasn't sure if the star had shifted in the sky or blown up into bits like a meteor diving down to earth from a celestial epoch now over. I suspected the star had only budged more to the right, lost from sight.

CHAPTER 23

I rode into morning light and watched clouds flecked by rising sun turn from rose and orange to white wisps of strands like fingers signaling my way home. At noon, I dozed in my saddle but would not stop to rest. Patting the pocket of my jacket, I felt the crumpled document that bore my name and wondered if my mother would be pleased with my offering. In the distance, I saw a steer chomping on mesquite grass but the nearer I rode the clearer became a white-tailed buck with antlers tangled and impressive like some rare Medusa. I drew nearer guessing the animal would run but instead it bowed its head and ate. I dismounted and saw the iron claws clasped around the creature's front leg where blood had dried and the flesh wound gaped open all the way to the bone of its thin shank. The buck glanced up at me with forlorn eyes and I felt sad for the creature. Down on one knee, I pulled apart the teeth wrapped around the raw wound and the beauty did not move but instead glanced again perhaps relieved that my peculiar proposal had resulted in freedom instead of captivity. "Go on now." I tapped its rump lightly. "Go on. No need to stay here alone. Go on and find your own kind." But the buck stood still and glared directly into me. "Someone's going to come along and have you for dinner if you don't get going." The creature finally limped into the oak forest.

"You gotten soft on me, Micaela."

It was Jedidiah Jones on his horse, Moreno. A gust of wind blew through the trees and he held tight to his hat. "Darlin, ain't you gonna greet your cousin?"

"You're not my relation."

"Well now. How about that? Not your relation. Just give me back my land grant then since we ain't relations."

"I won it."

"You won it? Darlin, I told ole Jake to let you win."

"I don't care. I still won it."

"Dang, Micaela, all this time and you still as young and innocent as ever."

"I wish I was."

"Well, you are."

"What are you up to, Jed?"

"Me? I just want my paper, that's all."

"Not yours no more."

"Tío left it to me."

"And I won it."

"I let you win it."

"Too bad 'cause it's mine now."

"It's ours. Mine and yours."

"I'm not sharing nothing with you."

He paused, thumbed his hat and grinned. Another gust came along and his hat tumbled from his head and blew away. "Don't you worry. You'll see her again."

"Who?"

"I don't got to say her name, you know who."

"I never want to see her again."

"And if she's waiting for ya?"

"Waiting for me?"

"Yeah, if she's waiting."

"It don't matter 'cause she's not."

"Like I said, you as young and stupid as always."

"What do you want from me, Jed? What did I ever do to you? Huh? I was born your cousin is all and you want to torture me my whole life like I deserve to be tortured. Well this time, you're not taking what you say is yours. You know why? 'Cause it's not. It's mine. Always been mine."

"I'm just protecting you, Micaela. And that is all. Can't kin protect their own kin?"

"Protecting me?"

"Protecting us both. From them boys. Don't you see?"

"You're not making sense, Jed."

He slid down off his horse and walked toward me. I reached for my rifle that poked out from behind my saddle and lined up the barrel toward my cousin's chest but he wouldn't stop. He kept coming at me so I cocked the trigger to show him I was serious but all he did was grin at me the way he always did when he thought he was the winner of some game.

"I swear, Jed, I'll shoot you."

He kept grinning and approaching and my gut got queasy and I almost started to cry knowing I would do what I had to do but right then a blast came from the forest and my cousin soared in the air and landed at my feet. The hole in his back spurted blood. I was so weary of looking upon blood. I fell down beside him using his body to shield me and when I peeked into the forest I saw Rove strolling toward me scooping his beard into a stiff point giving him the manifestation of an imp or a devil.

"Well hell. That bullet was for you, son."

He was so close to me that I could have shot his face off but I didn't because someone behind me pressed a gun barrel against my neck. Rove tapped Jedidiah's body with the toe of his boot, then held out his hand to me as if to help me up but I didn't take it.

"Give it here," he said.

"What?"

"The deed. Give it here."

The gun at my neck pressed in harder and so I reached inside my pocket and handed Rove the land grant.

"See, now. That's all I wanted. It's his own fault. He shoulda never let you have it."

Rove nodded and the butt of the gun slammed against my head and I lay there bleeding until the stars shined above. I studied the constellation Orion thinking back to papi, Lucius and Pete. Then Clara came to mind and I cried. Lying beside my cousin's corpse, I bawled out loud in a way I never thought I would cry for Jedidiah Jones.

CHAPTER 24

I could no longer explain even to myself the onus of all that had occurred on a journey I begged to be over but instead persisted as if to prove that something vast, yet inferior, was in charge of my destiny. I rolled Jedidiah's body in my saddle blanket and tied the tube with a worn rope to the back of my saddle dragging the corpse behind me and Lágrimas. I didn't think of the vestige I carried as my cousin. Jed would continue to be the thing that reminded me of my shortcomings before every woman and man who ever loved him and considered loving me.

When I was close to the ranch I dismounted Lágrimas and took his reins and we both ambled through grassland leading to la casa grande with Jedidiah's corpse furrowing a trail behind us. The remaining few of papi's criollos wandered about chewing on mesquite beans drooping from trees and I suspected rustlers had helped themselves to cattle that wandered beyond designated borders. At the sight of the double wooden doors leading to the patio, I wept and wiped my eyes and cheeks with my sleeve, then settled Lágrimas in the barn and spread hay before him, untied my cousin and let him rest in a corner of the barn.

A cold drizzle froze the path from the barn to la casa grande and on this late morning I slid skidding across the thin layer of ice in a dance that sustained my footing square on the path. When I looked up, I saw Jed on his horse, grinning down at me. I wiped my eyes and he was gone.

The house was silent and with no one to greet me, I sank into a kitchen chair with a bottle of papi's well-hidden brandy as my only company until I heard the winds pick up and the howling disturbed me. I walked out through the patio, bottle in my hand, to witness the disturbance shuffling through the trees and even the river coursed louder. I peered out into the distance and my imagination must have been fooling me or maybe it was just the brandy. I saw images unrecognizable ride toward la casa grande. Not knowing who they were, I snuck out the back way and climbed up to the barn's hayloft, hiding and observing from above.

In that merciless windstorm, three men on horses rode nearer. Their hats blew off and the small one of the bunch plunged down from his horse and chased the hats stomping each one on the brim then holding them tight against his chest and handed them up to each owner, who laced a strand of leather through a hole in the band and tied the hat to his saddle. They rode hunched over, saluting nothing and no one before them except the dust and the muck that blew in their eyes. When they pulled in to the ranch, the one who gave orders kicked open the patio doors and poked his head in empty rooms and the other two headed for the barn.

"Where the heck is everbody?" From the hayloft, I heard the horseman who wore a tin star on his chest.

The other two poked around lazy and undesiring of finding whoever or whatever they were looking for in the barn but when they kicked Jed's corpse in the corner, they unrolled the blanket and screamed out loud. They didn't bother to look up or they might have seen me. I watched them run from the barn and inch up the path to la casa grande. The man they called Sheriff met the two on the path and they huddled with backs to the chill gusts and pointed to the house and then to the barn. They walked back to the barn and the Sheriff kicked the corpse, then looked up at the hayloft.

"Come on, darlin. We got to take you in," said the Sheriff.

"Nope," I yelled.

"Micaela, come on down now."

"That a girl up there?" The small one spoke.

"Micaela. It's time to pay for the damage you been doing."

"You're not taking her." My mother suddenly appeared and I wasn't sure where she had come from. "You're not taking my daughter, Walker."

I came out from behind a haystack and saw Walker Stephens wearing the badge of Sheriff. He and the sorry men with him peered up at me.

"Now, Ursula. Don't give me no trouble. Micaela here is a murderer and that don't surprise me none. Shouldn't surprise you neither. Always had a mean streak, that one." He tossed his head back and his hat nearly tumbled from his head.

"You got proof?"

"We got all the proof we need," said Walker. "We got someone says he saw everthin."

"Well, he's a lying sonovabitch," I yelled down.

"Got no reason to lie," said the smaller one but he didn't speak to me.

My mother glanced up at me as if to signal to stay quiet and then proceeded to reason with Walker. "Ever since the battles, everybody lies 'cause they want what isn't theirs and I'm betting whoever you say this man is—"

"Rove."

"Rove?"

"Yes ma'am. Old Rove."

My mother stood pensive and although I couldn't see her face I sensed what was evolving in her mind.

"He's lying," my mother whispered and her throat choked.

"Well, tell it to the judge, Ursula. We got to take her in for murder."

"Who'd she murder?" She cleared her throat.

"Well now, that's the thing. She's accused of murdering ole Oscar, a friend to our new judge, then she did in a couple of boys over in New Orleans and if that wasn't enough, your own daughter up and murdered your nephew and my son. Seems to me you, Ursula, would care that she murdered your one and only nephew, Jedidiah Jones."

"Jed died a long time ago." I screamed from above.

My mother narrowed her eyes and placed her hands on her hips. "Since when did you call Jed your son, Walker?"

"He was my son. Everbody knows that, Ursula. And I aim to see that justice is done. Cain't go around killing innocent boys."

"How do you know he's dead?" she asked.

"His body's lying over in that corner. Where she done put him." It was the small one again.

She walked to the corner and saw Jed's corpse. I couldn't see the tears in her eyes from where I stood. Mamá kneeled down and wiped Jedidiah's face clean with her apron and hugged him close as if she was crooning a baby to sleep. I guess she was praying.

"Billybo, get on up there and bring that girl down," said Walker.

From inside her bosom, my mother pulled a six-shooter, cocked the gun and fired at Billybo's kneecap. As he screeched and dropped to the ground, Walker aimed at mamá and a bullet nicked her hand. Her pistol flew across the barn floor. Blood gushed from her thumb and from Billybo's kneecap and chickens scurried and poked at the red puddles.

"Leave my daughter be, Walker, I'm begging you, leave her be." My mother squeezed her wounded thumb between her knees.

"Now, Ursula, you know I can't."

"Why the hell did you have to go and shoot Billybo?" The one who wore a tin star squatted and ripped his shirttail, then wrapped it around the hole in Billybo's knee.

Walker tore a piece of his own shirttail and bound it around my mother's right hand. "Hold that tight." He shook his head. "Elmer, git on up there and git that girl."

When the tin star one started up the ladder, I climbed down and held out my wrists to be cuffed. He shoved my arms behind me and that's when I recognized him as one of the boatmen who had chased me in New Orleans. He pressed his body against my back and whispered into my neck, "We gotcha now."

"Elmer, git that girl's horse," said Walker. "Climb on up, darlin." He glanced over my body and chuckled. "Elmer, help Billybo with his horse and let's git. Wasting time is all we're doin."

Walker led us in single file back into that unforgiving windstorm and the tin star one pulled on Lágrimas's reins, giving me no choice but to drag close behind. Mamá's voice trailed us until she was out of sight and I heard her screaming through the wind gusts that she would come for me. No matter what, she would come for me, she said and although I believed her I knew she would not have the authority to triumph over the sorry deeds committed by the likes of Rove and the boys who protected him. But Rove was to be the least of my troubles.

CHAPTER 25

"How long you been sittin here like this?" Miss Elsie rested her hands behind her back, one hand patting the other.

Inside the jail cell, I hummed and rocked back and forth. I must have looked like a crazy creature.

"Darlin, I'm talkin to you. I ain't about to put up with this kind of craziness neither. Now, git on up from there and let's get you fed. Your mama is worried sick about you."

She grabbed my wrist and studied my eyes as if to be sure I was still inside somewhere.

"I done brung you some of Byron's chicken soup. Come on and eat. Dang if it ain't coldern a witch's tit in here." She sat with her legs wide open and rested an elbow on her knee. "How long you gonna sit here and feel sorry for yourself?"

I slurped up the soup and didn't look at Miss Elsie although I wanted to. I was too ashamed of all I had become.

"Fine. Don't matter to me if you expect to sit quiet while these ole boys plan to hang you for things that needed doing. The Micaela I used to know would be acting mad enough to swallow a horn-toad backwards knowing them ole lawmen is protecting the man who killed her sister, her brother and her cousin cuz I tell you what, I ain't sitting back knowing my Jed is gone."

"Nothing I can do," I said. "I'm done caring for anybody or anything. Don't matter what I do or how I do it, it all comes to pieces anyway."

"Dang, if I ain't seen it all. You telling me that you're the only poor girl ever suffered a lick in this world? Why, I seen it all now. Lemme tell you something, girly girl. Your mama works hard on your farm. Your papa worked hard too. And now you're just gonna quit them both cuz you think you got it rough? Don't you know what happened to your mama when you left?"

I was silent and I could tell she didn't care. Once Miss Elsie got to talking there was no intervening.

"Everbody leaving her alone. Do you know how she is? Do you even care? No. Course not. You ain't been here to help her out. Never you mind. That ain't what I come here to chew on. I come here to tell you somethin about your mama and you gonna listen. Ursula is a strong woman. Ain't nothing she cain't do. And the day you left, riding out on that pinto after your papa and my Jed, well, that's the best thing you coulda done cuz, darlin, you didn't have the guts to have in your memory the thing she's been carrying around."

I wrinkled my eyebrows and said nothing.

"The day those dang marauders come to the house, the same day your papa died at that dang battle, that's the day that changed everthing around here. You never stop to ask yourself what them ole boys done to her? All you done cared about is accusing her of this and accusing her of that and never askin her. Never caring."

"I asked. She just wasn't telling." My voice was faint.

She shook her head and pulled a tobacco pouch from her skirt. She rolled a thin cigarette, struck a locofoco on her shoe, and lit the cigarette. The smoke furled around her face as she leaned back in the one lone chair that Walker had placed in the jail cell for her. Sucking on her cigarette, she paused as if settling on the right words. "It broke her heart. What happened that day. It broke her heart and dang near broke her spirit."

"I know it broke her heart, I can see, old lady."

Miss Elsie giggled. "Dang if you don't remind me of her sometimes. She's a good soul, your mama, a right good soul. Not like most folks who judge a man or a woman by the color of skin or the size of a purse. Not your mama. She looks inside. Clear to the soul." Miss Elsie patted her chest with her fingers and cigarette smoke wound around her face. "Ursula and me, we fight, dang if we don't say some mean things but deep down, I know and she knows we could say those things cuz we trust one another. We do. Trust is a important thing, Micaela. Sometimes more important than anything."

"Maybe. I don't know."

"You don't know. Course you know." Miss Elsie giggled again and the wrinkles on her face looked like a plowed field ready for seedlings. "That day, after that danged battle, when y'all come to see me, we fought. We up and said some mean things but I don't regret what I said and I know she don't regret I said them. Them things needed saying. After that day we didn't speak for a long time, but then, when you was gone, I guess she couldn't stand it no more and she come back to see me. And that's when she told me."

I didn't interrupt her.

"About the twins. And what happened to them. Well, about Ifigenia."

"Why you telling me this now, Miss Elsie?" My voice remained soft.

"Cuz you got a right to know. The whole story. The bad and the good. Everthing. Danged if I didn't tell Ursula more than once she shoulda told you. That woulda kept you close but she would have none of it. No, she had to carry on like some martyr or saint. If that don't beat all."

I started to feel that hollow in my gut, the one that warned me of depravity I didn't want in my memory but was about to learn anyway and I'd have to find some way to make my peace with the evil about to be told.

"Maybe I don't wanna know," I heard myself whisper.

"Oh, you wanna know and you're gonna know. Shut on up and listen." The wrinkles on her face furrowed wider as if the plowing and planting had been done.

I fiddled with a thread on my shirtsleeve, unstitching the cloth. "Go on," I said.

"I mean to." She sucked on her cigarette. "I guess it all musta caught up to her cuz when she come to see me she was talkin crazy. Made me feel sad for her. And mind you I know your mama is strong as a ox. Still is. Ain't nothing she cain't do once she puts her mind to it. 'Cept for this one thing. She couldn't forget. She just couldn't forget what happened on that day. I swear it made her crazy. Hell, I woulda gone crazy myself if I seen what she seen. I swear I woulda gone crazy too."

I unraveled the thread to a hole in my sleeve.

"All right. I done wasted enough talk. I got to git to the point, don't I?"

I unstitched the cloth and the hole got bigger and bigger.

"Sweetheart, what I got to tell you is foul. Plenty foul. But you got to promise me something."

"I can't make promises."

"You can and you will. Now promise me you ain't giving up."

"I'm hanging, Miss Elsie."

"Not while I'm alive you ain't. While I'm alive, you gonna be set free.

Ursula and I gonna see to that. Don't you worry none. But first, you got to promise me you ain't goin loco on me after what I tell you. Like you mama did."

She inched toward me with her face so close that her smoky breath calmed me down. I released the thread and buried my hands in my pockets.

"Here's the way your mama told it. Them boys, them ugly boys, they took your baby sister and they done things to her. You can guess, I don't got to spell it out for ya. They done things that no child and no woman should have to go through but they done those foul things. With your mama watching and there weren't nothin she could do cuz they was doin it to her too. They was doin it to her, taking turns with her and with her little baby. With Ifigenia. Your baby sister."

A shame so vile came over me that my face must have reddened. I felt my stomach grind with pain and I ran to the corner and threw up. I wiped my face with my shirttail and gazed at the dirt floor.

"When they was done raiding everthing, they run off. Even took some old rusted farm tools. Ursula, well, they give her a good beatin too but she got on up and picked up your baby sister and took her to the river to wash her. Ifi was knocked out. She was bleedin too. Poor child. Ursula washed her good but she said she felt the life go out from under her baby. She said she could not forget that one moment. Felt like her baby's soul just up and flew away that one moment her little legs went limp. Course, she talked to her. Told her how much she loved her and then she let her go. Down the river. Just let her go cuz she didn't have the strength to bury her baby. When she come to see me after you disappeared, she cried and cried and said, I got to find my baby, I got to find her. Well, I thought she meant you. She went crazy, just crazy as a loon. And I just thought, well, no harm in that, I guess. I mean, nobody never asked us women what we thought or how we think things around here should be run or what the laws oughta be but those same somebodys who do all the thinking for poor souls who ain't got the means to fight them that make the laws, well, them lawmakers never cared none what it meant for us poor souls scraping by. Just scraping by is what we ever done." She looked down on the floor as if she was trying to remember what she had meant to say next. "The way I seen it, so what if everbody thought she was crazy? Women got to be crazy to live in these parts. If Agustín had just a smidgen of sense maybe things woulda been different. But I guess not. I guess nothin woulda changed for

Ursula. She lost her husband in a battle nobody had no business fighting and she lost her babies to the kinda men who obey their own laws. Make them up even. Then, she had the likes of you running off thinking you was gonna fix what got broke. If that don't beat all." She lit another cigarette with the butt of the one she had finished.

I sat quiet, tears smudging my cheeks, digging fingers into my pockets. "And Rusty?" I whispered.

"They strung him up. Your mama brung him down from that tree. Let him float on down the river with his little sister. Two little souls free from the evils of this new republic."

I wiped my face with my good sleeve. "It was Rove."

"Course it was. With his good bud, the Colonel."

"What Colonel?"

"The Colonel, the Colonel, that's who. The one and only Colonel who makes his way in these parts and acts like a danged hero. That Colonel."

"What do you mean, the Colonel?"

"Dang, Micaela, ain't you listening? I said a man goes by the name Colonel. He was with Rove that day."

"How do you know that?"

"I know because your mama heard them call each other by name."

"I'm gonna kill him. I swear this time I'll kill him."

"You've done enough of that for one lifetime."

"Jed was riding with him. I saw. Murdering the innocent."

"Now, don't go talkin that way. What Jed done is between him and his maker. Not for you or me to judge and anyways, you don't believe he killed innocents any more than I do. Not in him. Not my Jedidiah. Not Byron's Jedidiah and not Lena's Jedidiah and not Ursula's Jedidiah and not your cousin neither. He was a good boy and now he's gone and I ain't even gonna blame you for letting him get killed, Micaela, cuz I'm thinking, well, I know how he got hisself into messes just for gambling. But that's all right. I know he's got a lot to do with why he got hisself killed. Let's just leave his memory be. I done cried for my boy and that's all a mother can do. Other things to think on right now and we got a lot to do."

CHAPTER 26

Mamá and Miss Elsie came into town to assist the lawyer who was to represent me at the trial. I thought it was unlikely that some stranger from the east could set me free from accusations true to those without a speck of wisdom that truth may be more than two-sided. What I had come to realize was that only two sides of things mattered in my homeland anymore and after all I had seen, I knew life was more complicated even if I couldn't abide by complexities myself. Thing is, the time for discussion about more than one way of seeing things was over and I wondered if there would ever be a time for free thinking in this so-called republic.

As I ate a foul dinner of rancid pork watered down into stew, my musings were preoccupied with that stub-nosed demon that I should have killed when I'd had the chance. The meal caused me to upchuck into the concoction's bowl and that's when Elmer, the tin star horseman who had helped arrest me, entered my cell and removed the bowl.

"Tell me, Elmer, why are you so kind to me?"

He snorted and stood above me. "Doing my job is all."

"Your job to follow me?"

"Maybe."

"How long you been following me, Elmer?"

"As long as it took."

I dropped to the floor to rest on a urine-stained blanket, or at least I hoped it was only urine. "You followed me all the way to New Orleans? Without pay?"

"I didn't say nobody paid me."

"Well, who then?"

"I reckon I don't got to tell you nothing." He stepped outside and locked the cell behind him.

I fell into a deep sleep and saw Jed laughing in his customary manner with his back to me. Beside him was Rove acting like he owned the world and I swear right then I wanted to execute the sonovabitch, thinking on what he had done to Ifi and Rusty. I looked around and was disappointed I was only in a dream of my own making. It was dark out, darker than I'd ever seen. No stars, no constellations, no moon and no sounds either and yet in all that murkiness I still saw his pink stub of a nose marking his face with that same eerie disposition. When he caught a glimpse of me, we faced off in that gloomy night and he said something but I didn't listen. I turned and tracked an unlit path and with only darkness before me and nothing behind me except his breath hissing through his nose, I readied myself. From inside my coat, I plucked my six-inch pearl handle dagger and when Rove's chest bumped my back, I whirled around and grabbed his whiskers like a plump bouquet and sliced the throat's spongy flesh, then sidestepped the gush of blood still clutching the bloodred nosegay that was his beard. His hiss became a cough then a gurgle and his body plunged into a muddy river like a creature who may or may not comprehend he was soon to be forgotten. I felt myself returning to the jailhouse and when I looked down, I saw that I wore a dress and it glistened cherry red in the candlelight. The lines in my palms were ruby streaks.

Suddenly I awoke and gazed beyond the window's iron rods and the sight of Orion appeased me into a slumber without torments or imaginings for the rest of the night.

I heard Miss Elsie's voice and I woke up. "Micaela, get on up now. I done brought you a surprise."

Miss Elsie giggled and coughed at the same time but mostly she giggled from the apprehensive look I gave her as I anticipated the worst of realities about to be personified before me.

"Walker, get on over there and let that girl in here," she said.

"I ain't your danged servant, Miss Elsie."

"If that don't beat all. I swear ever since they pinned you Sheriff it's like you forgot who you are or where you come from."

"Don't be giving me no lectures," he mumbled as he turned a page of a book on his desk.

Walker rose up from behind his wooden desk and without taking a step stretched his arm toward the door and cracked it open. He had no need to signal her. The door flung wide from a gust of wind and while I noted her physical presence, the specter of her spirit had long before taken hold in my gut. Poised on the other side, clutching her wool coat at her neck where a button was missing, Clara strolled into the jailhouse and my knees buckled, but only a little.

"Come on over here, darlin," said Miss Elsie. "You two have yourselves a good visit. Don't you worry, I'll be comin back, Micaela."

On her way out she nodded at Walker. "Thank you kindly, Walker" and he tipped his hat without lifting his head from his book, the title of which I could not discern from my distance and I have to say to see Walker reading was as unusual as anything but things had been changing before me and I couldn't really know what was true or right or usual anymore. My stomach fluttered and I stood back at the other end of my cell so Clara could not reach me if she was so inclined. I was not going to offer her the opportunity.

"Micaela." She announced my name as if she had to assure herself that I stood before her. "Pleased to see me?" She smiled and her plump lips curled at the corners of her mouth.

"I don't know, Clara." I studied her belly that protruded out into an expanse so wide I understood what I was seeing.

Clara unfastened her coat and rubbed her belly with one hand, holding the other out to me. "Come here," she said.

"No. Gracias."

"Micaela, I said come on over here and meet your baby cousin. Now."

She had said it and I guess that was its own emancipation for me. To be delivered from suspicion I was harboring was its own freedom.

"Jedidiah Jones is dead." I announced this so emphatically that Walker looked up for a second.

"I know."

"That why you're coming around me now?"

She squinted the way she did when she was annoyed but assumed if she talked fast she could possibly convince me of the thing she thought was crucial to modify my point of view.

"Dead, dead, dead. My cousin Jedidiah Jones is dead, Clara. What have you got to say about that? Looks like you got yourself a baby without a father." From the corner of my eye I saw Walker shake his head but he kept on reading, meaning he was either disagreeing with a passage, disbelieving my pride or maybe he was even thinking he didn't want to have to claim a grandchild born of black, Indian, Mexican and white blood. Who knows what Walker thought anymore. Mostly I didn't care.

Clara blinked and her eyes became tiny slits. She raised her chin up into the air and held it high. We stood for a minute, maybe longer, staring each other down, waiting for the other to speak but I was feeling as stubborn as I ever would and no matter what she said to me I wasn't going to fall into her spell again.

"Come here, Micaela." She reached through the bars and thrust her hand toward me.

I had come closer without being aware of cutting the distance between us and then without strength of will I touched her face and rested my hand on her belly. Tears rolled down my face and I felt sheepish of how much I had made known to Walker, who by now was watching us and no longer reading.

"I miss him," I whispered. "I swear, Clara, sometimes I miss that sonovabitch cousin of mine."

"I know."

"Do you?"

"Miss Jed?"

"Yeah." I wiped my face to dry it.

"Micaela, how can I miss someone I barely met?"

"Not the way he told it."

"I don't care how he told it."

I smiled and rubbed her belly.

"From now on, things are gonna be different."

"From now on? Clara, look around. Where do you think we're both standing right now?"

She smiled big and waved her hand as if to wave away a backdrop at a musical revue in some saloon. "This is temporary, Micaela. Just like life. It's all temporary. Haven't you learned that yet?"

I bent toward her and inched as close as I could, trying my best to resist her smell, relying on my words to sustain the fight in me. I spoke softly but she knew me well enough to know a part of me was still fuming inside. "What I've learned is that my journey to make things right put me behind these bars. There's no justice, Clara. That's what I've learned. I killed men thinking the killing of them would make me feel better but I don't. All I feel is empty inside. Things I've seen I don't want to remember and I sure don't want to repeat the reality of them, not to anyone and sure as hell not to myself. I caused deaths too. Of my loved ones. I'm responsible 'cause I wasn't there or 'cause I was there. Either way, I caused those deaths, Clara. Me. Now you sure you want me touching this baby? 'Cause that might jinx it and you don't want it getting jinxed too, do you?" I cried and rubbed her belly.

She cocked her head sideways and smiled again, "You silly girl, Micaela. I never knew what a silly girl you are and now I know. All those lies you told me. Why'd you have to tell so many lies?"

"What lies?"

"About being a hero. About how you got that cut on your face."

"Jed told you, didn't he? I knew that sonovabitch wanted me to look like a fool."

"Miss Elsie told me. And your mother. These women around you. They know the truth, Micaela." She brushed my cheek, the scarred one. "You think I needed to hear those lies?"

"I don't know. Wasn't sure if you'd love me just the way I am, I guess." I wiped my face dry with my shirttail. "Look at me, Clara. I'm pitiful. I'm about as pitiful as anybody can get. No further down the line for me. This is it. All I am. All I'm ever gonna be. A woman like you. She deserves more, Clara."

"Come closer." She pulled on my arm and held my face between her hands and the feel of her along with the scent of her made me go shaky and weak. She kissed my lips so tender I felt I could die right then and my life would be complete.

"This baby will be needing her big cousin coming around. Teaching her things."

I pulled away from her and moved to the center of my cell. "You're talking to a dead man," I mumbled.

I faced the window to an alleyway outside. If I strained I could see from the upper left corner the street parallel to the jailhouse. Men on horses and women with children in buggies rode by quietly embracing the day's errands. I thought back to days at El Paraíso when I first met Clara and envied those people who performed ordinary chores, repeating them daily or weekly with those they loved. That is what real sweetness in life is made of—common days with the ones you love. I heard Clara's footsteps and the door closed behind her. When I turned back around, the jailhouse was vacant. Walker's book was tilted toward me and the title glinted in the sun. *Don Quixote.* It was as if my father had entered the room to keep me company for the rest of the day and I was grateful.

CHAPTER 27

Either he felt compassion for me or he was just plain happy to see me caged because when Walker returned to the jailhouse and I asked how he liked the adventures by Cervantes, he handed me my father's book.

"Too much foolishness," he said. "I like a real story. None of that imaginary foolishness." He squeezed the book between the bars. I took his gesture as an opportunity and decided not to probe as to why he had papi's copy of *Don Quixote*.

"You got anything to drink around here?"

He threw his head back and I thought he was about to break out in an evil laugh but he was really looking up at some shelves so close to the ceiling that they were clear out of sight unless you happened to gaze up. He climbed a chair and scavenged around with his hand until he brought down a dusty bottle.

"I been saving this."

He pulled off the cork and guzzled a bit, then handed it to me. I guzzled until my insides felt raw and I could stand myself again and he was agreeable enough not to object to how much I drank from his bottle. I pushed the bottle back through the bars.

"Appreciate it," I said.

He sat at his desk, legs strewn across the top, cradling the bottle.

"Your pappy gave me this brandy."

"My papi gave you too much, if you ask me."

He took another drink and smiled. "We had plans, your pappy and me. Lots of plans but, well, things happen different from what you plan. Ain't nothing we can do about that except go along to get along."

He paused, waiting for me to respond but I refused to speak with him any more than I had to.

"We rustled ourselves some cattle together, Agustín and me. Working on your abuela's ranch. That's how we met. You weren't born, hell, he didn't even know Ursula till I pointed her out. I used to tease him. Tell him that Ursula was never gonna look at him, all scrawny and dark with that curly hair of his. Looked like a damn darky, your pappy. I bet him. I bet him some cattle that Ursula was gonna marry ole Barrera 'cause your abuela wanted it that way. So I bet him. If he could take her away from poor ole Venustiano, well, Agustín would be the owner of all the cattle I rustled up for the next year."

Walker laughed and shook the bottle of brandy until bubbles slid down the sides of glass. "Poor ole Venustiano. Didn't know what hit him. Day of their wedding, Agustín done give me this bottle of fine brandy and thanked me. Said he'd never gone after Ursula if I hadn't bet him. Your pappy, he liked a challenge, that is for sure."

He pointed the bottle's neck toward me and I nodded. He strolled over and I swallowed as much as my belly could hold without coughing it up. I drank so much that I nearly emptied the brandy but he didn't object and I reasoned that he was feeling guilty finally that my father was dead and he wasn't. Or, maybe he was done saving a filthy bottle for nothing in particular. He leaned a shoulder against the iron posts and looked down at the ground. The silence disturbed me and I couldn't abide having him stand so close that I could hear his breathing. I wanted to choke him just for being Walker, the same monster who gave Jedidiah and me hell on our farm. And Juana. I couldn't forget what we all suspected he'd done to Juana.

"You like being sheriff, Walker?"

"Hell yeah. Least work I ever done. Running things."

"What about your scrap of land?"

"Don't you worry. All that's gonna get taken care of. Soon enough." He threw his head back and sighed deep.

"I got only one thing to tell you, darlin."

"I ain't your darlin."

"I know, I know. Just listen up. The Colonel ain't your friend, ain't nobody's friend. And nobody, I mean nobody, fools with the Colonel. As for old Rove, well, he just follows orders. You watch yourself at the trial. All hell's gonna break loose."

I held the bottle out to him. "Finish it. Go on, finish it," he said.

Miss Elsie walked in and when she saw me drinking the remains of a crusty brandy bottle she stared at Walker with such disdain that he left the jailhouse.

"What in the hell are you doing, Micaela? You been listening to that fool Walker? That man ain't nothing but a liar and his mama, God rest her soul, was ashamed to call him her own, all the danged lying he did to get by."

She eyeballed me up and down and handed me a pile of folded clothes. "You got to wear that tomorrow. At the trial. And no more drinking, you hear?"

I sat on the floor and tossed a dress on the blanket thinking to myself that these women were crazy. All of them. Miss Elsie, mamá and Clara. Especially Clara. I bunched the dress into a ball and placed it beneath my head and dozed into drunken sleep for no other reason than to pass the time.

Dress or no dress, when I entered the courtroom I might as well have saved them the effort and brought my own rope. I did as Miss Elsie asked and showed off my slim hips in the calico dress with silly yellow flower print, maybe hoping I could be saved from impending death, as if a dress could conjure such power or luck. The townspeople sat in the pews of the church that served as courtroom, turned and stared at me seemingly prepared to make me the obligatory scapegoat for all their misfortunes and conquests. I was the virgin to be sacrificed to their gods; I was the culprit to be punished for their crimes and the Colonel himself stood erect at the pulpit priming himself to lead the pack into his own accord. Seated in the choir's pews on the far right side of the church was a group of twelve men, either Irish or Anglo or French with ancestors and birth rites from an old world beyond this town. Dogs, wild-eyed and scrawny, scratched their hairless bellies and townspeople tripped over the dogs' whirling hind feet as they searched for empty seats closer to the pulpit. In the front row, Miss Elsie sat up crumpled and bleary-eyed having made her stake the night before. My mother and Clara sat on each side of Miss Elsie and I felt them all stare at me as I was escorted to my seat beside a man I'd never met and yet entrusted with my life because these women did.

"When we gonna git started here?" yelled someone.

"Yeah, we ain't got all day. Let's see that little meskin hang today," yelled another.

The Colonel stood behind the pulpit and banged the butt of his pistol against a wooden platform. "Shut up, boys. Ain't nobody gonna hang to-day so you might as well get going if that's all you come here for. We're here to see justice done in the name of a good friend. Jedidiah Jones has been murdered. By his own kin. Stand on up, little lady."

"What about Oscar?" someone hollered.

"Leave Oscar be. It's Jedidiah Jones we can prove she murdered."

I twisted around in my chair and stood.

"Hell, we got to hang her now, Colonel," yelled someone.

"It ain't that easy. We're gonna have a trial here. A fair trial. You all know that the laws are changing mighty fast in these parts. Now, I'm sure you're wondering why I got to go on about this but it's important to what we're doing here today. All eyes are on Texas, boys." The judge faced the twelve men who sat in the choir pews. "It's up to you to be sure that we run a fair trial. We're entering a new time in our history. A great time. The laws of great men who founded this republic are being tested today and that's a great thing, boys. Now, I'm gonna trust you to do right by their memory. We even got ourselves a slick city lawyer. Mr. Lloyd, are you ready to start?"

"Yes, your honor," Mr. Lloyd said.

Everyone laughed, including the Colonel.

"You don't gotta address me that way. Call me Colonel. That's mostly how I'm known in these parts." He searched the room. "Y'all seen Elmer? Elmer, where the heck are you? He's supposed to be here on behalf of the murdered. He's representin Jed. He's your opponent here, Mr. Lloyd. Where in blazes is he?"

"I seen him ride out early, Colonel."

"Well, he's late," said the Colonel. "Let's get started anyway. He can catch up when he gets here."

"Colonel, that is irregular," said Mr. Lloyd.

"Son, so long as I'm judge and not to mention mayor around here seems to me that I got the right to say what's regular and what's not. You got a case to state or don't you?"

"Yes, Colonel. But the family of Mr. Jedidiah Jones would like to make a statement."

"What you got to say, Miss Elsie?" said the Colonel.

"I'm that boy's mama and I say you got no right to try to hang anybody for killing Jed. Least of all his own cousin cuz we know she didn't do it," said Miss Elsie.

"She's right, Colonel. Let my daughter go!" My mother shouted from the front pew.

"We're having our trial and that's all there is to it. Everybody knows what side of the law you two favor. Now shut on up and let the fine men of this court do their job. State your case, Mr. Lloyd. These fine people're waiting."

"My client, Micaela Campos, will testify," said Mr. Lloyd.

"Go on then," said the Colonel.

"Miss Micaela Campos. Please come forward," said Mr. Lloyd.

I traipsed to the front of the church, stood next to the pulpit and faced the town of people, many that I no longer recognized.

"Is it a she or he?" someone yelled.

"I think it's a he/she," someone else yelled.

Miss Elsie spoke out, "Leave her be. She lost her papa at San Jacinto."

"A thing like that ain't got no pappy," someone yelled.

"Hell, let's save everbody the trouble and hang the he/she. That oughta take care of a couple of sins and laws that been broken here," someone yelled.

The Colonel laughed and banged the butt of his pistol against the pulpit where he stood above the townspeople. "All right, all right. Quiet down," he said.

Mr. Lloyd stepped forward, took my arm and sat me down in a chair next to the Colonel's pulpit. I held my right hand over a bible and swore to say the truth even though I knew no truth would save me.

"Rove shot my cousin. In the back. I saw him do it." My voice echoed to the ceiling, then dropped to the back pews where people stretched their necks to get a look at me.

"Thank you, Miss Campos. You may step down," said Mr. Lloyd.

"Wait just a minute." Elmer shoved through the crowd. "I got something to say, Colonel."

"Elmer, it's about time. Come on up and state your case," said the Colonel.

"You ain't gonna like what I got to say, Colonel, but I got to say it," said Elmer.

"Well come on now. The suspense is more than we can handle." People laughed and the Colonel chuckled.

Elmer faced the pulpit, removed his hat and placed it over his tin star. "I went out looking for Rove like you asked me to."

"Well, where is he?"

"Gone."

The crowd mumbled and I saw fingers pointing at me.

"Well damn. How we supposed to hold a trial without old Rove?"

"We don't need Rove," said Walker.

This was the first time I'd seen Walker since I'd been escorted into the church.

"She killed ole Rove." Walker pointed at me. "Slipped out in the night when Elmer left the jail cell open."

People in the pews gasped and stared at Elmer.

"I did no such thing, Colonel," said Elmer.

"You did and you know it, Elmer. You and this girl, why you been knowing each other since you was after her in New Orleans," said Walker.

"The Colonel paid me to find her, Sheriff. You was in on it."

"Quit your lying, Elmer." Walker thumbed his hat and rested his fists on his hips.

"It ain't true, Colonel. Not a word of it. I swear." Elmer inched his way closer to the pulpit.

Walker pointed to my lawyer. "Mr. Lawyer, ask that girl if she knows Elmer."

"Judge—I mean, Colonel—this is irregular."

"I don't care what's regular or irregular, you ask her, hell, I'll ask her myself." The Colonel placed his hand on his hip and faced me. "Now you tell me, girly girl. You and Elmer know each other before today?"

"You know we did," I answered. "You sent him after me."

"Just more lies from both of them," said Walker.

The crowd hissed and some of the men spit in my direction.

"Just wait a minute." The Colonel held his palm out toward the crowd. "When did you first set eyes on Elmer?"

"On a boat, to New Orleans," I responded.

People stood and hollered and I could only make out what the loudest of the hecklers were saying and by now I was less and less hopeful about my future.

"Looks like they been planning all this, Colonel," said someone.

"Some mighty suspicious things going on here, Colonel," someone yelled.

"Well, darlin, looks like you finally been caught," said the Colonel.

"She's a dirty meskin," someone yelled. "Time to hang her."

"She's got savage blood too, Colonel."

"Ain't nobody gonna hang today. That ain't the kind of court we're running here," said the Colonel.

"Elmer's been planning this. He's even got the deed to Jedidiah's ranch, don'tcha, Elmer?" said Walker.

"I don't got it. The Colonel's got it," he said.

"Now quit your lying, Elmer. You ain't gonna hang anyways," said the Colonel.

"Elmer, what have you been up to?" someone screamed out and laughter rumbled through the church.

"Yeah, Elmer, what have you been up to?" asked Walker.

"Nothing, Sheriff. Just taking orders. That's all." He looked like he was about to cry.

"The way I see it, the very one who murdered Jed must have wanted the only one who could point the finger at her out of the way. You got the murderer of two men right there," said Walker.

"Looks that way, don't it?" said the Colonel. He looked toward the choir pews where the jury sat. "Now, I want ever one of you to think on that. You got yourselves a double murder and that ain't even accounting for what she done in New Orleans but we can't hang her for that. I'm counting on you boys to help the hand of justice today."

"I'm not done here, Colonel," said Mr. Lloyd and I was grateful at least one man in that church had not lynched me yet.

"Oh, you're done all right, Mr. Lloyd. The evidence has been presented. You're no longer needed. Go on back to Kansas or New York, wherever you come from. Your dealings here are herewith over. I declare it. As judge and mayor of this town."

"But, Judge, you have no evidence. For all you know your witness, Mr. Rove, has left town."

"Now see here, Mr. Lloyd. You don't understand our kind of folks. We're good, God-fearing boys here and we don't need no fancy-talking lawyer to set us right. We know our kinda right from your kinda right," said the Colonel. "And our kinda right is led by the hand of our Christian God."

He banged his pistol against the pulpit. "Now, boys of the jury. Get on to the back room and come back with your verdict. We ain't got all day. Should be clear as daylight what you gotta do today."

After the jury left the room, the crowd rose from their pews and gawked at me. Miss Elsie, mamá and Clara were quiet and when I turned around

Clara smiled at me and I found myself smiling back in that nervous way you smile when something bad is about to happen. The jurors, not a one from Tejas, came back in five minutes and declared my guilt.

"Hangin's in the morning," shouted the Colonel. "At dawn."

I heard cheers and more name-calling but by then I was not listening much to those who had determined my guilt long before today.

"One more thing," said the Colonel.

I gazed up at him and wondered what else he could possibly decree since I was already set to die.

"Jedidiah Jones was willed a lot of acres. And now he's gone. The court will seize those acres on his behalf."

Walker stood in a corner, crossed his arms and tipped his hat far back on his head the way Jed used to do.

My mother rose to her feet. "You've got no right to do this," she said.

"Oh yes I do," said the Colonel. "I got all the rights from here on out, missy. I am the law. Get used to it or get yourself on back to Mexico. If you don't like it."

"You can't take away my home," she said and turned to look at Walker.

"Ain't your home no more. You got till the end of the week," said the Colonel.

My lawyer stuffed papers in his bag, shook his head and walked out of the church without a word to any of us.

CHAPTER 28

"You recognize envy when you see it?" Walker led me to the jail cell and locked me up.

"What?"

"Do you recognize envy? When you see it?" He hovered on the other side of the bars with his hands on his hips.

"I know what you said, I just don't take your meaning."

"Here's the thing. Look on out at that spread of land. Well, what used to be your pappy's land." He grinned when he made the announcement.

"You planning to take me there, Walker? 'Cause I'd be pleased to get out of here."

"Just imagine it in your head, Micaela. You already know what it looks like. Just imagine it. Now, you see all the mesquite trees, full and plump, and the criollo cattle by the hundreds wandering on them acres? You see how the house is bigger than it ever was, it ain't the same house no more, it's a three-story mansion, made of wood and the porch wraps around and guess who's sitting on the porch smoking hisself a pipe and daydreaming cause the sky is so blue you can paint a pretty picture on it. And the corn and cotton are as high as the horizon stretching tall to touch that blue sky. And this same someone who is smoking his pipe and painting pictures in the sky, well, he's holding someone's hand. His wife's hand, Micaela. And this happy pipe-smoking sonovabitch is holding his wife's pretty white hand and they're looking at all their pretty white babies playing in the cornstalks, just running and playing and laughing. Now you tell me. Who is that man?"

"I guess it's you."

"Me? Hell no, girl. Not me."

Walker threw his head back and laughed. I could see the dark hollow of his throat.

"Uh-uh. Not me. Better than that. It's the generations, Micaela. Way on down the line. Populating this land. The generations of good, God-fearing, white folk, that's who. Ursula never could handle your pappy's spread. Hell, thing is, Agustín couldn't handle that much land neither."

"This is still our home, Walker."

"See now, that's what I mean. That's the envy I been talking about. Don't it make you down right envious thinking on how that land's gonna get passed on to someone who is not your kin? Not no dirty brown greasers or red-skinned no-goods and not no nigger-blood neither. Things are changing around here, Micaela. With God-fearing folks who speak the right kind of language. Not that meskin-sounding trash I hear you and your mama speaking and not them red-skinned grunts that don't sound like no kind of language no how. Yessirree, it's all changing, Micaela. And your pappy, well, he'll be turning over in his grave."

My hands balled into fists behind my back. I reasoned on how I could grab his neck and choke him through the iron bars. I had nothing to lose. Tomorrow I was dying. My thoughts must have shown clear to him because he stepped away from the jail cell, beyond my grasp.

"I tell you what, darlin. It's time to do something useful with all them acres your pappy left behind."

"You won't get away with this."

"Won't I? Hell, I ain't the one hanging come sunup."

"That deed don't mean nothing anymore."

"You're right about that. That deed's just a piece of paper."

"My mother won't let go of that land, Walker. You know she's going to fight you on that."

"It ain't me she's fightin. Hell, I'm no match for your mama, but the Colonel, well now, he's got friends in high places. I think you know he's a man used to getting his way. Lots of land around here is fixing to change hands, thanks to the Colonel."

"Don't count on the likes of us disappearing, Walker."

"Like I said, things are changing and ain't one thing you can do about it." He slapped dust from his pants with his hat, then put it back on and walked out of the jail.

I sat alone. A clock on the wall ticked so loud I couldn't ponder my situation. None of my circumstances had become real to me. I sat and stared at my hands and listened to the clock's ticking.

How it all happened I'm still unsure because the swiftness of the action still has me wondering. All three women were in my midst and I'm assuming that no one suspected Clara, my mother or Miss Elsie capable of scheming or successful of any such scheme. Long past midnight I was awakened in my cell when I heard keys jingling and boots scraping on the floor. Elmer was fast asleep but then I realized he had been knocked out and Miss Elsie was dragging him inside the cell and laying him down next to me. Mamá was shaking me awake and helped me stand, quieting me from any talk or the asking of any questions and of those I had many. Outside Clara sat in the driver's seat of a wagon and tied to the wagon was Lágrimas. He spit and bobbed his head when he saw me and that he was saddled and packed for a long journey perplexed me but only momentarily. Mamá handed me papi's rifle that I'd left on the farm and inside my jacket she placed an envelope of pesos.

"Don't worry. We'll be fine." She dipped her chin toward Clara and I assumed she meant she would be caring for Clara and the newborn.

Miss Elsie handed me a small pint of whiskey and hugged me hard. "Don't go and drink it all at once, you hear? You got to learn to treat it like medicine."

I stuffed the pint inside a pocket and mounted Lágrimas. I felt Clara's eyes on my back but I couldn't turn to look at her. I rode south, fast and fortunate.

EPILOGUE

The thing is, so many years have passed since the time of my cousin Jedidiah Jones and the circumstances that led those scavengers to accuse me of his murder, that I've let rest the disdain I carried in my heart for my less fortunate cousin. I am the lucky one now. Although I am exiled from my home, I am the lucky one. But you got to know this other thing about me. Each time I think back to my papi's land and realize that Walker and the Colonel are getting fatter by the year and that Rove is still roaming the countryside doing harm, my conviction grows stronger and my will is unmovable. I'm going back for good one day and on that day our hallowed home will be ours again but not through the same kind of murdering and hate. I'm not going back like that. I can't. Not anymore. Something inside me has changed and I guess it's a feeling for the generations coming upon us, the generations that need a legacy of truth to keep them going 'cause sometimes truth is all we got on our side. I'm not saying the battles ahead won't be hard on us. They will. But it's like Eagle Mother said, nobody can take away memory in our flesh and nothing can take away the spirit in our blood 'cause that spirit is guiding us to new days no matter how much men like Walker, Colonel and Rove lie and cheat and murder their way through everything they touch. We don't got to be like them. I've been sitting here among holy ones in a convent hidden far from anyone who may think he recognizes me and I've been here long enough to realize I never want to murder another sonovabitch again. Maybe it's all those prayers and meditations these nuns have me doing. Maybe we can change all the evil in the world. I'm not real sure but I got to try in my own way.

I did want to kill again. To have my revenge. I went back to the farm once and I held a knife to Walker's neck and just when I was about to slice clean through, I stopped. I stopped when Walker made his confession to me. "I'm the one drove a knife into your pappy," he said, and right there, knowing he had nothing to lose by telling me, I stopped and I turned around without any fear in my heart and body 'cause I knew he had to live with himself for the rest of his days and I knew that by confessing to me, he thought he was free of his sin. But he wasn't. He killed a man who loved him. Least I never committed such treachery.

I will move ahead of my story to confess one more thing because this is a happy part and I believe we got to leave ourselves with a few happy measures of our lives. It is the thing that I must say aloud if only to feel myself sharing something so removed from where I am now. When Clara had the baby twins, a girl and a boy, I saw their birth as a sign of good things to come. I started to cross the border north to my home almost yearly. Quietly, I sneak up the path to Miss Elsie's where mamá, Clara and the babies live strong and steady. Clara always looks at me as if she's expecting me, and the twins, Ifigenia and Aristus she named them after my sister and brother, always seem to recognize me. Their giggles make me giggle and when I hold them I can't let go. That is the effect babies have on the human heart and I am no exception. That regard from those babies gives me hope for myself because I know now I am not so evil as I thought I was during those horrific times of the Tejas battles. I greet my baby cousins and see my eyes, Jedidiah's eyes, in their tiny faces and Clara leans against me and we both laugh and cry. I kiss each baby and pull Clara closer, then leave in the night before anyone else awakens.

Here in this holy place, this convent where I am protected from those who might pursue me, I meditate daily on the next time I may see them, Clara and the twins, mamá and Miss Elsie too. As winter approaches, I plan my journey to celebrate with the twins another year of their lives and I raise each child above me and my infinite love for them enters my body and I see the future. It's a strange and satisfying thing, the power of future generations in one's arms and I guess that's part of the change inside me I've been trying to explain. That another war is coming doesn't dishearten me as much as before because so long as men like Walker and the Colonel occupy our land, there will be more wars. Maybe the only justice we'll ever know is in surviving to tell our own side of things. Maybe that's enough for now. Telling our own stories so we won't be forgotten.

CPSIA information can be obtained
at www.ICGtesting.com
Printed in the USA
FFOW02n0441110817
38672FF